Two minds with but a single thought. . . .

Leah watch   se all
to herself.   rself.

Water   mped
by a windm   tank,
and waited   pigot
that let the   then
stepped ove   lown
into the wat

Oh, the   ainst
her naked b   x.

When John t   iced
the family bu   ere.

An ideal

With a c   up
the stairs. W   was
greeted with   iful
young woma   her
eyes closed. J   go
back to his ap   ted
to the spot.

HER
AMISH
MAN

ERIN BATES

Gallery Books

New York   London   Toronto   Sydney   New Delhi

Gallery Books
A Division of Simon & Schuster, Inc.
1230 Avenue of the Americas
New York, NY 10020

First Gallery Books trade paperback edition September 2012

GALLERY BOOKS and colophon are registered trademarks of Simon & Schuster, Inc.

For information about special discounts for bulk purchases, please contact Simon & Schuster Special Sales at 1-866-506-1949 or business@simonandschuster.com

The Simon & Schuster Speakers Bureau can bring authors to your live event. For more information or to book an event contact the Simon & Schuster Speakers Bureau at 1-866-248-3049 or visit our website at www.simonspeakers.com.

Designed by Davina Mock-Maniscalco

Manufactured in the United States of America

10 9 8 7 6 5 4 3 2 1

Library of Congress Cataloging-in-Publication Data

Bates, Erin.
  Her Amish Man / Erin Bates.—1st Gallery Books trade paperback ed.
    p. cm.
  1. Murder—Investigation—Fiction. 2. Life change events—Fiction.
3. Amish—Illinois. 4. Grandparent and child—Fiction. I. Title.
  PS3602.A856H47 2012
  813'.6—dc23   2011051760

ISBN 978-1-4516-6209-2
ISBN 978-1-4516-6210-8 (ebook)

HER
AMISH
MAN

CHAPTER ONE

St. Louis, Missouri

When Leah McKenzie came out of the drugstore, there were two men sitting on a bench just across the sidewalk from where she had parked her cherry-red Mustang convertible.

"My oh my, Johnny, look at that," one of the two men said. "If God ever made anything any better to look at than a pretty girl in a red convertible, He sure kept it for Himself." Leah smiled as she got into the car, and because it was a warm September day, she put the top down before backing out of her parking spot.

A few minutes later she was driving south on Memorial Drive, listening to Vivaldi's *Four Seasons* on her satellite radio. She passed the Edward Jones Dome on the right, while just ahead of her on the left, gleaming in the midmorning sun, rose the Gateway Arch. The wind was ruffling her hair, which meant she would have to comb it before she went into the office, but she didn't care. She loved driving with the top down.

Leah was a first-year associate with the law firm of Blanton, Trevathan and Dunn, and as she whipped into the firm's parking lot, she suppressed a momentary thrill at having landed the job of her dreams. Pulling into the spot that had her name on it, Leah put the top up on the car, then worked her blond hair back into shape before getting out. She locked the Mustang remotely and smiled at the cheerful "beep" it gave in response.

"Good morning, Miss McKenzie," the smiling security guard said as she walked by. Mike Stratton had played college football, and though he carried a Taser, his six-foot-seven-inch, 320-pound frame was enough to intimidate anyone who might try to force their way into the office.

Leah smiled back at him. "Good morning, Mike. Is Tommy feeling better?"

"Yes, ma'am. The doctor said it was nothing but a case of chicken pox."

"Part of growing up," Leah said.

Leah took the elevator to the third floor, where it opened into the reception area of the law office.

"Good morning, Millie," Leah said brightly as she checked her in-box. Picking up the mail and case folders, she walked purposefully down the long hallway toward her office. Though it wasn't large and grandiose like the offices of the partners, she at least had a real office, with a door and a window. She knew lawyers in other companies who were at about her level but were still stuck in cubicles.

Leah sat down and started reading her e-mail. She scrolled down through them, deleting the spam, including the daily offer from an overseas "businessman" who just wanted her bank account to hold a small fortune for a bit.

"Not today, Mr. Ogombua," Leah said with a chuckle.

When all of her e-mails were taken care of, Leah headed to the break room for her first coffee of the day.

"Don't you know that stuff will stunt your growth?" Marilyn Summers, one of the law clerks, asked. "At least that's what my daddy says."

"If stunting my growth means keeping the weight off, I'm all for it," Leah replied.

"Is Mr. Trevathan ill? I haven't seen him this morning."

"He's at the federal court building, filing a brief," Leah said.

"Listen, there's going to be a get-together tonight at Westborough, and every clerk has to bring a real-life lawyer. Would you be my lawyer? I'm told there are going to be several single man-type lawyers in attendance."

Leah chuckled. "Ha. The last thing, the absolute *last* thing, I want would be to hook up with another lawyer."

"Oh," Marilyn said, looking crestfallen.

Leah held her hand out. "That doesn't mean I won't go with you tonight. I'm just not in the market for a lawyer boyfriend."

Marilyn smiled. "Great! I'll meet you there at seven."

With coffee in hand, Leah returned to her desk. That was when she saw a new e-mail.

To: Leah.McKenzie@BTD.com
From: Carl.Trevathan@BTD.com

Leah,
As soon as you receive this e-mail I want you to access the
Harrison file on my computer. Access is restricted. Password is

Gashousegang. Print out all forty pages and bring it to me now.
I am on the 24th floor of the Eagleton courthouse. Say nothing
about this to anyone in the office. Please permanently delete
the file after you download it, and this e-mail after you read it.

Leah thought the e-mail was a little strange. First of all, she wasn't aware of any client named Harrison. And why did he not want her to say anything to anyone else in the office? And for that matter, why did he send her an e-mail instead of calling?

She picked up the phone and dialed five of the numbers to his cell phone, then she hung up without completing the call. She started toward Blanton's office but stopped. Mr. Trevathan had asked her not to mention this to anyone else.

Carl Trevathan was the one who had recruited Leah right out of law school. He was a wonderful boss and mentor, and she had learned more about law while working for him than she had all three years of law school.

Leah had her own key to Trevathan's private office, so the locked door was no impediment. Letting herself in, she closed and locked the door behind her before settling at his desk. Leah smiled as she sat behind the computer and saw a baseball moving back and forth as the screen saver. His password, "Gashouse-gang," referred to the 1934 St. Louis Cardinals baseball team. Trevathan's office was a testament to his passion for baseball. In his youth he had been a good high school and college player, and he'd once shared with Leah his regret that he had never tried to make it in the major leagues. He had autographed photographs, baseballs, and bats all over his office. His proudest possession was one of the baseballs used in Bob Gibson's 1971 no-hitter game against the Pittsburgh Pirates. It wasn't just any ball; it was the last pitch of the game, and it was signed by Bob Gibson himself.

Leah opened the Harrison file and printed it out. It always made her nervous to delete a file because often Mr. Trevathan would change his mind and ask her to find it for him. Several months ago she'd started backing up deleted files on a thumb drive, and she did the same thing to this file.

Fifteen minutes later, she was walking through security at the Eagleton building. Issued a temporary badge, she took the elevator to the twenty-fourth floor, watching the numbers flash by. When the doors slid open at twenty-four, Leah could see Carl Trevathan standing there.

"Mr. Trevathan," she said. "I was just—"

"Go back! Go back!" Trevathan shouted.

"Hold it right there!" someone shouted from the far end of the hall. Leah stepped out of the elevator to see who was shouting and saw a slender man with black, unruly hair and a narrow, pinched face. She also saw the gun pointed at her, and she froze in shock and fear.

"Back in the elevator!" Trevathan said, shoving her physically toward the open doors.

That's when Leah heard a sound, more like a burst of air from a high-pressure hose than a gunshot. Blood squirted from the front of Trevathan's shirt as he staggered into the elevator and hit a button on the panel. The doors slid closed.

"What's happening? What's going on?"

"Get down, he may shoot again!" Trevathan grabbed Leah and

pulled her down to the floor, but it was unnecessary. The elevator was already moving.

"Mr. Trevathan, what . . ." Leah said. It wasn't until then that she realized she had blood all over her. Then Trevathan sat up, his hands clutched to his chest. Blood streamed through his fingers.

"*Ad astra per alia porci,*" he muttered.

Trevathan opened his mouth as if to speak again, but this time there were no words. He took one last rasping breath, then collapsed.

Leah was looking down at Trevathan when the doors of the elevator opened on the ninth floor. There were two young women there, laughing and talking as they were waiting. When they saw the bloody scene in the elevator both women screamed and ran.

"Wait!" Leah called, but even as she shouted, the elevator doors closed and the elevator continued down.

When the elevator doors opened in the lobby Leah began shouting to the security guards.

"Help him! Help him!" Leah pleaded.

Two of the guards ran into the elevator and knelt beside Trevathan. One of them put his hand on Trevathan's neck, then shook his head.

"Miss, you had better come with us," one of the security guards said.

"But Mr. Trevathan!" she said, reaching back toward him.

"He's dead, miss. Come with us," the security guard said again.

Stunned and saddened, Leah let herself be led away, still clutching the black leather file folder.

She was in a dingy room somewhere in the court building, and had been there for half an hour answering the same questions over and over again, when she saw a rather smallish man in his late fifties, with a few strands of gray hair combed over a balding head. A particularly unattractive man, he had a red nose and prominent ears. Leah had never been so happy to see anyone in her life.

"Mr. Blanton! Thank God you're here. Mr. Trevathan is dead. I saw someone shoot him."

"Who are you?" one of two U.S. Marshals asked the man.

"Keith Blanton. I am Miss McKenzie's lawyer. Have you taken her statement?"

"Yes, we have."

"Is she being charged with anything?"

"Not at this time."

"Not at this time?" Leah gasped. "What do you mean, 'not at this time'?"

"If you have taken her statement and you are not charging her with anything, then I'm taking her out of here."

The two marshals stepped over to one corner of the room for a private consultation.

"Leah, forgive me for not asking before—you have blood on you. Were you hurt?" Blanton asked.

"No," Leah said. "This—this is Mr. Trevathan's blood. Oh—" She began crying. "Does Annie know?"

"Mr. Dunn and his wife are with Mrs. Trevathan now," Blanton said.

One of the marshals came back. "All right, you can take her. But, Miss McKenzie, please stay where we can get in touch with you."

Wiping her eyes with a handkerchief Blanton provided, Leah nodded.

There were TV cameras and reporters in the lobby, and as soon as they saw Leah, especially the blood on her clothing, they rushed to her.

"Miss! Miss! Who are you? Were you a witness to the murder of Carl Trevathan?"

Blanton stepped in between Leah and the cameras and reporters. "Please, Miss McKenzie has been through quite an ordeal. She is quite shaken. Please respect her privacy."

"Who are you?" one of the reporters asked.

"I'm Keith Blanton."

"You were a partner of Carl Trevathan, weren't you?"

"Yes. Please, let us go now. I promise you, we'll release a statement later. Right now, Miss McKenzie needs some time to compose herself."

With the police and U.S. Marshals helping to part the crowd, Blanton led Leah out of the building and into the parking lot. She started toward her car.

"No," Blanton said. "I don't think you should drive just now. I'll have someone come get your car. You ride back to the office with me."

Leah acquiesced without resistance. Blanton and Leah got into the backseat of Blanton's Cadillac. Although Blanton did not normally use a driver, Mike Stratton was driving today.

"I thought that, given what happened, it might be a good idea to bring Mike along," Blanton said.

"Yes, sir. I don't mind telling you, seeing him here makes me feel a little better."

"I know you told the police everything," Blanton said. "But I'd like you to tell me."

"There isn't much to tell," Leah said. "When the elevator doors opened on the twenty-fourth floor, Mr. Trevathan was standing there. A man down at the other end of the hall shot him. Mr. Trevathan got into the elevator and managed to get the doors closed before the shooter got to him. But he died in the elevator on the way down."

"What were you doing there?"

"Oh, Mr. Trevathan asked me to bring him the Harrison file."

"The Harrison file? What Harrison file? Is that something Carl was handling on his own?"

"I don't know. To be honest, I'd never heard of it before. He just asked me to download it from his computer, print it out, and bring it to him."

"Did he call you on your cell? Because he didn't call through our switchboard."

"No, he sent me an e-mail."

"An e-mail? That's rather odd, isn't it? You'd think he would want a more immediate response than that. Did you find the file he asked for?"

"Yes, sir."

"Where is that file now?"

"I have it right here." Leah pulled out the pages she had printed earlier that morning and handed them to Blanton.

"Did anybody else see this? Did you show it to the police?"

"No. They didn't ask for it and when everything happened, I forgot about it."

"Well, don't worry about it. I'll keep it."

They pulled into the parking lot of the law office building.

"Mike, if you would, drive Miss McKenzie home so she can clean up," Blanton said. Then to Leah he said, "You don't need to come back in today if you don't want to."

"Thank you, but if Mike drives me home, I won't have my car."

"Give me your car keys. I'll have it brought to your condo."

"Thanks, Mr. Blanton. And thank you so much for being there this afternoon. You don't know how happy I was to see you."

"You are part of the firm, Leah. That makes you family, and we look out for family."

Leah started to hug him, then, with a self-conscious smile, pulled back. "I don't want to get blood on you."

Blanton got out of the car and took Leah's address, then Mike drove her home.

"Miss McKenzie, you sure you're all right? If you'd like, I'll come up to your apartment with you just to take a look around, Mike said."

"I—yes, thank you, I would like that."

Leah's apartment was on the second floor. She fumbled for her keys but was too nervous to find them, so, silently, she gave her purse to Mike. He found the keys, opened the door, then went in first. He came back a minute later. "I've looked everywhere—closets, out on your balcony, even under your bed and behind your sofa. There's nobody here."

"Thank you, Mike. You don't know how much I appreciate that."

Ten minutes later, with the door to her apartment double-locked, Leah sat in her whirlpool tub. She remembered then the strange thing Trevathan had said just before he died. "*Ad astra per alia porci.*" As a recent graduate of law school, Leah was pretty well versed in Latin legal terms, but she had no idea what that meant.

CHAPTER TWO

Arthur, Illinois

John Miller stepped out of the workshop for a few minutes. Mr. Collins's cabinet shop was at S. Vine and Route 133, which gave him an unrestricted view toward the setting sun and the nearby Amish houses. Houses belonging to the non-Amish, or "English," began to glow brightly with lights and television screens. The English houses scattered among the predominately Amish neighborhood looked like fireflies scattered in the night.

The Amish houses were considerably darker than the English houses, illuminated only by gas or kerosene lanterns. Here, buggies, not cars, were parked in the driveways, and horses grazed in nearby pastures. Dogs and cats wandered around, but the neighborhood was free of the noise of evening newscasts, reality shows, blaring music, and even the hum of air conditioners. The only intrusions in the silence were those of nature: the lowing of a cow, the snort of a pig, the singing of tree frogs and night insects. From time to time the sound of a trotting horse, its hooves clopping loudly against blacktop pavement, would ring out in the growing darkness. John Miller was a part of this world, and he waited outside for a long moment before he went back into the shop to resume his work.

Farmland had become very scarce among the Amish, so many had to find other means of employment. John was one such person; he worked for Glen Collins, an English cabinetmaker whose shop was not far from John's family home. John was a master carpenter who enjoyed working with wood and very much liked making beautiful and useful things.

When John went back into the shop, he saw Glen with a clipboard, taking an inventory of the cabinet-building material.

"What was it you told me we needed?" Glen asked as John came back in.

"Flat-head screws and drawer slides," John replied.

"Ah, yes, the drawer slides. That's what I forgot," Glen said as he made an entry on the clipboard.

Glen went back into the front office as John picked up the piece of wood he had been sanding, using a grade so fine as to barely make an impression. All of the pieces of the cabinet had been cut out and sanded. Now he needed only to assemble it and apply a hand-rubbed stain.

After assembling the cabinet, John stood up and stretched to his full six feet, two inches. Holding his hands high over his head, he could almost touch the overhead beams in his workshop as he loosened muscles cramped from a long day's labor. He brushed a shock of sandy hair from his gray eyes, then began to clean up his workbench for the night. He'd come to look forward to the evening ritual of cleaning and organizing, reverently returning each tool to its proper place. Some nights, though, his tools seemed to shift under his fingers into the service rifle he'd once cleaned nightly.

Unlike the average Amish man, John had gone to college, and after college, he went into the army, winding up in Afghanistan.

Although it had been almost three years since he left active duty, sometimes even now, in the quiet of the night, he could hear the thump of distant artillery, the rattle of machine-gun fire, and the screams of the wounded.

John knew about PTSD. They had been briefed about it when they came back to the States. He hadn't paid that much attention to it, thinking that because he was sound of mind and strong of body, he would not be affected by it. But nothing in his youth had ever prepared him for anything like what he went through during his two combat tours.

No one in the Amish community had shared similar experiences, and John felt he had no one he could talk to. How could he tell anyone that he had seen men blown apart right beside him? How could he tell someone that he had, himself, killed?

There might be some among the English who would understand, but none of them knew his history—because he didn't want to talk about it. All he wanted to do was forget about it. To anyone in town who came into contact with him, John Miller was just another Amish man in plain clothes.

He was gradually coming out of it; he had these episodes with decreasing frequency now. Working with the wood, seeing beautiful things emerge from his efforts, was therapeutic. And at this precise moment, as he held what was going to be one of the sides of the cabinet, he felt nothing but satisfaction with a job well done. There was peace in his soul.

"John," Glen Collins called back to him. "I just got off the telephone with Mrs. Crabtree. She loves the table so much she's going to have us make her a hutch as well. You did a great job, my boy. An absolutely great job."

"Thank you, Mr. Collins."

"What are you still doing here, anyway? You need to get on home before it gets dark. I'll close down here."

"I stayed a little longer so I could finish this piece." John rubbed his fingers along the smooth board once more. He loved the tactile sensation, like tracing his fingers over silk. He took great pride in his workmanship, though he knew that such pride was strictly forbidden by the Ordnung, the rules that governed the lives of the Amish. But it seemed to him only a small sin, really. Turning from the finished cabinet, John headed out into the night.

CHAPTER THREE

Keith Blanton had several pages laid out on the desk in front of him. The pages came from the forty-page file that Leah had printed from Carl Trevathan's computer, and though they were labeled "Harrison," they had nothing to do with anyone named Harrison. They were detailed, and they were damning.

> Information for Agent Robert Coker
>
> May 17—Learned today that our client, MP, has been falsifying documents to hide a one-hundred-million-dollar loss. I approached K and J to point this out, only to learn that our firm not only knew about this but is complicit in it. Following is a report on the specific losses and how they have been covered.

What followed were fifteen pages of very detailed accounting, showing how losses were being covered by subsequent investments.

I have seriously underestimated the amount of money involved
in Martin Pigg's scheme. It is nearly one billion dollars, fifty million
of which has been channeled through Blanton, Trevathan and Dunn.
God help us; we could all wind up spending the rest of our lives in
prison.

Blanton picked up the phone and speed-dialed Dunn.

"Yes?"

"Better get in here, Jim. Looks like we just dodged a bullet."

When Dunn stepped into Blanton's office a moment later, Blanton signaled to him to close the door. "I think you should take a look at the Harrison file."

"The Harrison file? What is that? Who is Harrison?"

"You might as well call it the Martin Pigg file. This is the document Leah was taking to Carl Trevathan. He was selling us out. Here, you don't have to read the whole thing, just this couple of pages."

Dunn skimmed through the pages quickly, then whistled. "How did you get these?"

"Leah gave them to me."

"Has anyone else seen them?"

Using his hand as a comb, Blanton arranged his few hairs across his head. "I don't think so. In fact, I'm sure no one else has seen them, because this is what she was delivering to him on the day he was killed. That means he didn't get to show them to anyone, and the way things happened, I'm sure that Leah didn't get a chance.

Also, I've checked Trevathan's computer—there's no trace of a Harrison file there."

"What are we going to do with them?"

"Burn them."

One week later, Leah was watching the local morning news on television as she ate her breakfast.

"A perusal of the security cameras have been futile, and the police still have no leads in the brutal slaying of Carl Trevathan. Trevathan, a well-known St. Louis attorney from the firm of Blanton, Trevathan and Dunn, was gunned down last week while he was visiting the Thomas Eagleton federal court building. Keith Blanton, of the firm, gave this statement."

The image of the senior partner came on-screen as he addressed the reporter. *"Carl Trevathan was a brilliant attorney and one of the finest men I have ever known. My heart goes out to his family at this time. I have no idea why anyone would want to shoot him, but our firm stands ready to help the police in any way we can."*

On-screen, the picture returned to the studio anchor, who moved on to the traffic report. Picking up her remote, Leah turned the TV off, then grabbed her keys and went downstairs to her car. In the week since Carl Trevathan had been killed, Leah had not left her apartment except to attend the funeral. She thought staying home for a while would help her get over it but discovered that being alone just made it worse. This would be her first day back to work since it had happened, and she hoped that getting back in the routine would help her cope with the horror she had witnessed.

* * *

She parked in her assigned space and automatically glanced over to see if Mr. Trevathan was there yet. She had to remind herself that the slot would remain empty until it was reassigned.

"Welcome back, Miss McKenzie," Mike greeted her. "How are you?"

"I'm all right, thanks, Mike."

"That was a terrible thing with Mr. Trevathan. He was one fine man, I tell you."

"Yes, he was."

When Leah went into the office, she was greeted by the other lawyers, the legal aides, and Keith Blanton and Jim Dunn.

"How are you doing?" Blanton asked solicitously.

"I'll be all right," Leah said. "It was just such a shock, not only that Mr. Trevathan is dead but that I saw it happen. I don't know that I will ever get over that."

"You will," Blanton said. "The mind is a very resilient thing."

"I hope so."

"Oh, uh, Miss McKenzie, would you—that is, if you are up to it—would you clean out Carl's desk today? You can make the decision as to what needs to stay here with the firm and what should go to Mrs. Trevathan."

It took Leah more than an hour to go through Trevathan's desk and credenza, separating personal items from the office material. She found this more difficult than the funeral had been, because everything reminded her of him. She held the Bob Gibson baseball, then another baseball that was covered with names.

"My high school baseball team," Carl had told her the first time she saw that ball. "We were Missouri state champions that year, and I went four for four in the final game."

With all his personal belongings out of the way, Leah started on the work-related items. This, she believed, would not be quite as hard to do. Sliding open the top drawer, she gasped.

Holy crap! A gun? There was a pistol lying on top of a file folder. What was it doing there? She was pretty sure she had never seen this before. No, she was positive she had never seen it before. *Why would Mr. Trevathan have a gun? Did Mr. Trevathan suspect someone was after him?*

So, what to do with it? Should it go with his personal items or with his office material? Finally, she decided that seeing a gun would just make it worse for his family, so she put it in the office pile.

When everything was done she stacked all the office items on a service cart, then pushed it through the labyrinthine hall to Blanton's office. Linda Martin, Blanton's personal secretary, smiled at her.

"How are you doing, kiddo?" she asked.

"It was . . . hard," Leah said. She blinked a couple of times as tears welled in her eyes. "Having to handle all those things that were so important to him and know that he—he won't ever . . ."

"I know," Linda said. She took a tissue from a box on her desk and handed it to Leah just as Blanton came out of his office.

"That's Carl's stuff?" Blanton asked, indicating the material on the cart.

"Yes, sir."

"Bring them in. Linda, you wanted to pick up your daughter after school? You can go now."

Leah pushed the cart into Blanton's office. "I've got all of his personal things packed in boxes in his office," Leah said.

"Good, good, I'll have Mike take them to Mrs. Trevathan."

"And this," Leah said, reaching for the gun. "I found it in his desk. It's funny, I never saw it before."

"Yes, I think he only bought it recently." Blanton got a small box and held it out. "Put the gun in here."

Leah put the gun in the box, then Blanton closed the lid.

"I know today was hard on you," Blanton said as he opened a desk drawer and put the box containing the pistol away. "If you want to, you can take the rest of the day off."

"No, I'm having a harder time at home than I am here. Besides, I have a few things to take care of in my own office."

"All right," Blanton said. "Do whatever you feel you have to do until you're over this."

Leah went back to her office, where she sat for several minutes, cleaning up her e-mail in-box. Then, on a whim, and because she knew the password to get into Trevathan's computer, she decided to check his e-mail. One stood out.

To: Carl.Trevathan@BTD.com
From: Lowball@Murvau.com

Ad astra per alia porci

That's odd, Leah thought. *That's what Mr. Trevathan said just before he died.* Leah had not told the police about the odd comment, nor had she mentioned it to Blanton or Dunn. Maybe Blanton would know what it meant.

Leah hurried back down to Blanton's office. Linda was already gone, but the door to Blanton's office was slightly ajar. As she drew near, she could hear Blanton and Dunn talking.

"If Carl had gone along with us, this wouldn't have had to happen," Blanton said. "I hated to have it done, but there were millions, literally millions of dollars involved."

"Who knew that old Carl had such an honest streak? I mean, if he was such a straight shooter, why did he become a lawyer in the first place?" Dunn laughed.

"Yes, well, the deed is done, and now we need a designated fall guy or this thing is going to explode in our face," Blanton said.

"Who do you have in mind?"

"The obvious. Leah McKenzie. She was his protégée; we'll claim she was sleeping with him, and when she learned he wasn't going to get a divorce, she killed him."

"But there was no gun in the elevator."

"Ah, that's the beauty of it," Blanton said. "I have the gun that killed Carl. I put it back in Carl's desk for McKenzie to find, and this afternoon when she cleaned his office, she brought the gun to me. I had a box all ready for it." He laughed. "I had wiped it clean before putting it in Carl's desk, so now it has her fingerprints—and *only* her fingerprints—all over it."

"Good move!" Dunn said. "You think of everything."

"I've already called the police; they should be here any moment now. Of course, we will offer to defend her in court."

"Of course," Dunn added with an evil chuckle. "Where is she now?"

"She's back in her office. As soon as the police arrive I'll convince her, as her attorney, that she would be better served to surrender."

"Missouri does have the death penalty for murder," Dunn pointed out.

"Oh, I'm sure we can avoid the death penalty for her. After all, it's like I told Leah—we're family here. Just one big happy family," Blanton said.

It was all Leah could do to keep from crying out. Blinded by tears of betrayal and fear, she ran quickly back to her office to grab her purse. She had other personal things there that she wanted— her diploma; a photograph of her mother and father; the collar of her dog, Suzi, whom she'd had to put down six months ago. She wanted those things but was afraid to stay in her office long enough to gather them.

When she stepped back out of her office, she heard Blanton's voice, and another voice that she didn't recognize.

"She's back here in her office, detective," Blanton said. "She's not expecting you, but I don't think she'll give you any trouble."

"You were right to call us, Mr. Blanton."

"Yes, well, you can imagine how shocked I was when I found out. And I intend to act as her counsel. You might call it an affair of the heart. She's a young and impressionable woman who couldn't deal with a broken heart. I'm sure it was a spur-of-the-moment thing."

Blanton and the police officer were coming down the hall; they were just around the corner. She ran to the rear staircase and hurried down three floors. She saw a police car parked in front of the office, its red and blue lights flashing. Another policeman leaned against the side of the car with his arms crossed over his chest, looking toward the front door, away from her. The car window was down, so she could hear the radio. There was a pop when the static was broken.

"Unit six, what is your ten-twenty?"

"Lindell and Grand."

"We have a ten-fifty at Page and Grand. Can you cover?"

"Unit six, ten-four."

There were at least ten or twelve people standing around in front of the office, gawking. Using a parked van to shield her, Leah managed to get into her car. But how was she going to be able to drive out of the parking lot without arousing anyone's suspicion? She was driving a red Mustang convertible, which was about as subtle as a flashing neon light.

A Federal Express truck drove up, and when the driver went in to make his delivery, Leah managed to move her car, keeping the FedEx truck between her and the policeman out front. When the FedEx driver pulled way, she matched his speed until they reached the exit. Then she flashed her prettiest smile at the driver; he smiled back and made a motion with his hand telling her to go first. Even if the policeman out front had been looking in her direction, he would not have seen her.

Her first impulse was to drive away as far as she could, as fast as she could, but she knew she would need money. And it would have to be cash—she wouldn't be able to use an ATM or a credit card, and even if she could have used a check, no one wrote checks anymore, anyway. She drove directly to the bank to empty her checking and savings accounts, hastily filling out a withdrawal for a total of eleven thousand dollars. She pushed the two documents across the counter to the teller.

"My, this is quite a large sum. Are you closing your account, Miss McKenzie? Are you dissatisfied with us?" the teller asked.

"No, I'm going to leave six hundred dollars in the account, but I'm going to buy a car from a friend who's leaving town, and he won't be able to cash a check right away."

"Good, I'm glad to see that we aren't losing you. Are hundreds okay?"

"Hundreds are fine."

A few minutes later, and with eleven thousand dollars in cash in her purse, Leah was back in her car. She drove to her father's house, but when she saw a police car out front, she kept going, wandering around the city for a while, trying to decide what she should do next. Then, realizing that the police probably had a description of her car, she decided it wasn't safe to stay in St. Louis much longer.

But where to go?

Then Leah got an idea. She began driving southwest on I-44, and just before she reached Eureka, she called the office. Millie Thompson answered the phone when it rang. "Blanton, Trevathan and Dunn."

"Millie, I want to talk to Mr. Blanton."

"Miss McKenzie!" Millie said. "Where are you? Everyone is looking for you."

"Please, Millie, just put me through to Mr. Blanton."

Detective Sergeant Gary Hellman was in Blanton's office when Blanton received the telephone call from Leah.

"Leah, honey, where are you?" Blanton asked. He held up his finger as a signal to Hellman, and the detective called the station to locate the phone.

"Why are you trying to pin this on me?" Leah asked.

"Leah, I don't know what you're talking about. What do you mean pin it on you? Why don't you come in? Come to the office and we'll go to the police together. Believe me, it will go much better for you, and it will make it much easier for me to defend you."

"After what you did, I have no intention of using you."

"After what I did? Whatever are you talking about?"

"You know what I'm talking about. I overheard you and Dunn plotting to make me the 'designated fall guy' for the shooting."

Blanton laughed. "You just heard snatches of the conversation. That wasn't what I meant at all. I said that the *police* were looking for a designated fall guy, and since you were the last person to see Carl alive, it would probably be you. And, of course, that is how it's turned out, isn't it? It was a joke, a poor joke under the circumstances, I admit. But it was a joke. Leah, I told you, you are a part of our family. Please, come on in now and let us see what we can do to help you. The longer you run, the more difficult it's going to be to construct your defense."

"I don't need a defense for something I didn't do."

"Leah, even the innocent need defending in court. Especially the innocent. Please, trust me. Trust us. We want to . . . Leah? Leah? Are you there?" Blanton looked up at Detective Hellman. "I think she hung up on me."

Hellman was on the phone, and he smiled, then hung it up. "No problem, we have her located. She was calling from I-44, near Eureka."

"Ha!" Blanton said, snapping his fingers. "I bet I know where she's going! Trevathan told me her father has a cabin at Lake of the Ozarks."

"Do you know where on the lake?"

"Not too far from Camdenton."

"We'll get the sheriff on it."

"Detective, I think I should warn you," Blanton said. "Jason McKenzie is an avid deer hunter, and he keeps a rifle in his cabin. Leah is a hunter as well, and an excellent shot. If I were you, I would tell the sheriff to approach her with extreme caution."

"Thanks, I will."

Hellman started to leave and Blanton walked to the elevator with him. "This is a terrible thing," he said. "Carl was like a brother, and when I found out he was, uh"—Blanton looked around to make certain none of the employees were close enough to hear him before he continued—"fooling around with Leah, I tried to warn him. I told him, he had a family, he had no business doing anything like that. Oh!" he suddenly said, putting his hand to his forehead.

"What is it?" Hellman asked.

"I'm to blame for this, aren't I? I mean, I told Carl to break it off and when he did, Leah probably couldn't handle it, and she—" He ended in midsentence. "But of course, I will be defending her in court, so I've already said too much. But I must confess that the thought that I might be, somehow, responsible for this is almost more than I can take."

"You did what any concerned friend would do, Mr. Blanton. You can't be responsible for how an unstable person may act."

"That's just it. There has been absolutely nothing in Leah's past to suggest that she would react like this. I do hope you can bring her in before she does anything foolish, like take a shot at the sheriff's deputies who'll be apprehending her. I'd hate to be responsible for yet another life, be it that of one of the deputies or Leah herself."

"I'm sure they've handled situations like this before," Hellman said. "I wouldn't worry about it now."

"I can't help but worry. This is like some terrible family squabble gone mad. So tragic, so tragic."

The elevator doors opened and with a final nod, Hellman stepped in, then pushed the button for the first floor.

A check of county property records enabled the sheriff's department to locate the cabin belonging to Jason McKenzie. Once they found it, the sheriff and three cars of his deputies arrived on the scene to make the arrest.

The cars stopped about fifty yards from the cabin. There was no red Mustang convertible visible, but of course anyone on the run would hide their car, so that didn't deter them. As the six deputies approached the house with weapons drawn, one of them suddenly pointed toward the structure.

"Sheriff! There's a rifle barrel sticking out the window!" he shouted.

Without warning, a shot was fired, and the sheriff and his

deputies quickly scattered, then began firing at the cabin. They fired for several seconds and the forest rang with the sound of repeated gunfire until, finally, the sheriff called for them to stop.

"Hold your fire, hold your fire!" he shouted.

The shooting stopped, though the echoes rolled back from the hills and across the lake for a few seconds more.

The cabin had been decimated by the gunfire. The windows had been shot out, a rainspout had fallen, and there were bullet holes in the door and the front wall.

"I don't believe that's a rifle. Who fired that shot?" the sheriff asked.

"I guess I did, sheriff."

"Jasper, do you want to tell me just what the hell you were shooting at?" the sheriff asked.

"Well, I mean I thought I—uh—thought that was a rifle."

The sheriff returned to his car and retrieved a bullhorn.

"Leah McKenzie, if you are in there and uninjured, come out with your hands up." *Hands up, hands up*, the echo rolled back.

"If she's in there, sheriff, you can bet she's wounded, or more 'n likely dead," Jasper added helpfully.

"I'm going in; keep me covered. And, Jasper, do your best not to shoot me, okay?"

There was a scattering of nervous laughter as the deputies held their guns at the ready. The sheriff, his own pistol returned to its holster, started toward the cabin with his hands held out to show that he was unarmed. After cutting the distance by half he stopped, lowered his hands, then laughed out loud.

"What is it, sheriff?"

"The rifle we saw? It's just a piece of pipe. I doubt there's anyone in here at all." The sheriff walked up to the front door. Although riddled with bullets, it was still locked. He kicked it open and stepped inside. He let out a low whistle as he surveyed the damage. Lamps were shattered and the TV had a dozen bullet holes in it, as did the sofa and chairs. There was nobody there, and it looked as if nobody had been there for months.

CHAPTER FOUR

There was nobody there," Hellman said.

"Maybe she was there and she got away when she saw them coming," Blanton suggested.

"I doubt it. They had all the approaches covered, including the lake. If she had been there, they would have found her."

"I would have sworn that was where she was going."

"I'm going to have to have the computers, external hard drives, thumb drives, and computer disks for Miss McKenzie and Carl Trevathan."

"Why would you need all that? It's obvious she killed him out of jealousy," Blanton said.

"Mr. Blanton, you're a lawyer. You know that nothing is ever the way it appears at first glance. I don't intend to leave any bases uncovered, so I'm going to need those computers. They are germane to this investigation."

"I'm sorry, detective, but you can't take them; you can't even look at them. There are confidential files on those computers. It's a matter of attorney-client privilege, and that privilege is backed up by a ruling of the Supreme Court."

"As I said, they are germane to a murder investigation. If you won't give them to me willingly, I'll get a warrant."

"That will do you no good."

"I will be back, with a warrant," Hellman said. "I expect those computers to be here."

After Hellman left, Blanton and Dunn held a quick conference.

"We need to know what's on those computers, and we need to delete anything incriminating," Blanton said.

"Deleting won't do it," Dunn said. "We'll just have to fight it in court. They can't access the files without violating attorney-client privilege. The court will support us on that."

"I'm not so sure," Blanton said.

"What do you mean? The precedent is well established. Let me show you." Dunn got a book down from the shelf, opened it, looked at it for a moment, then smiled.

"This is perfect," he said. "This finding fits us perfectly." He began to read. "*Swidler and Berlin v. United States,* 524 U.S. 399 dash 1998, a case in which the Supreme Court of the United States held that"—he looked up at Blanton and raised his finger—"and listen to this part—held that 'the death of an attorney, or the client, does not terminate the attorney-client privilege with respect to records of confidential communications between the attorney and the client, even though these records may have been subpoenaed.'

"We're solid on this, Keith; they ruled that the privilege is *in esse* postmortem. Trevathan's right of privacy still exists."

"Let me see that book," Blanton said.

Dunn handed it over to him.

"Yes, but listen to this. 'There are a number of exceptions to the privilege in most jurisdictions, chief among them being if the communication was made for the purpose of committing a crime.'"

"Martin Pigg," Dunn said.

"Martin Pigg," Blanton repeated.

Blanton snapped the book closed. "If the feds are able to make a case against us, they'll have every right to access not only Carl Trevathan's files, but ours as well."

"That leaves them in a catch-22, doesn't it? They need to find us guilty of a criminal conspiracy in order to access our computers, and they need to access our computers in order to find us guilty of a conspiracy," Dunn said.

"We need to get into Carl's computer and delete any incriminating files."

"That won't do any good. If the police get permission to go into the computer, they have computer geeks who can access files that have been deleted, almost as easily as if they were still active."

"Wait a minute, if a geek can access the files, can't a geek totally erase them?"

Dunn smiled. "Yeah, he can."

"All right, so we hire our own geek. He'll not only permanently erase Carl's files, we'll have him hack into Leah's computer. Maybe it will give us an idea as to where she might be."

The computer geek they eventually found looked like a teenager and dressed like a homeless person, but within hours he'd completely erased all the files on Carl's hard drive, then accessed every file, every e-mail, and every posting on Twitter, Facebook, and LinkedIn on Leah's computer before turning it over to Blanton, who paid him five thousand dollars to keep this particular job a secret. Blanton read all the postings, hoping he might get an idea from them about where to look for her, but most were innocuous, friendly exchanges.

"This was the last e-mail she got from Trevathan," Blanton said, giving a printed copy to Dunn. He chuckled. "This one wasn't hard to get. She deleted it, but not permanently." While Dunn read, Blanton continued to flip through Leah's old e-mails.

To: Leah.McKenzie@BTD.com
From: GK@Nstar.com
Touching Base

Hi, Leah, visited the Wash U campus yesterday with my nephew.
Brought back a lot of memories. Do you remember the party
at the TKE house when the police came? I was scared to death
Daddy was going to find out. But all they did is tell us to tone it
down a bit.
Gail

To: Leah.McKenzie@BTD.com
From: Martha.Gooding@VCU.edu
Frannie's trip

Took little Frannie up in the Arch for the first time. I thought she
might be frightened up in the top, but she wasn't. You know

what scared her? Those little egg-shaped elevators, the way they
jerk and tilt going up. The claustrophobia of being in those things
bothered her too, but I can't blame her. I don't like that part
either.

Martha

To: Leah.McKenzie@BTD.com
From: Doghome@dogrescue.com
Looking for a dog?

I know you are still grieving over Suzi, but when you get ready
to have another dog, come see us. We have several rescue
dogs looking for someone to love them like you loved Suzi.

"You've found nothing to give a hint as to where she might be?"
Dunn asked Blanton.

"No. I checked her e-mail and her social accounts but found
nothing helpful."

"Listen, as long as there's a possibility that the police are going
to have access to her computer, I have an idea," Dunn said.

"What?"

"Since we've managed to hack into it, why don't we plant some
incriminating evidence? You know, maybe an e-mail, or a post or
something about how angry she is with Carl for not getting a divorce?"

Blanton shook his head. "Do you think I haven't already thought
of that? Unfortunately, it won't work. The computer keeps an accu-
rate date for everything you put in it. If we put something in after
she disappeared, it would be obvious."

"Can't our geek fix that?"

"I asked him about it, without telling him what I wanted, and he said that even if we faked it, someone like him could find out that it was faked."

"Well, there goes that idea," Dunn said.

"Where in the world did she go?"

"That's not the only question. The other question is, how did she know to leave? Mike didn't see her exit the building, but when the police got here, she was gone."

"When she called, she mentioned the 'designated fall guy' comment. She overheard us."

"Yes, I can see how that might get her a little suspicious. The police checked her bank," Dunn said. "She took out eleven thousand dollars in cash just before she left."

"She had it all planned out, that's for sure. I wouldn't be surprised if she called from I-44 on purpose, just to lead us astray. She wasn't at her old man's cabin, and her phone hasn't been turned on since then."

"Well, she can't disappear forever," Dunn said. "She's got to come up sometime."

"Really? What about D. B. Cooper? Heard from him lately, have you?"

"Yeah, I see what you mean. Maybe she crossed the river over to Illinois."

"Or Kansas, or Iowa, Oklahoma, Arkansas, Tennessee, or Kentucky," Blanton said disgustedly. "Or New York, for that matter. There's only one thing to do."

"What's that?"

"We need to hire a private detective to find her."

"What makes you think a private detective can find her if the police can't?"

"If she isn't in the St. Louis metro area, the St. Louis police have no jurisdiction. The murder happened in a federal courthouse, so the FBI can get involved—but to them she would just be one more case in thousands. We need someone who is one hundred percent dedicated to finding Leah McKenzie—and who won't ask too many questions if she meets with an unfortunate accident."

"Do you have someone in mind?"

"Yeah. Frank Stone. He's a combination bloodhound and bull-dog. He'll get on her trail, and he'll stay on it until he finds her."

"Frank Stone? Isn't he the one who had his license suspended for a year for being too rough on his subjects?"

"Yeah, he is."

"Well?"

"Well what? Is there a downside to that?" Blanton asked with a malevolent smile.

"I see what you mean. All right, let's get hold of Stone."

"I thought you might agree. I haven't hired him yet—I wanted to talk to you first—but I did give him a call telling him of our interest in his . . . services."

Leah had turned her phone off immediately after making the call. She knew that cell phones could be tracked, and she knew, also, that Blanton was aware of her father's hunting cabin on the lake. With luck, Blanton would tell the police about it and lead them there, which would give her a chance to put her idea into play.

She had a grandmother in Arthur, Illinois, a grandmother she had never seen. Leah's mother had been born and raised in Arthur, among the Amish there. But Sarah McKenzie, née Lapp, had been shunned when, at the age of eighteen, she left the Amish to marry Leah's father, Jason. Leah knew little about Miriam Lapp, only what she'd pieced together from occasional conversations over the years—her mother rarely spoke of her and had passed away two years ago without ever reestablishing a relationship with her Amish family. The question was, even if Miriam Lapp was still alive, would she have anything to do with Leah?

Leah turned left off I-44 and followed Route 109 to Route W, which took her over to I-55.

While the police would be concentrating all their effort on locating her at the hunting cabin, she would be going in the opposite direction. She put Arthur, Illinois, into her GPS.

Leah had no idea what her grandmother's address was, or if she was even still alive—but even that, she reasoned, could work in her favor. Since she had never met her grandmother, that would be the least likely place for the police to start looking for her.

The police *are* looking for *me*. Just thinking the words made her shudder with fear. How had it come to this? Fugitives on the run were the stuff of movies and television dramas or mystery novels, nothing that had ever touched her life. Even her experience as a lawyer was with corporate law, not criminal.

Maybe she should turn herself in. Maybe if she could just talk to someone, she could tell them that . . . that what? That the murder weapon with her fingerprints on it had been planted by Keith Blanton, one of the most famous and respected lawyers in the country?

Leah was well aware of the concept of fight or flight. She wanted to fight, but for the moment, flight seemed like the wisest option.

As she was crossing the bridge into Illinois, she rolled the window down, then tossed her phone into the Mississippi. Coming off the bridge into a new state, she felt a little safer. She knew the feeling was illusory, but at this point she would take what she could get. She turned on the radio.

"St. Louis metro police are looking tonight for Leah McKenzie, a lawyer with the firm of Blanton, Trevathan and Dunn. She has been named as a person of interest in the murder of Carl Trevathan, and police are asking all citizens to be on the lookout for her. She is believed to be driving south on I-44 in a 2010 red Mustang convertible, with a Missouri vanity plate that says Le Gal. That's L-E space G-A-L. If you spot this vehicle, do not approach, as police believe the suspect may be armed and dangerous. Instead, contact the police at once."

Oh! Leah thought. *My* license plates! She had just gotten them a month earlier, and her friends had laughed at her play on words. But now she felt as if those too-cute license plates were a homing beacon just calling out to the cops.

The good thing was that the police thought she was on I-44, which meant that her ruse had worked. She could only hope that not everyone on I-55 was listening to KMOX. Also, it was getting darker, and cloudy, and that had to help as well.

She punched her radio mode from AM to satellite and let Dvorak's Symphony Number 9, *From the New World,* help her keep her composure.

"John, I hate for you to stay late, especially tonight," Mr. Collins said. "Looks to me like it's going to rain, and I'd hate for you to have to drive your buggy home at night and in weather like this."

"I can close it up, and driving a buggy on rain-slick roads is safer than driving a car," John said. "Besides, what if I do get wet? I'm not made of sugar."

Collins laughed. "There may be a lot of things in your makeup, John Miller, but I'm dead sure that sugar isn't one of them. Jalapeño peppers, maybe, but not sugar."

"I'll make sure everything is secure before I leave," John said. "But I promised this cabinet would be done tomorrow, and I intend to keep that promise."

"You're a good man, John. Just be careful going home tonight."

Collins left, and John returned to work on the cabinet. He didn't have that much left to do, but he wanted it finished before they opened for business the next morning. He put the knobs to the doors in the center of each outer panel, then used wood putty to fill in all the visible screw holes. After that he used sandpaper to smooth the surface of the cabinet, then applied lacquer. He turned on the drying lamps, set the timer to turn them off at midnight, and made certain that everything else in the shop was ready to close. He let himself out through the back door, locked it, then hurried through the rain into the barn, where he connected his horse, Prodigal, to the buggy. Climbing into the seat, he clucked at the horse and snapped the reins.

"*Kommen, lass uns nach Hause eilen,* Prodigal. It'll be a nice dry barn for us when we get there."

John activated the battery-operated caution lights on the back of his buggy, then turned onto the narrow blacktop road that led out to his farm. He had gone about a mile when he saw car head-lights coming up fast behind him.

Leah had never seen a road quite this dark. There were no lights anywhere, and because it was raining, there was not even the ameliorating effect of a moon or stars. She hadn't seen another car since turning onto this road off Route 133. Then, dimly, through the rain and the dark, she saw something flashing rhythmically in front of her. A beacon of some sort? Then as she drew nearer—it was a buggy!

Leah slammed on her brakes and jerked the wheel to one side.

Hearing the squeal of tires as the car tried to stop, John looked back and saw the Mustang fishtailing before leaving the road and heading down into the ditch.

"Whoa, Prodigal, whoa!"

John set the brake and tied the reins onto the crossbar, then ran to the car. It was nose-down in the ditch with its air bag deployed. The driver was a woman, and she was out cold. He didn't see any blood, and a quick examination didn't suggest that there were any bones broken.

He looked in the car for a cell phone to call 911—but he could find nothing.

"You don't have a cell phone? What kind of *Englischer* are you with no cell phone?" he muttered, more to himself than the unconscious girl before him.

He was getting soaked by the rain, and because he had the door open, so was she. He couldn't very well leave her there in her broken car. And with no other way to call for help, John was, at least for now, her only hope. He picked her up and carried her to his buggy, then laid her down in the back. He formed a quick prayer that in moving her he had done no further injury. But at least now he knew what he would do.

He would take her to his *mamm*.

CHAPTER FIVE

L eah heard a cock crow. That was strange. What was a rooster doing in downtown St. Louis? When she opened her eyes, the sun was streaming in through a large window. She was aware of an earthy smell coming in through the window. The odor was vaguely familiar, though she couldn't quite place it. Then the cock crowed again and she knew what it was. It was a barnyard.

A barnyard? What was she doing here? Where *was* here? Where was her car? And how did she wind up in this nightgown?

She looked around the room, which contained only the double bed she was lying in, a chest of drawers, and a table on which sat a porcelain vase and washbasin. The wide-plank wood floor was bare except for a small woven rug. The large window, which was sparkling clean, had a green shade drawn halfway.

Was she dreaming?

Leah managed to swing her legs over the edge of the bed. She tried to stand but got very dizzy and had to sit back down again. From this position she could look through the window, and she saw a barn, a windmill, and two men connecting a couple of horses to some sort of wheeled farming implement. The men wore dark blue pants, light blue shirts, and straw hats. One had a beard and one didn't.

Just then a smiling woman who appeared to be in her midsixties, wearing an ankle-length gray dress and a white cap, came into the room, carrying a tray.

"*Guten morgen,* miss. *Frühstück für sie?*"

"I beg your pardon?"

"Would you like breakfast?"

"I—who are you? Where am I? How did I get here?"

"I am Mrs. Miller. You were in an accident last night. My son John brought you here."

All at once the disjointed and jangled memories of the night before flooded back. She recalled a man—big and strong, because he had physically pulled her from her car and carried her through the rain to get into a horse-drawn buggy.

"Why didn't he take me to the hospital?" Leah asked.

"He said you are not so badly hurt that you need the hospital, and it is thirty miles. Too far to go in a buggy. So he brought you here for me to care for."

"I—thank you. Where is here?"

"Here is the Miller farm. I think you should eat now."

One plate couldn't hold all the food Mrs. Miller had brought, so there were three plates on the tray. There were scrambled eggs, bacon, home-baked bread, fried potatoes, sliced fresh peaches with sugar and cream, coffee, milk, and apple cider.

"If you are still hungry after your breakfast, there is more in the kitchen," Mrs. Miller said as she set the tray down.

Still hungry? Leah thought. If she ate all this, she wouldn't be hungry for a week.

Leah ate as much as she could, but when a young woman came for the tray a short while later, it looked as if there was as much food on the tray as there had been when it was delivered.

"You did not like?"

"Oh, no, don't think that," Leah said. "It was delicious. But evidently, it was meant for an entire family."

The young woman laughed. "John said that the *Englische* don't have good appetites."

"John? The one who brought me here?"

"*Ja.* John is my brother. He knows the *Englische.*"

Leah knew that "English" meant any outsider, someone like her. Her mother had never been too vocal about her Amish background, but from time to time she had talked a little. Leah was fascinated by her mother's unusual, even exotic, background, so she had paid close attention to the little she had been told.

"What is your name?" the young woman asked.

"My name is Leah McKenzie."

Almost as soon as she gave her name, Leah had reservations. Because the police were after her, her name would be recognized. But her mother had told her that very little knowledge of the outside world got into the Amish community. So many cultural elements that Leah had taken for granted as a child—Jay Leno, *Sesame Street,* MTV—had been completely foreign to her mom.

"What's your name?" Leah asked.

"My name is Ada Miller."

"Well, Ada, I am very thankful to you and your mother for your hospitality. But I don't want to be a burden."

"You are welcome to stay for as long as you need."

Leah began looking around the room. "Are my clothes here?"

"They are being washed."

"Oh! My purse? Do you see my purse anywhere?"

"A purse? You mean a pocketbook?"

"Yes. I had one with me. Have you seen it?"

"No."

"It must be in the car. I—the car? Where is my car?"

Ada smiled. "I can tell you where that is. Sam and Jacob brought it in, and it is in our barn."

"How badly damaged is it?"

"I don't know. John said he thinks it is maybe not very bad."

"My purse must be in the car. I'll go look . . ." Leah got up but again was swept by a wave of dizziness. She fell back onto the bed.

"I will go look in the car for you," Ada offered.

"Thank you."

There was a small, round mirror over the washbasin. Leah managed to get out of bed and, moving very slowly, walked over to the mirror to examine herself. There was a bruise on her forehead, no doubt the cause of her dizziness. She also discovered a bruise on her left thigh and a cut on her right arm. Why didn't she have a clearer memory of what happened last night? Had she been knocked out?

She was a little sore but realized that the man who'd rescued her was right in his assessment of her injuries. They weren't severe enough to require hospitalization, and now that she thought about it, she was very glad. A hospital was the last place someone should go if they were trying to stay out of sight.

About half an hour later, Ada came back into the bedroom.

"Did you find it?" Leah asked anxiously.

"No, I found nothing, Leah. I'm sorry."

"Thank you for looking."

What was she going to do now? She needed that cash if she was going to survive. She had a money market account with her broker, and she had credit cards, but she couldn't access either without giving away her location. For all intents and purposes, without her purse, she was flat broke.

Leah did not leave the bedroom for the rest of the morning but had another meal delivered to her.

"The man who brought me here . . ."

"That was John, my brother."

"When will I see him?"

"Maybe tonight."

"Good, I want to thank him." Though she didn't say it, she also wanted to question him about her purse. Eleven thousand dollars was a lot of money.

"I'm back, Mr. Blanton, and I have a warrant. I'll be searching the offices of both Carl Trevathan and Leah McKenzie," said Detective Hellman as he arrived at Blanton's office.

"I thought you already did that."

"I was just looking in general then. This time I intend to be more specific."

Blanton and Dunn looked at each other. Dunn nodded, and Blanton spoke.

"Sure, go ahead, search all you want."

Half an hour later, every piece of paper in Leah's office had been scrutinized, and not one sent up any red flags.

"My warrant also allows access to the computers, towers, thumb drives, external hard drives, and all means of electronic data storage."

"I thought it might, so I won't try to keep you from taking the equipment," Blanton said. "But please understand, Detective Hellman, that we have filed in both state and federal court to prevent you from accessing any of the data. And there has been an injunction issued to prevent that. Besides which, we have already examined the data."

"Who gave you permission to do that? You knew that the status of the computers was in question. You could very well have compromised critical evidence."

"Detective Hellman, you need to remember something. Leah McKenzie was a lawyer with our firm. If we are to continue to serve our clients, we needed to know the status of some of the cases she was handling."

"What about Trevathan's computer?"

"Same thing; we needed to know what he was working on. But when we tried to access his computer, we got an unpleasant surprise."

"What sort of unpleasant surprise? I don't like any surprises, much less unpleasant ones."

"His computer had been wiped clean. There's nothing on it," Dunn said.

"We think Leah may have erased everything before she left, to make certain there were no compromising e-mails from her to him," Blanton added.

"That's no problem," Hellman said. "I'll take the tower back to headquarters and see what our people can do with it."

"I hope you can find something on it. I'm going to be her defense counsel, and she isn't here for me to question, so whatever you find useful for you will be equally as useful for me. Just make certain you share everything with us."

CHAPTER SIX

It was after dinner, or "supper" as Ada called it, and already dark outside when there was a knock on the door to Leah's room and Mrs. Miller entered. She was carrying a dress that looked very much like the dresses she and Ada were wearing.

"John is here and would like to meet you," Mrs. Miller said. "But first, I think, this dress you should wear."

"Oh, Mrs. Miller, I don't want to put anyone out." But even as she spoke the words, she knew that she had no clothes of her own, except for what she had been wearing yesterday. She'd left town so quickly that she didn't have time to go back to her apartment to pack.

"You have no more clothes, so I think it is only hospitable to offer you something to wear. And all we have are plain clothes. I know it is not what you wear when with the *Englische*."

If she was going to stay there, hide there, she might as well look the part.

"Thank you, Mrs. Miller."

"I give you a few minutes."

The dress was dark blue, with a black apron and overblouse. There was also a white cap. She put on the clothes, then looked in the mirror. As she examined herself, she smiled. This was certainly not the Leah McKenzie anyone knew. She could walk right by Keith Blanton now, and he'd never recognize her.

There was a knock on the door.

"Leah, are you dressed now?"

"Yes," Leah answered.

"*Kommen,* John is here."

Leah opened the door and stepped out into the hall. Mrs. Miller was there, and so was a man.

"This is John," Mrs. Miller said. "*Kommen,* we can go to the parlor."

"Well, you look none the worse for wear," John said as he led the way down the stairs.

Her impressions of the man who had pulled her out of the car, formed on a dark and rainy road, were confirmed. A powerful-looking man, he wore dark trousers and suspenders over a collarless white shirt. He was also wearing a low-brimmed straw hat. This was hardly the dress of the men she was familiar with, but despite—or perhaps because of—his bucolic apparel, she found him ruggedly handsome.

She also noticed that he was clean shaven, and she knew from the few stories her mother had shared with her that this meant John was not married.

The living room had neither cushioned chairs nor sofa. John held his hand out in invitation, pointing toward a rocking chair.

"I think you will be more comfortable there."

"Where is my money?" Leah asked as soon as she sat down. Her anxiousness made her voice sound harsher and more challenging than she intended.

"You almost kill me, and the first thing you ask me is where is your money?" John replied. The tone of his voice, even his accent, was different from Ada's. "You were driving much too fast on that road, given the time of night and the weather conditions."

"And just what would you know about driving too fast? How fast can you get that buggy to go, anyway? Eight, nine miles per hour?"

"Oh, fifteen, at a gallop," John replied with a disarming smile.

Leah pulled her fangs in. "I'm sorry if I sounded harsh. My money was in my purse," she said hopefully. "And I haven't seen my purse since I got here."

"Oh, that's my fault. I left it in the buggy, under the seat."

"Oh, my God! I have eleven thousand dollars in that purse! Please, bring it to me right now!"

John held up his hand. "There is no way that I will be seen carrying a purse. But don't worry, I'll have Ada get it."

"Good."

"As soon as my buggy gets back."

"Back? Back from where? What are you talking about?"

"I let Jacob and Sam take it to go to the singing."

"I can't believe you left so much money lying loose in the buggy so anyone could take it. And now it's who knows where! At some singing, whatever that is."

"I had no idea there was that much money in your purse. Anyway, don't worry about it."

"How can I not worry about it? That's everything I have in the world."

"It is safe," John assured her. "None of the churchmen will take something that doesn't belong to them. And the *Englische* don't go through our buggies because they think we have nothing of value."

"I hope you're right. But I'm going to worry until I have the money in my hands."

"Tell me, Leah—"

"Are all Amish so free and easy with other people's first names?" Leah asked.

John chuckled. "We have to be. How else could we tell each other apart? There are so many Millers and Yoders."

Leah laughed as well. "Are you sure you're Amish?"

"Don't I look it?" John asked, inviting her appraisal with a sweep of his hand.

"Yes, you look Amish, but you don't sound Amish."

"*Wäre es besser, wenn ich nur in Deutsch zu sprechen?*"

"*Now* you sound Amish."

"I'm curious. What were you doing out on that road at that time of night? To be honest, we rarely get cars on that road even during the day."

"I came to find my grandmother. She's Amish and from here— that is, if she's still alive. I've never met her."

"Your mother's mother, or your father's?"

"My mother's mother."

"Shunned, was she?"

"I thought the Amish were supposed to be good people. How could they do such a thing?"

"Shunning is as old as the Amish," John replied. "What is your grandmother's name?"

"Lapp. Miriam Lapp. Have you ever heard of her?"

"Oh yes. I know her very well."

"You do? You actually know her? Oh, wonderful! Then that means she's still alive?"

"We are a close-knit group. I know all the Amish here."

"What's she like? I mean—do you think she'll see me?"

"I don't know. I cannot speak for her or tell you what she will do. But if you would like, I will take you to meet her tomorrow."

"Oh, would you? Yes, thank you, that would be wonderful. And, uh, will you check in your buggy for my purse?"

"I will."

The next morning Leah went downstairs for breakfast. This was the first time she had seen the entire family: Mrs. Miller, Mr. Miller, Ada, Sam, and Jacob.

"Our guest has come to join us," Mrs. Miller said. "*Das ist mein Mann,* Isaac Miller."

At his wife's introduction, Mr. Miller nodded cordially to Leah, but Ada greeted her with a broad smile.

"Do you feel well enough to be up?" Ada asked.

"Yes, thank you." She looked around the table. "John isn't here?"

"John has an apartment in the barn. Shortly he will—"

"Is everybody up?" a voice yelled from the front of the house. Leah recognized it as John's voice.

"*Ja,* we do not sleep all day like you," Mr. Miller replied in a teasing voice.

John came in and hugged his mother and his sister. "Oh, Ada, before we eat, on the seat of my buggy is Leah's purse. Would you bring it in, please?"

"You found it!" Leah said happily.

"Yes, and everything is there."

"Oh, what a relief!"

"If you want, after breakfast I will take you to visit your grandmother," John said.

"You have a *grossmamm* in Arthur?" Isaac asked.

"Miriam Lapp," Leah answered.

"Ach! Mrs. Lapp! What a wonderful lady she is," Mrs. Miller said.

"You are Sarah's daughter," Isaac said. It wasn't a question, it was a statement.

"Yes! You know my mother?"

"She is dead," Isaac said.

"Yes, she died two years ago. How did you know?"

"She died many years ago," Isaac said again.

"Daad, Leah is not one of us. She does not understand such talk," John said.

"Oh, no," Leah said. "I do understand. You mean because my mother was shunned."

"We will speak no more of her," Isaac said. "Let us pray."

Leah bowed her head, expecting Isaac or someone to give a blessing. Instead, everyone was silent for a moment, and the silence was broken when Isaac said, "Amen."

The rest of breakfast was passed in silence, an uncomfortable silence for Leah, though the others around the table took it in stride. Only John seemed discomfited by his father's comment, and he gave Leah a comforting look. But Ada, too, reached out to her, giving Leah's arm a squeeze.

After breakfast, all the men left the house. As Mrs. Miller and Ada began clearing the breakfast table, it seemed only natural for Leah to join them, and her help was accepted without comment.

"Your chrysanthemums are so beautiful, Mrs. Miller," Leah said. Leah was washing the dishes, Ada was drying, and Mrs. Miller was using a pumice block on the stove.

"The flowers are all Ada's," Mrs. Miller said. "Ever since she was a little girl, she has planted chrysanthemums."

"You must be very proud of them, Ada."

Ada looked down. "'Pride goeth before destruction, and a haughty spirit before a fall,'" she said.

"It is not our way to be prideful," Mrs. Miller said. "Ada but planted the seeds. God arrayed the flowers in their beautiful colors."

"Of course, I didn't mean anything by it. But still, the flowers are beautiful."

"Leah, the buggy is hitched," John called.

"John, it is an open buggy, *ja*?" Mrs. Miller asked.

"Yes, Mamm, it is an open buggy."

"Oh, a convertible," Leah said. "How delightful. I love to ride with the top down."

John chuckled. "It's not that."

"What do you mean?"

"We are not married. An unmarried man and an unmarried woman cannot ride together in a closed buggy."

"Oh." Leah smiled. "How did you get me home the other night?"

John chuckled. "That was an emergency. I think our Ordnung will allow that. Besides, you aren't Amish, so I'm not sure it even applies to you anyway."

"Ordnung?"

"Rules of the church."

Outside, Leah was able to get a closer look at where she'd been staying. The house was large, two stories, with what looked like a fresh coat of white paint. The lawn was green and perfectly cut, and she got a closer look at the flower garden. She also saw the open buggy they would be riding in.

"Well, Ordnung or not, I do love to ride without a top," Leah said.

"Yes, I noticed that your car is a Mustang convertible."

"Oh, my car! I almost forgot. How is it?"

"There is no visible damage outside, but when you went into the ditch the underneath of your car hit a rock and the oil pan was pushed into the timing gear. It was making a terrible racket. I took off the oil pan, knocked out the dent, and put it back on. I checked the timing gear, and it doesn't appear as if any of the gear teeth were compromised. As soon as you replace the oil you lost, it will be as good as new."

"That's funny," Leah said.

"What is funny?"

"That you know so much about cars."

"We may dress, talk, and act like we are in the nineteenth century, Leah, but we actually do live in the twenty-first century."

"Yes, of course, I didn't mean to be . . ."

"Patronizing?"

"Was I? I'm sorry."

"Hello, Prodigal," John said as he approached his horse. He rubbed the horse behind his ears, and Prodigal bobbed his head.

"Your horse is named Prodigal?"

"Yes."

"What an unusual name."

"Perhaps," John said, with no further explanation.

John helped Leah into the buggy, then he clucked at Prodigal and they started out at a brisk trot. The horse's hooves made a rhythmic and almost musical sound as they clopped hollowly against the hard surface of the blacktop road.

"Oh, this is wonderful!" Leah said. "It reminds me of Central Park."

"You've taken a carriage ride in Central Park, have you?"

"Yes, but only once. It costs a fortune. Fifty dollars for half an hour."

"Really? I was only going to charge you twenty dollars this morning. But if you *Englische* are willing to pay that much, perhaps I should raise my fee."

"What?"

John laughed. "Don't be so gullible, Leah."

"You're a strange one, John. Except for how you're dressed, you certainly don't fit my idea of an Amish man."

"So my *daad* has said."

John turned off the hardtop onto a dirt road, and Prodigal's hoofbeats grew more muted. The road passed through fields of towering corn.

"I love your farm. I'm a city girl, born and raised. But there must be something in the blood—something I must have inherited from my Amish mother."

"Except now there are more Amish than there is farmland available," John said. "If we are to keep our group together, we have to find other ways to make a living."

"You don't farm?"

"No. My father and my brothers are the farmers. I'm a carpenter. I make cabinets, tables, desks, anything for the home or office."

"Oh, then you're much more than a carpenter. You're a craftsman."

"There is the Lapp place," John said, nodding toward the white house in front of them.

The house was a large, two-story wood-frame house, not unlike the Miller house, and with paint that hadn't weathered. But this house was boxy, without any particular personality—no cheerful flowers in the windows like the Millers had.

"How long has my grandmother lived there?"

"For as long as I can remember," John said. "I'm sure she has been there for at least sixty years or more."

"So it's possible that my mother was born and raised here?"

"Oh, it's much more than possible. I would say it is probable."

Leah examined the house and yard in greater detail as they grew closer, the leisurely approach of a horse-drawn vehicle giving her time to peruse the layout. She looked at some trees and tried to imagine her mother playing in and around them.

They stopped out front and a young girl of about fifteen came out to meet them.

"Hello, John," she greeted them.

"Hello, Mary. Is your *grossmamm* in?"

"Yes."

"Her grandmother? Then she must be . . ."

"Mary is your cousin," John said.

"My cousin? I know all of my cousins," Mary said.

"Well, here is one you don't know," John said as he tied Prodigal to the hitching rail.

Miriam Lapp greeted John with a broad smile, then she turned her smile toward Leah. "And is this your girlfriend?" Mrs. Lapp asked.

"No," John said. "She is just a friend—and"—he paused for a long moment before he continued—"your granddaughter."

"My granddaughter?" The smile turned puzzled.

"Yes. Grandmother, I'm Leah. I'm Sarah's daughter."

Now the smile left the old woman's face entirely. She began shaking her head and became very agitated.

"*Nein, nein. Die Frau namens Sarah starb, als sie aus der Kirche ausgetreten. Ich habe keine Tochter Sarah, darum ich nicht über eine Enkelin namens Leah.*"

Unable to understand her grandmother's response, Leah looked toward John.

"Mrs. Lapp says that when your mother left the church, she died to her. And since she has no daughter named Sarah, then she has no granddaughter named Leah."

"My mother *is* dead," Leah said. "She died two years ago at Barnes Hospital in St. Louis. She and my father were very happily married for twenty-five years."

Leah was surprised to see her grandmother's eyes well with tears.

"Grandmother, please. I know my mother loved you; she loved

her whole family with all her heart. Sometimes she would cry because she knew she could never see you again."

Mrs. Lapp didn't answer.

"Mrs. Lapp, look how Leah is dressed. She is wearing plain clothes. She didn't leave the church, her mother did. How can you punish her for something her mother did?" John asked.

"Please go now," Mrs. Lapp said.

With tears flowing down her cheeks, Leah turned and walked toward the door. John waited for just a moment, then he joined her. Mary came with them.

"I'm sorry, Leah," Mary said. She smiled. "But I am happy to have you for my cousin."

Leah smiled through her own tears. "And I'm happy to find a new cousin I didn't know I had."

"I won't shun you. You will be my cousin."

"Thank you."

John was quiet as he helped her back into the buggy, and he didn't speak until they were on the way back.

"That was my fault," he said. "I'm sorry."

"How was it your fault?"

"I could have warned you that this might be her reaction. I *should* have warned you."

"I—I suppose I wasn't shocked by it. I know how my mother hurt, over the years, because of the *bann*. I know too how much she wanted to come back to see her parents. Her father died, and she wasn't even able to come to the funeral. Then, when my mother died, not one member of her family came to the funeral. I should have known."

"What will you do now?"

"I think I'd like to stay here for a while, if that's possible. It might be hopeless, but I'd like to try to become a part of my grandmother's life again."

Leah did not add that she needed to stay there to hide out from the police. How could she explain that to John? She barely understood exactly what happened herself.

"Do you know where I might be able to rent a room?"

"My parents will rent you the room where you are staying now."

"Do you think so? I hate to be taking up someone's room."

"It was my room," John said. "They have rented it before, they will rent it again."

"Wonderful. Oh, and I'll have to buy some clothes. Plain clothes," she added.

John smiled but said nothing.

The Millers' kitchen the next morning had a warm, inviting scent of stewed cinnamon apples, sizzling bacon, and freshly baked bread. The morning sun streamed in through the window, laying squares of light on the wood floor. Leah thought about her mother growing up in an environment just like this and felt closer to her than ever.

Mrs. Miller, who now insisted that Leah call her Emma, not only agreed to rent John's old room to her, she also arranged for Leah to buy clothes from some of the Amish ladies who supplemented their family's income by sewing. Within a few days Leah had an entire wardrobe, though as every dress and apron looked the same as the next, it wasn't difficult to choose what to wear each day. The hardest thing to get used to was the cap, or *kapp,* as Ada called it. In order to wear it, she had to keep her hair swept up and tied in a bun.

Even though Leah was paying rent to stay in the house, she knew that she was expected to help with the household chores. Nobody had said so, but when she began working alongside Emma and Ada, neither of them made the usual demurrals one usually hears as a houseguest. And in truth, she didn't mind the work. It kept her busy, and it kept her mind occupied with something other than Carl's murder.

Leah and Ada, carrying tin kettles of water and drinking cups, walked out into the cornfield, the golden-brown stalks rising higher than their heads. Isaac drove the team that was pulling the corn picker, while Jacob was driving the team pulling the wagon. Sam walked behind, picking up those ears that didn't make it into the wagon.

The three men stopped when they saw the women coming and gathered around them for a welcome drink of water.

"Do you make a farm woman out of our guest?" Isaac asked as he wiped sweat from his brow.

"She asked to come with me, Daad."

Isaac nodded. "*Ja,* I think she is a good woman."

When the three men's thirst was slaked, Leah and Ada returned to the house with the empty kettles.

"How often do you have to take them water when they're in the field?" Leah asked.

"Two times in the morning and two times in the afternoon," Ada said. "It is an important job and I have been doing this since I was a little girl."

Leah's mother had told her once that she was a "water girl" for her father. Leah had never met her mother's father, and because of that was never able to mentally construct a picture of him. Now she imagined a strong, stoic man like Isaac, but with her mother's sandy hair and lively eyes.

She saw airplanes and an occasional helicopter flying overhead, and cars and trucks would drive past on the road, so the outside world was still there, but it was as if some invisible wall separated them from the farmers they passed. In her new plain clothes, Leah felt detached from all her "real world" worries.

Hiding out in an Amish community had its advantages and disadvantages. She was so cut off from the rest of the world that she could have been in another country. That would keep her out of sight, but it also kept her cut off from any news from the outside. There were no radios or TVs among the Amish.

"The television antenna is the devil's tail, and the screen is the devil's tongue," Ada told her. They didn't even read newspapers, except for a monthly bulletin that was printed in Ohio and contained only Amish news, such as marriages, births, and deaths. There were no reports of suicide-bombing attacks in the Middle East or the latest political scandal—or missing witnesses in sensational murder cases. Were the police even still looking for her?

Other than her complete isolation from the outside world, the most difficult thing Leah had to get used to was the lack of a shower. Lord, how she wanted to take a shower, to stand under the stinging spray and let it play on her naked skin! She had no idea that she could absolutely lust over something so ordinary. There was a bathtub in the house, in a bathing room, as opposed to a bathroom, at the end of the upstairs hall. But the men who worked in the field every day had first access to it. Then, shortly after Leah and Ada returned from taking water to the field, a wonderful opportunity presented itself.

"Mamm and I are going to call on Mrs. Martha Yoder. She has been ill of late," Ada said. "You will be fine here alone?"

"Yes, I will be fine. Have a good visit."

Leah helped Ada connect her horse to the buggy, not because Ada needed any help but just because she thought it would be interesting to do so. When the horse was hitched to the buggy, Emma came outside carrying a covered bowl of sausage-and-sauerkraut soup.

"We will be back in time for dinner," Emma said as she got into the buggy.

"Should I fix lunch for the men?"

"You do not need to take food to them. We will be back for dinner," Emma repeated, and Leah realized that she was talking about the noon meal.

"I see. Well, have a nice visit."

"*Ja,* we will."

Leah watched them leave, then realized that with Isaac, Sam, and Jacob in the field, and Emma and Ada gone, she had the house all to herself. Which meant that she also had the *bathtub* all to herself.

Water was brought into the house from a deep well, pumped by a windmill. The hot-water tank was gas-heated, but there was no thermostat, so Leah had to light the burner, then wait until the water was at just the right temperature. Then she turned on the spigot that let the water into the tub.

The soap wasn't the small, white, perfumed bar she was used to, but a big, brown, rough block of lye soap. But at this point, she didn't care. Taking off her dirty clothes and putting them aside, she laid out her clean clothes, then stepped over the edge of the big porcelain tub and slipped down into the water, which was now the perfect temperature.

Oh, the luxury of it, the delightful sensation of warm water against her naked body. She giggled, then lay back in the tub to just relax. She couldn't do this in a shower. Who needed a shower anyway?

John could hear the television in Mr. Collins's office; he always left it tuned to one of the cable news channels. John was filling out paperwork when the anchor introduced a story from Afghanistan.

"In Kandahar today, fourteen people were killed when a suicide bomber, disguised as an Afghani soldier, detonated a bomb at a training facility. Four of those killed were Americans."

John put his pen down and pinched the bridge of his nose to help him force the memories out of his head. He could hear the explosion, picture the sights—he thought for a moment he could even smell the acrid scent of charred flesh. Mr. Collins chose that moment to come into the office.

"Do you have a headache?" Mr. Collins asked.

"A little one. Nothing serious," John said. He didn't want to share his memories with Mr. Collins.

"You've put in a lot of overtime over the last few weeks. Why don't you take the rest of the day off?" Mr. Collins suggested.

"I wouldn't want to leave you shorthanded," John said.

Collins chuckled. "I once owned a small business in Decatur. You know what the hardest thing was about owning that business?

Getting dependable help. If every company in America would hire only Amish, our country wouldn't be in the financial mess it is now."

"Do you think every company in America should just make furniture?" John teased.

"You know what I mean, John. I didn't know what to think when I first moved into Amish country, what with all the plain clothes, horses, and buggies." Collins laughed. "First time I heard the term 'plain clothes,' I thought they were talking about a police detective."

"You are sure you don't mind my taking off for the rest of the day?"

"I'm positive. You've more than earned it."

"All right, maybe I will."

"Good. And when I say take the day off, I mean take the day off. Don't relax by picking corn or mucking out one of the stalls, or something like that."

John chuckled. "I'll take the day off."

During the drive home, snippets of the news report ran through John's head, and he thought of Master Sergeant James Wyatt, one of the NCOs who had been under his command.

"Amish? No kidding, you're Amish?" Master Sergeant Wyatt asked. "I thought the Amish didn't come in the army."

"They don't," Captain Miller replied. "Since I left the church, I'm no longer Amish."

"You can't really quit being Amish, can you? I mean, isn't that like saying you're no longer Chinese or something?"

"Amish isn't a race, sergeant."

"I guess. It's just that I never met no Amish before. But I've seen pictures of 'em. They're, well, I don't know what the word is."

"'Quaint'?" John suggested.

"Yeah, quaint. And don't they talk in German and stuff?"

"And stuff."

"You sure don't seem like what I thought an Amish would be."

"That's what my daad says."

"Your what?"

"My father."

Master Sergeant Wyatt laughed and pointed at John. "There you go, cap'n. That was one of them quaint words, wasn't it?"

"Yes," John said. "That was one of those quaint words."

When John turned down the road that led up to the house, he noticed that the family buggy was gone. Unhitching Prodigal, he went into the house, but neither his mother nor Ada was there. With his father and brothers out in the fields, and the buggy gone, he decided the women must be either in town or visiting somewhere.

An ideal time to take a bath!

John hurried to his room in the barn, then, with a change of clothes draped across his arm, came back and started up the stairs. When he opened the door to the bathing room, he was greeted with the sight of a totally nude and extraordinarily beautiful young woman. Leah was running a towel through her hair with her eyes closed, and she was completely unaware of John's presence. John knew that he should shut the door quietly and go back to his apartment in the barn, but he couldn't. He was so transfixed by the sight that he stood rooted to the spot.

Leah opened her eyes and saw John standing there, staring at her. For a moment she seemed as stunned as he was, simply gazing back at him. Then her face flushed bright red as she hastily wrapped the towel around herself.

"You should have knocked," Leah chided.

"You should have locked."

She chuckled at that. "I didn't think I would have to. Everyone's gone."

John thought she was amazingly calm under the circumstances. "Yes, that's what I thought as well. I'm sorry, but I saw the buggy gone, and I thought you had gone with Mamm and Ada. It is so difficult to find time to take a bath that I take every opportunity to do so."

"Are you just going to stand there and stare? Or are you going to be a gentleman and allow me to recover some modesty, if not dignity?"

"Oh, yes, yes, I'm sorry, I'm sorry," John said. "I'll, uh, I'll just go now."

"You do that."

"Again, I'm sorry."

John started to put his clothes down, thought about it and pulled them back up, then put them down again.

"I thought you were going now," Leah said, clutching the towel more tightly around her, wondering how much it was covering.

"Yes, I'll, uh, just go now," John repeated. He backed out of the room and Leah dissolved into giggles, muffling her laughter with her towel. She would have given anything to have had her cell phone with her—she'd have loved to have a picture of the expression on his face.

* * *

Thirty minutes later, Leah was sitting on the porch swing when John came back outside, freshly bathed. When he saw Leah sitting in the swing, he stopped.

"I'm sorry I barged in like that. I didn't mean to."

"So you said."

"I mean, I wouldn't want you to think that I—"

"It's an understandable accident," Leah said, interrupting him. "And I know what you mean about finding time to take a bath. I thought I had the bathroom all to myself today."

John chuckled self-consciously. "Yes, so did I."

Without being invited, John sat beside her on the swing. She was very aware of his masculinity, the clean smell of him—lye-soap clean, not perfumed. She thought back to earlier when he had seen her naked. Her reaction had surprised her. Rather than being angry, or frightened, or even that embarrassed, she'd been . . . titillated. And even as she thought of it now, a warmth suffused her body.

"John, you've lived on the outside, haven't you?"

"Have I been so corrupted by the English that it is obvious?"

"Corrupted? Do you think living anywhere but among the Amish is a form of corruption?"

"For me, it was."

"How long were you out?"

"Nine years."

"Nine years? You were on the outside for nine years, living with electricity, showers, television, radio, cars, movies, the Internet—you were there for nine years and you gave all that up to come back here?"

"Yes."

"Why? What did you do that was so horrible, so corruptive, that you were willing to turn your back on everything?"

John gave a little shake of his head but said nothing.

"If you don't want to talk about it, I understand."

"Why are you here?" John asked.

"I told you. I'm trying to reestablish a relationship with my grandmother. Well, establish a relationship with her, since we've never had one in the first place."

"Are you willing to turn your back on all those things you mentioned—electricity, television, showers?"

"Showers," Leah said. "Oh, what I'd give for a shower!"

"Yes. Now that I've seen you bathe, I think it would be more fun to watch you shower," John said with a teasing smile on his lips.

"Oh, you're awful!" Leah said, hitting him on the shoulder, though the blow was ameliorated by laughter.

"Well, I do miss television during March Madness," he said.

"March Madness? You mean basketball?"

"College basketball. That's what I miss. I played basketball at SIU Carbondale. And I got forty-two points against Murray State. I can't brag about it to anyone, because Amish must be modest in all things. And I'm not sure who would understand anyway, so what's the fun of bragging if the person you are bragging to doesn't appreciate the enormity of it?"

"I appreciate the enormity of it," Leah said. "And if I had been at that game, I would have cheered my head off for you."

"How could you cheer for someone you don't even know?"

"You've seen me naked, John. How much better do I need to know you?"

John laughed out loud.

Keith Blanton waited at police headquarters with Detective Hellman for the results of the computer download, which the judge had authorized that morning.

"I can't believe you haven't found Leah McKenzie yet," Blanton said.

"We have followed up on every lead we could, but so far, nothing," Hellman said.

"She can't just have disappeared into thin air."

"We're doing all we can, Mr. Blanton. The FBI is on the case, and like you say, she can't just disappear."

An attractive young woman in large round glasses entered the room, carrying two folders.

"What have you got for us, Miss Margrabe?" Hellman asked.

"I've printed out everything there was on the McKenzie computer."

"And the Trevathan computer?"

"Nada. It was wiped clean."

"What do you mean 'wiped clean'?" Blanton asked. "I thought you could recover anything that was deleted."

"Deleted material, sure," she said. "But this wasn't just deleted. The hard drive was electromagnetically erased."

"What did you do to it?" Blanton asked. "There's material on that computer that we need."

"I didn't do anything to it, Mr. Blanton," Miss Margrabe snapped. "Whatever was done to the computer was done before I saw it. Also, the thumb drives and CD-ROMs are clean."

"Nothing from the computer will give us *any* information?" Hellman asked.

"I'm sorry, detective. Not a thing."

"All right, let me have the material you got from McKenzie's computer," Hellman said. "Maybe something there will give us a lead."

"I made two copies of everything," Miss Margrabe said, handing one folder to Hellman and the other to Blanton.

"When will we get the computers back?" Blanton asked.

"I'm through with them," Miss Margrabe said. "You can have them any time you want."

CHAPTER SEVEN

It was halfway through October before Leah felt comfortable enough to go with the Miller family to church. Their buggy was but one of nearly two dozen horse-drawn vehicles rolling down a long, narrow dirt road that stretched between flanking fields of corn. Ahead lay Aaron Brenneman's farm, where today's service would be held. To the left was the house; like nearly all the Amish houses, it was two stories high, a functional building without cupolas or dormers, but with a chimney on each end. In the same compound was a large barn and several other smaller buildings that Leah couldn't identify. There were also two silos. Behind the farm, fields led up a low rise to a great collection of trees.

It was a beautiful picture, like something Norman Rockwell might have painted, and Leah marveled that there could be such a place of peace and harmony in the world today.

When she heard they were attending services, she thought

that meant they were going to a church building. She didn't know until they actually started their trip that morning that their worship service wouldn't be held in a church building, but in the living and dining room of the Brenneman house. In order to stretch the seating, long wide boards were placed between two chairs to make benches. Leah thought she would be sitting with John, but that wasn't the way it happened. All the women sat on one side of the room and all the men sat on the other side. The way the seating was arranged, they were looking across a center aisle at each other.

Shortly after they were seated, someone, Leah didn't know who, called out, "*Dreihundert und fünf.*"

The worshippers turned to page 305, then began to sing. The singing was without piano or organ accompaniment, but the voices of the singers blended, not in harmony, but in tone and in timbre, and Leah thought the result was quite beautiful.

Then came the second song, which, Leah learned, was also the second song in every Amish church service except for funerals. It was *"O Gott Vater wir loben dich"*—"O God the Father, We Praise You."

After the second song was sung, Leah could hear the sound of footsteps on the stairs as the deacon, minister, and bishop came down to sit together in the front row. Deacons, ministers, and bishops, Leah was told, were not elected, but selected by lot. This way, it was believed, God Himself had done the choosing. Being selected to serve as a bishop or a minister was cause not for congratulations but for pity, because those chosen had to take on a tiresome burden.

The pastor, who John had already told her was Elam Lantz, got up, then stepped into the center aisle between the men and women and began. He opened the service with a few remarks in English.

"Is today different from any other day? Today we go about our appointed rounds. We tend to our horses and sheep, we milk cows, fill the silos, haul the manure, and walk behind the plow turning up God's earth so that we may sow the seeds that sustain us.

"Has there ever been a time in history when we were more envied? Many of you work with the *Englische,* so you are aware, in a way that many of us in the past have never been before, of the events of the outside world. There is strife, bitterness, and unimaginable evil. Against such a dark picture, it is no surprise that many would seek the peaceful life of the Amish.

"Now they write books about us, and they make movies about us. But what do they know of us? How should we react to this? We should strive to lead Christian lives, not for the *Englische,* but for ourselves. We should give all honor to our Heavenly Father, for while the *Englische* ponder our clothes and our buggies, we should show by our lives the width and depth of our faith."

From then on, and for more than two hours, the service continued in German, and Leah had not the slightest idea of what was being said. And because she couldn't understand what was being said, she studied the others in the room. It was easy to see John because he was seated directly across from her and he, like all the other men, and all the other women that Leah could see without being too obvious, was concentrating on the pastor. Once, John caught her looking at him, and he smiled at her, causing her to blush.

The service concluded with the reading of a passage from the Bible, one that supported the lifestyle followed by the Amish. It was

1 John 2:15: "Love not the world, neither the things that are in the world. If any man love the world, the love of the Father is not in him."

After church, Caleb and Daniel, Aaron Brenneman's sons, who were acting as hostlers for those who had come to the service, brought all the horses back out of the barn, matching them up to the correct carriages. Leah thought she noticed a few glances exchanged between one of the Brenneman sons and Ada.

"You were supposed to be watching the pastor during service," John said with a teasing grin.

"Yeah? Well maybe if he would preach in English so I could understand what he's saying, I would pay attention to him. *Supposons qu'il avait donne le sermon en Français?*"

"*Puis je l'aurais écouté ses paroles en Français,*" John replied. "If he had given the sermon in French, I would have listened in French."

"You speak French?"

"Yes."

"John Miller, you never cease to amaze me."

"Good. I enjoy being a source of amazement for you."

"John, here's your horse," Caleb Brenneman said.

"*Danki,* Caleb."

This was the young man who had been showing interest in Ada.

As John and the other men were connecting their horses to the buggies, the women and younger children gathered in conversational groups to wait. The older girls gathered together in their own little groups. Leah wandered over to stand next to John's mother and sister. They smiled as she approached them, then Emma spoke to the other women, who were obviously curious as to who Leah might be.

"*Dies ist ist Leah. Sie hat hat ein Zimmer in meinem Haus getroffen,*" Emma Miller said, introducing her to the other women, explaining that Leah was living with her.

Leah was welcomed by the others.

"Are you *Englische*?" one of the others asked.

"Yes, I am English."

"If you are *Englische,* why are you wearing plain clothes?"

On the outside, that question would have been considered rude, but Leah knew that it was not asked with any intent, except one of innocent curiosity.

"I want to understand what it's like. My mother was Amish, but she . . ." Leah looked toward Emma, seeking help in explaining her situation.

"*Leah's Mutter verliess die Kirche vor langer zeit. Aber Leah's grossmamm lebt noch immer hier. Miriam Lapp ist ihre grossmamm.*"

"Miriam is a woman who is set in the old ways," one of the younger women said. "I think maybe she will not accept Leah as her granddaughter."

"That is exactly what's happened," Leah replied.

"But why?" another asked. "It was not Leah who left the church, it was her mother. And now, Leah is trying to come back. I think Miriam will open her heart."

"We can but pray that it will be so," Emma said.

"Hello, Cousin Leah," Mary said, coming up to her with a broad smile.

"Hello, Cousin Mary." Leah's smile was just as large. "At least I am accepted by some of the family."

Looking across the yard, Leah saw her grandmother. Miriam had been studying her, but when she saw Leah return her scrutiny, she turned away and broke eye contact.

Emma saw the silent exchange, and she put her hand on Leah's shoulder. "Give her time. I think one day she will see that she has another granddaughter."

At that moment Isaac drove up.

"*Kommen,*" he said. "We must go."

With good-byes to her cousin and the other women, Leah, Ada, and Emma got back into the carriage. Isaac snapped the reins, and the horse started out at a brisk trot, moving into the long line of buggies that were now reversing their pilgrimage of the morning and leaving the farmhouse where they'd had their service behind them.

In addition to the numerous buggies, there were scores of young people walking along the road, the boys in their black suits with white shirts and black hats, girls wearing dark blue dresses that were held together not by buttons, or hooks and eyes, but by pins. The dresses were covered by white aprons. All were wearing white *kapps,* but with the strings dangling, untied. Some of the boys had the brims of their hats folded up.

"Look at those girls," Emma said. She clucked her tongue. "Not one has the *kapp* strings tied."

"And the boys are as bad," Isaac said. "Do you see how their brims are turned up? What are our youth coming to?"

Leah had to fight back a laugh. She had heard her father make the same comment about "youth" after seeing on TV a group of young people arrested when a victory celebration got out of hand one night and they began vandalizing cars and buildings. Hardly a valid comparison to a group of girls not tying their cap strings or boys turning up the brims of their hats.

She thought of her father. He had had a difficult time dealing with her mother's passing. He had no brothers or sisters, and Leah was his only child. No doubt the police had gotten in touch with him by now, to tell him that she was wanted for murder. How she wanted to call him, to let him know that she didn't do it and that she was safe. But she was certain that, by now, the police were monitoring his phone.

"You are thinking of your *mamm, ja*?" Emma Miller asked.

"Yes," Leah replied. It was better to have Emma think that than to know that she was concerned about the police.

"I know it was difficult for her."

"Did you know my mother?"

"Yes, we were childhood friends."

"Tell me, Emma: everything I have seen about the church has been so wonderful—the people are generous, kind, and loving. And yet, my grandmother will have nothing to do with me because my mother was shunned. How can the church do such a thing as shun one of its own?"

"We are bound by Jesus to do this," Emma said. "For in Matthew chapter eighteen, verses fifteen through eighteen, Jesus says: 'If your brother sins against you, go and tell him his fault, between you and him alone. If he listens to you, you have gained your brother. But if he does not listen, take one or two others along with you, that every charge may be established by the evidence of two or three witnesses. If he refuses to listen to them, tell it to the church. And if he refuses to listen even to the church, let him be to you as a Gentile and a tax collector. Truly, I say to you, whatever you bind on earth shall be bound in heaven, and whatever you loose on earth shall be loosed in heaven.' These are the words of Christ himself."

"But for a mother to shun her own child? I remember that sometimes, on her birthday, or at Thanksgiving or Christmas, my mother would cry because her family had turned her out."

"She turned herself out, child," Emma said. "It was she who left the church. She who went to live with the *Englische* and marry an *Englische* man."

"My father is a wonderful man," Leah insisted.

"Your father was not shunned."

"That doesn't make sense."

"It is hard, I know. It was hard when John was lost to us."

"But nobody shuns John."

"John has come back. If Sarah had come back to the church, the *bann* would have been lifted."

CHAPTER EIGHT

Blanton studied Frank Stone. His head sat on his shoulders with no visible neck. He was completely bald, but whether naturally so or whether he kept his head shaved, nobody knew. His head looked like a cannonball. Blanton found him more than a little intimidating. It wasn't just because Stone was a big man—Mike Stratton was a big man. No, it was something else, something more than just his size. Frank Stone exuded a sense of danger.

At one time, Frank Stone had been a St. Louis policeman whose record could only be described as "spotty." He received the Distinguished Service Citation, which was the highest award for bravery, because, according to the accompanying citation, *When a murder suspect purposely drove his car at high speed toward a group of pedestrians, Officer Stone placed his car in front of the speeding car, deliberately bringing about a collision that killed the suspect and injured Officer Stone. By his action, Officer Stone saved the lives of the pedestrians.*

But he had also received several official reprimands: *Officer Stone, in violation of approved procedures for handling suspects, used excessive force in subduing suspects.*

When the reprimands began to greatly exceed the meritorious mentions, Frank Stone was dismissed from the force. That was when he became a private investigator. Two times since becoming a PI, his license had been revoked. He was, though, except for a tendency to be more physical than necessary, an investigator with an excellent record of accomplishment.

"I don't know," he said after Blanton told him what he wanted. "Most of the time when I get involved in a case, it's a civil case, someone wanting to find someone because they owe them money, or they ran out on an obligation or something. If I understand you, this woman is a murderer, so she already has the police after her, doesn't she? And not only the police, but the FBI as well, since the killing took place in a federal court building."

"True. But I'm her lawyer; I want her found and brought back for her own good. I mean, she's going to be caught eventually. But if I could find her, talk to her, and convince her to turn herself in, I feel like things would go better for her in court."

"I see there's a one-hundred-thousand-dollar reward for her," Stone said as he examined her file.

"That's only if you turn her over to the police."

"Well, who else would I turn her over to?"

"To me. I told you, I want to convince her to turn herself in. But don't worry. I'll pay you the one-hundred-thousand-dollar reward in addition to your fee."

"My fee is five hundred dollars per day, plus one hundred dollars per day expenses, and that's every day, beginning today. That is whether I find her or not. And if I find her, I will expect you to pay the one-hundred-thousand-dollar reward."

"I can live with that," Blanton said.

"You must really want her found."

"I do."

Stone smiled, then stood up and extended his hand across his desk. "As of now, I am on your payroll," he said.

"Good."

"I mean as of *now*. I will expect my first five hundred dollars before I leave the office."

Blanton pulled open one of his desk drawers and took out a checkbook. Writing the check, he tore it out, then handed it across the desk to Stone. "I expect results."

During the night, Emile Zook's barn burned down. As soon as neighbors saw the night sky being painted orange, they realized what was happening and got to Zook's farm as quickly as possible. John, Isaac, Sam, and Jacob were among those who hurried over to the farm in the middle of the night.

Now the four men, their clothes still smelling of smoke, were back home, sitting at the breakfast table.

"We were able to save Emile's horses, but not his buggy. It was destroyed along with his barn."

"Oh, my goodness," Leah said. "I certainly hope Mr. Zook has insurance."

"*Ja*, he does. It is us," Isaac said without further elaboration.

Seeing Leah's baffled expression, John explained further.

"What we do have is a mutual-aid fund," John explained. "Once a year everyone contributes to this fund, so there is enough money on hand to buy the material needed to replace a barn or house that has burned down. We provide the physical labor."

"Oh, yes, a barn raising," Leah said with a big smile. "I know about barn raisings."

"Have you ever been to one?"

"No."

"Well, you are about to. That is, if you want to go. We'll be getting started on Mr. Zook's barn within the next few days."

John, his father, and his two brothers went on ahead, leaving the house even before dawn. Leah joined Emma and Ada in another buggy, taking with them enough food to feed an army.

And when they reached the site of the burned-out Zook barn, Leah thought she had happened onto an army. There was a large gathering of buggies, much larger than the gathering that had been at the church. Already the burned rubble had been moved away, and the men were working. They had just finished assembling the frame for one end and several were in position to lift it up.

"*Wir brauchen jemanden, hier heraufzukommen und eine Hand zu leihen,*" someone called from the bare eaves of the barn.

"What did he say?" Leah asked.

"He asked someone to go up to lend a hand," Ada translated.

"*Ich kommen,*" John answered, and he scurried up one of the ladders, then got into position. Half a dozen ropes were thrown to the men on top of the barn frame, and John grabbed one of them and pulled with the others as the end frame was raised into position.

"*Kommen, kommen,* we must get the food on the table," Emma said. "The men will be hungry."

When Leah had seen the food Emma brought that morning, she had the idea that perhaps they were bringing enough food to feed everyone. That wasn't the case, because she was amazed to see how much food was actually there. Several long tables had been created by stretching one-by-eight boards across sawhorses. The boards were covered with cloth and absolutely laden with food. This was the breakfast meal, so there were several bowls of scrambled eggs, fried cornmeal mush, oatmeal, fried potatoes, sausage, ham, and bacon. In addition there were several loaves of freshly baked bread, butter, jelly, jams, and apple butter.

Looking back toward the barn, Leah saw that the entire framework was up now, and there were at least forty men crawling around on it. Leah was reminded of hornets building a nest, all of the worker hornets climbing around on the nest as it grew larger and larger.

A woman that Emma had identified earlier as Mrs. Zook began to ring a bell, and all the men climbed down from the barn, then hurried over to the table. Leah wasn't quite sure how the seating arrangements were going to work, but she found out quickly enough. Not one woman sat at the table. Only the men, and, after a brief moment of silent prayer, the men began eating.

Ada laughed. "You are hungry, *ja?*"

To Leah's surprise, she was hungry. She had worked as hard as all the other women this morning and had built an appetite.

"Yes."

"Don't worry, we will eat. But the women do not sit until after the men have eaten their fill."

There were few words exchanged among the men, such conversation as there was being relegated to the task at hand or requesting that food be passed. With forty hungry men, their appetites whetted by the hard labor, there was very little left. Leah smiled. There was enough food to satisfy her, but this would be the first breakfast since she arrived where she didn't feel she was stuffing herself.

She had been sure she'd gained weight with all the food she was eating, but the mirror told her otherwise. Then she realized that the reason she hadn't gained weight was the same reason all the other Amish managed to stay thin, regardless of the amount of food they ate. Living there in Arthur, she was working *hard*.

Before arriving there, Leah had thought she knew what work was—staying late to find a precedent or to prepare a brief for an upcoming case. But she had never known real work before, the kind of work that had you falling into bed at night on the brink of physical exhaustion, and she wondered how these people could do it day in and day out.

"*Kommen, kommen schnell, es gibt viel zu tun*," Mrs. Zook called, and Leah smiled because she was able to translate the words. It was something her mother used to say: "Come, come quickly, there is much to do."

After breakfast, the women washed the dishes on an outside table with washbasins, then returned home to cook lunch, which most of them called dinner. As Ada drove the buggy away, Leah looked back toward the barn. Now the entire framework was in place and the only thing that remained was to fill in the siding and the roof.

Emma was riding in back of the buggy, keeping a close eye on the dishes, pots, and pans. Leah was up front with Ada.

"Is it hard to drive a car?" Ada asked.

"No, not really," Leah replied. "You have to be very careful of course, especially when you're out on the interstate driving seventy-five miles per hour and all the other cars around you are going just as fast."

"I would like to drive a car sometime."

"I'll teach you to drive."

Ada chuckled and shook her head. "The bishop and the elders would not let me drive. The Ordnung forbids it."

"Would the Ordnung allow me to drive this buggy?"

"You want to drive?"

"Yes. I think it would be fun."

Ada handed the reins over to Leah. "All right, here. But don't be trying to go seventy miles per hour, because Daisy can't do that."

Leah laughed out loud as she took the reins. She could feel the horse moving through the reins, saw Daisy's rear end swishing back and forth as she trotted in rhythm, the footfalls making hollow clomping sounds. She was surprised at how much she was enjoying it.

When she tried to turn up the long drive to the farm, Daisy stopped and Ada laughed.

"What happened?"

"You pulled too hard on the reins. You don't have to pull so hard. Daisy knows where to go."

Daisy started again, and Leah did as Ada suggested. With only the slightest pressure on the right rein, Daisy turned and trotted up the drive to the house.

"Whoa, Daisy," she said, pulling back on both reins.

Daisy stopped.

"Oh, that was fun!"

"You go in the house to help start dinner. I'll unhitch the horse," Ada offered.

When they returned to the Zook farm a couple of hours later with the buggy once more loaded with food, the siding and roofing were already completed. Leah was amazed. She had seen houses go up in her neighborhood, erected by professional carpenters using heavy equipment. It would take them weeks to get a house to the level this barn had reached in less than one day.

The men ate lunch as ravenously as if there had been no break-fast, then grabbed paintbrushes and buckets of paint, and even before all the dishes were cleaned and repacked in the buggies, the barn was completed—erected and painted, and all the leftover scrap lumber around it picked up and thrown into the back of the wagons.

As they drove back home that afternoon, Leah felt tired, but it was a different kind of tired from anything she had ever felt before. It was, if she had to describe it, a "good" tired, because she felt a sense of accomplishment.

In fact, Leah thought this was one of the most thrilling days she had ever experienced.

Driving through Chesterfield, Missouri, Frank Stone turned off Justus Post Road onto Walpole Drive. Entering a condo complex known as Windsor Manor, he easily found building 1623. He parked in a visitor slot, then crossed the parking lot to the building.

He was looking for unit D, and he was about to buzz when someone came out of the door. Smiling at the white-haired woman who
exited, he caught the door and stepped inside. A and B were downstairs, C and D were upstairs, so he climbed the stairs and knocked
on the door to unit D.

A tall, silver-haired, dignified-looking man answered the door.

"Mr. McKenzie?"

"Yes?"

"My name is Frank Stone, Mr. McKenzie. I've been hired by Mr.
Blanton to try to find your daughter."

"You say you were hired by Blanton?"

"Yes, sir. He is very worried about Leah. He's representing her,
you know."

"Leah isn't here, and I don't know where she is."

"Could we talk for a while? It may be that you know something
helpful."

"I don't know if I should help or not," Jason McKenzie replied.
"I mean, if she's run off, maybe she doesn't want to be found."

"She's probably just frightened and not thinking very clearly,"
Stone said. "Please, it will only take a few minutes of your time. And
I'm sure you would rather I find her than the FBI."

"All right, come on in."

A movie was on TV, and McKenzie picked up the remote to
click it off.

"What were you watching?"

"*Casablanca*. It's an old movie, I know, but I like old movies better than the stuff they're making today."

"I don't blame you. I do too. I'll try not to keep you away from
it so that you miss too much of it."

"No problem, it's a DVD."

"They don't make actors like Humphrey Bogart and Ingrid Bergman anymore," Stone said.

"You've got that right." Jason held out his hand, indicating that Stone should sit down. "Now, what do you want to talk about?"

"About your daughter, about anything that might give me an idea as to where to start looking. What can you tell me about her?"

"She's very smart. She graduated from Washington University with a 3.9 grade-point average."

"That's pretty good. Wash U is a tough school. When is the last time you talked to her?"

"Talked to her? Or saw her?"

"Either one."

"Well, I saw her at the funeral for Mr. Trevathan. And I talked to her on the morning of the day the police say she disappeared."

"Did she say anything, give you any hint that she was about to leave town?"

"No. In fact, she said she had tickets to the football game the following Sunday, and she was going to come get me in time for us to eat out before the game. Then the next I heard, the police were here asking me where she was."

"And you don't have any idea where she might have gone?"

"No, not the slightest. She's lived here in St. Louis all her life, and she went to school here. She doesn't have any other place to go."

"Does she have any brothers or sisters?"

"No."

"Do you have any brothers or sisters?"

"No."

"What about your wife?"

"My wife is deceased."

Stone got up and took a card from his pocket. "It may be, Mr. McKenzie, that your telephone has been tapped."

"What? Why?"

"I imagine it's because they expect Leah to try to get in touch with you. Anyway, if you hear anything from her, please, call me at this number. This is my cell phone, and I have it with me at all times. But don't call me from this phone or from your cell. If we're going to find her before the FBI does, then we need to keep them out of what we're doing."

"All right," McKenzie said.

CHAPTER NINE

The next Sunday, after the morning services, John asked Leah if she would attend the singing with him that evening.

"Singing? What's a singing?"

"It's when young single men and young single women gather for an evening of singing hymns. For the Amish it's almost the same thing as what you might call a hoedown."

"A hoedown? With dancing?"

"Um, not quite," John said. "But the young people very much enjoy the singings because there is no supervision of interaction between the sexes. Asking someone to go to a singing would be like asking someone out on a date."

Leah smiled. "What if I suggested we go on a real date? Maybe to dinner in town, then to a movie?"

"We couldn't do it in Arthur. There are too many people there who know us—or at least who know me."

"Decatur? We could take my car." Even as she asked the question, she wondered how smart an idea that would be. The police knew about her car.

"I've had a hard enough time being accepted back as it is," John said. "If I were to do something like that, I think I would be shunned for life."

"Oh," Leah said. "No, I wouldn't want anything like that. I saw what my mother went through."

"It could be worse," John said.

"Worse?"

John laughed. "I could be your brother."

"What?"

"My father and your mother attended singing together a few times. Who knows?"

"My brother?" Leah said. "Well, I've always wanted a brother."

John took Leah's hand in his. "I like it better this way," he said.

Strangely, the touch of his hand caused her to feel the same tingly warmth she had felt when he saw her naked. And as she looked at him, she knew that he was feeling the same thing.

"Yes," she said. "I think I like it better this way as well."

"So, you will go to singing with me?"

"Can I just move my lips and pretend to sing?" Leah asked.

John smiled broadly. "Your secret is safe with me," he said.

"All right, then I'll go."

"Oh, one more thing. We may get a few stares tonight."

"Because I'm *Englische*?"

"No, because we are old. The average age there will be about seventeen. Kids really, who come from all over, because this is where boys and girls meet, to become men and women."

"Well, how do they get to meet if everyone is singing?"

"You'll see."

The singing was held at the same house where church was held that morning, but there was no church service, as such. Young people were gathered around a long table, boys on one side and girls on the other.

The teenagers looked at John and Leah as they entered with a hint of concern. "No, we aren't your chaperones," John said with a laugh. "We are just like the rest of you, here to enjoy the company."

There were a dozen different types of cookies, doughnuts—which the Amish called *fassnachte*—and other pastries available. There was also fruit punch, and Leah took her first swallow cautiously. John laughed at her. "Trust me, it isn't spiked," he said.

In between the songs everyone visited. There were several people who inquired about Leah.

"This is Lena Lapp," John said. "She is my betrothed, from Missouri."

Leah wondered why he introduced her as Lena, then she realized that he needed to give her an Amish name. Later, after the singing, when the young men and young women paired up, then went for "moonlight walks," Leah went outside with John.

"So, I'm your betrothed, am I?" she asked.

"I hope you don't mind. It's easier than trying to explain why an *Englische* is here, living with us."

"I don't mind."

"Leah, why *are* you here?"

"I beg your pardon?"

"Did you come here just to try to establish a relationship with your grandmother?"

"Why do you ask that?"

"I—forgive me. I have no right to pry. It's just that sometimes you seem a little detached. I have to ask you this. You aren't married, are you? I mean, you aren't running away from a husband?"

Leah laughed. "No, John. I'm not married, and I never have been."

John let out a long sigh of relief. "I'm glad," he said. "I'm very glad you aren't married."

"Were you really concerned about that?"

"I confess that I was," he said.

"Glad I'm able to put your mind at ease."

They walked farther out into the dark so that the sounds of insects and frogs were now louder than the sounds of conversation and laughter from the others.

"You were out with the English for nine years?"

"Yes."

"Why did you come back? I know you didn't want to lose contact with your family. But Ada told me that she, your mother, and both of your brothers came to see you from time to time. And Ada said she was sure your father would come around as well. Maybe they couldn't welcome you back here, but you weren't completely cut off, the way my mother was."

"It had nothing to do with that," John said.

John was silent for a long moment, and Leah could tell that he was troubled.

"I'm sorry," she said. "I shouldn't have asked."

"No, I—I'm glad you did ask the question. I do need to talk to someone, someone from outside who might be able to understand."

As John told the story, he told it with such passion, and in such vivid detail, that Leah could almost see herself there.

"Four years ago I was in Afghanistan, leading a patrol through the streets of Gardez. Sergeant Wyatt, one of my NCOs, as tough a man as I had ever met, turned white as a sheet and pointed to the road ahead of us.

"What Sergeant Wyatt pointed out to me was more grisly a scene than any human should ever have to witness. The bodies of a headless man and a headless woman were lying in the street. The woman was naked. A young girl of about six was sitting beside them, and she was—" John halted in his narrative, fighting to hold back the tears that, even now, were just on the other side of his horror-filled eyes. "She was—" Again, he stopped in midsentence, then cleared his throat. "She was holding the severed, bloody heads of her mother and father in her lap."

"Oh, John, no," Leah said, her voice full of compassion as she not only recognized but felt the pain in John's words.

John cleared his throat again, then continued with his story. "There was a boy there too, who couldn't have been over ten years old. He was holding his right arm with his left. He had to be holding it with his left, because the right arm had been crushed and disfigured. The boy was in shock and unable to talk, but the little girl told us that the Taliban had killed her parents, then held her brother's arm under the wheel of a pickup truck and ran over it!"

"Why in heaven's name would they do such a thing?"

"I've asked myself the same thing a million times since then. I have no answer."

John was silent for a moment, and Leah's head spun as she imagined what an awful experience that had to have been for him.

"The medic had some morphine, and we gave the boy a shot, but I don't know if it was even necessary. He was in such shock that I don't think he felt the pain, anyway. I mean, think of it. He had seen his father decapitated, his mother raped and beheaded, and his own arm crushed.

"While we were tending to the boy, the Taliban attacked again. Turns out they had done this, then left them in the street as bait. And we took the bait. There were at least forty of them, and ten of us.

"I put my men into a final defensive fire position, and I assigned Master Sergeant Wyatt the task of looking out for the little boy and girl. The firefight that followed was the most vicious I have ever been in, before or since. They had us outnumbered, but we had them outgunned. They charged repeatedly, yelling, 'Allahu akbar,' and we poured fire into them. We killed over twenty of them before they broke off the attack and fled in pickup trucks. But by then we had called in C-130 gunships and they finished them off. The Taliban who attacked us were no doubt the same ones who killed the man and woman and crushed the little boy's arm. And of the forty, not one survived. I killed four of them myself. I had three wounded and one killed in the attack. The little boy was also killed."

John pinched the bridge of his nose and was silent for a long moment.

"One of the men killed was Master Sergeant Wyatt. He literally shielded the boy and girl with his body, taking rounds that were meant for the children. My assigning him the responsibility of looking out for them cost him his life.

"Every officer has an NCO they've taken under their wing. Master Sergeant Wyatt was that NCO for me. I held Master Sergeant Wyatt's head in my lap and squeezed his hand as I watched him die.

"I was not only responsible for Sergeant Wyatt's death, I killed four men myself that day. They weren't the first, and they weren't the last men that I killed. Do you know what it means for an Amish man to have taken a life? I forfeited my soul while I was in Afghanistan, Leah. And I've had to live with that, ever since I came back. This is not something I can tell my father, mother, sister, or either of my brothers. This is something I must deal with myself, and I intended to deal with it myself. But now, I have burdened you with it."

"John, you haven't burdened me. If telling me about it helps in any way, I'm here for you. And it isn't as if you murdered anyone— you were a soldier. I know that God forgives soldiers who are placed in such situations."

"But you don't understand. I am Amish. I shouldn't have been a soldier in the first place," John said. "I shouldn't have gone to college." He tapped himself on the chest. "Now I'll meet God with these scars on my soul."

John lowered his head, and Leah felt drawn to him as she had never felt drawn to another person in her entire life. She stepped up to him and put her arms around him. He wrapped his arms around her and they stood together that way, embracing in the dark.

And then, though Leah couldn't say for sure when it happened, the embrace grew beyond one of providing comfort and solace. She was aware of his muscular body against hers, and she leaned into him, enjoying the contact. They stood that way for a moment, then John stepped back from her and looked down. She could see his eyes, shining in the moonlight.

Leah was not surprised when he kissed her, but she was surprised by her reaction to it. She felt a tingling in her lips that spread throughout her body, warming her blood. When they parted, she reached up to touch her lips and held her fingers there for a long moment.

"I had no right to do that," John said. "I'm sorry."

"I'm not," Leah replied, and she leaned into him again, lifting her head toward his. He kissed her again, deepening the kiss as he pulled her more tightly against him. Then, gently, he tugged her head back to break the kiss. She stared up at him with eyes that were filled with wonder and as deep as her soul. Her lips were still parted from the kiss, and her cheeks flushed.

"I should get you back," John said.

A part of Leah felt a ragged disconnect, to be pushed this far only to be summarily pulled back. *No,* she wanted to shout. *Not now, don't stop.* But she knew that John was right. There was no future in this.

Leah remembered once reading an old Yiddish proverb: "A fish and a fowl may marry, but where will they live?"

She didn't know if she was the fish or the fowl. But she knew that she and John were worlds apart.

"Yes," she finally said. "We should go back."

CHAPTER TEN

It was raining, a cold, late-October rain, and when Detective Sergeant Gary Hellman stepped into the FBI building the warning bell sounded and the agent on duty looked up at him.

"You're going to have to empty your pockets, sir."

Hellman held out his hand, showing his police badge. "I'm Sergeant Hellman, SLPD, and I'm armed," he said. "I just don't want you to get excited when you see me pull out my gun."

"All right, if you would, please put your weapon in this container."

Hellman did as instructed, then, bending down, he pulled a second, smaller pistol from his ankle holster.

"Thank you, sergeant. And now, the purpose of your visit?"

"I called Coker earlier this morning. I would like to speak with him, please."

The door monitor picked up a phone and punched a number.

"Mr. Coker, there is a Sergeant Hellman here to see you. Yes, sir," he said. Hanging up the phone, he looked over at Hellman.

"He'll be right here."

Hellman stepped over to look at some of the photographs on the wall, pictures of current and past agents who had served in the St. Louis office. He found Agent Coker's picture and studied it for a moment—the photo showed a dark-haired, dark-eyed man looking sternly at the camera.

"Sergeant Hellman?"

"Agent Coker."

"Come along. We'll stop and get some coffee on the way."

Hellman and Coker stopped at the coffee station, each poured themselves a cup, then went on into Coker's office.

"Now, what can I do for you?" Coker asked.

"I'm working the Carl Trevathan homicide case."

"Oh, yeah, the lawyer who was popped by his secretary."

"She isn't a secretary, she's a lawyer. And from all I've been able to find out, a very good one."

"Do you think she did it?"

"I don't know. I suppose so. I mean, the evidence against her is pretty damning. We have two witnesses on the ninth floor who saw her with his body when the elevator doors opened. Then, of course, once the elevator reached the ground there were several who saw her. We've got the murder weapon, ballistics has already made the match, and the gun is covered with her fingerprints."

"Well, if she was seen in the elevator with him on the ninth floor, and he was dead on the ground floor, and she was standing over his body holding the gun, that seems pretty locked up, doesn't it?"

"She didn't have the gun."

"I thought you said you had the murder weapon and it had her fingerprints."

"Yes, that's true. But we didn't find the weapon on her. Somehow she got through without the gun being found."

"If you didn't take the gun off her, how did you get it?"

"That's where we got a break. The other two senior partners in the firm, Blanton and Dunn, found it in her desk, and they turned it over to us. They think she did it, but even so, Blanton is going to represent her in court, if we ever find her."

"What's the motive?"

"Blanton and Dunn think she might have been having an affair with him, and when he wouldn't agree to divorce his wife she went off the deep end."

"Sounds reasonable," Coker said as he took another swallow of his coffee.

"Yeah," Hellman said. "And it might be even more reasonable if I could find some evidence that there really was such an affair. That's where I'm having trouble."

"You mean you don't believe she was having an affair with one of the senior partners? Would that be such a rare thing?"

"Of all the people in the law firm, only Blanton and Dunn suggest that she was having an affair with Trevathan. The others I've interviewed say that if that was so, they didn't know anything about it. Marilyn Summers, one of the law clerks, knows Leah McKenzie very well, and she insists that there was no affair."

"Well, if anyone would know, wouldn't it more likely be Blanton and Dunn? I mean, after all, they're the senior partners, they would know more about another senior partner's private life than anyone else in the firm."

"Maybe. But you would also think his wife would know, wouldn't you? Or at least suspect? Mrs. Trevathan is absolutely positive there was nothing going on between them, and she also doesn't believe Leah McKenzie shot her husband. Which is why I came to you," Hellman concluded.

"What do you want from me?"

"Mrs. Trevathan told me that less than a week before he was killed, her husband contacted you."

Coker took another swallow of his coffee and studied Hellman over the rim of his cup. The two men stared at each other for a long moment before Hellman spoke again.

"Well?"

"Well what?"

"Did Trevathan contact you?"

"Yes."

"What was it about?"

"It was about an ongoing case. I'm afraid I can't comment on it."

"Damn it, man, this is an ongoing case as well!" Hellman retorted angrily. "Now, what was it about?"

"I'm not really sure what it was about."

"What kind of answer is that?"

"Trevathan said that he had a file pertaining to a case we've been working on. A file that would, to use his words, 'blow the lid off everything.' He wanted me to see it."

"What was in the file?"

"I don't have any idea. He was killed before I ever saw the file."

"Wait a minute," Hellman said. "Were you in the Eagleton building?"

"Yes."

"On the day he was killed?"

"Yes."

"I knew it," Hellman said, hitting his fist into his hand. "I knew you were there."

Coker didn't answer.

"All right, so you didn't see the file. But you must know what case it referred to. Tell me about that."

"I can't tell you that."

"Please, Agent Coker, you must understand. If I can connect Trevathan to the case you're working, I might be able to find a motive."

"I will say this, and this is all I can say until your boss clears it with my boss. It has to do with money. A great, great deal of money."

"So, it could be that if she did shoot him, her reason had nothing to do with, as the poets say, unrequited love."

"Yes."

"Thank you. I believe you may have just opened a new line of investigation for me."

Hellman's next stop was the Thomas Eagleton federal court building. Once there, he sought out Mr. Don Pratt, the senior security guard.

"You can ask me all you want, Sergeant Hellman," Pratt said.

"And you'll get the same answer every time. If she had a gun, I didn't see it. She wasn't holding it in her hand, and it wasn't on the floor of the elevator."

"I'm not particularly looking for how the gun got out now," Hellman said. "I'm interested in something else."

"What?"

"I don't want to influence your answer with a suggestion. I want you to just close your eyes and think for a moment, then tell me exactly what you saw when the elevator doors opened."

"I saw one very frightened woman and one very dead man. Both of them were covered with blood."

"Did you see anything else?"

"There was no gun."

"Did you see anything else?"

"I told you. There was no gun."

"I'm not asking if she had a gun. Did she have anything at all with her?"

"All she had was her purse and one of those flat leather folders. And there was no gun in the purse, because I looked."

"Aha! What was in the folder?"

"I don't know, I didn't look there. None of us did."

"Why not?"

"Why should we have? I mean, if there had been a gun in it, we would have seen it. When I say it was flat, I mean it was absolutely flat, and thin. Not a briefcase, more like, oh, maybe something like a leather envelope. Yes, that's it. It was like about a twelve-by-fourteen leather envelope."

"Could there have been several pages in the envelope? Something like a report, maybe?"

"There could have been, I suppose. I don't know. There weren't any of us looking for papers. We were trying to find the gun."

Sergeant Hellman interviewed every other security guard who was there when the elevator doors opened, but none had anything to add to the testimony of Mr. Pratt.

CHAPTER ELEVEN

W hen my *daad* was a boy, there were no rules against owning or watching television," Isaac said.

"There were no rules? Then you mean Grossdaadi watched television?" Jacob asked.

"No, he didn't watch."

"He didn't watch because he was a good man," Sam suggested.

"*Ja*, he was a good man. But that isn't why he didn't watch television."

"Then I don't understand, Daad. Why was there no rule about not watching television?" Sam asked.

A broad smile spread across Isaac's face. "Because there was no television," he said, and the others laughed.

"Do you like television?" Jacob asked Leah.

"It has its place," Leah said. "But I don't watch a whole lot of television anymore. There are so many reality shows that just show the worst in people."

"What is a reality show?" Jacob asked.

"I'm not sure I can even explain what it is. It has certainly caused a deterioration in what you get on television though."

"I have heard the *Englische* talking about news," Isaac said. "They say that when something very bad happens, others often do the same thing. It is called copycat."

"Yes," Leah said. "Unfortunately that is true."

"But I think that such a thing can have no effect on us," Isaac said. "As long as we live our lives and keep ourselves separate from the outside world, we will be safe from the crime and evil that plagues them."

"That isn't true," John said.

"But of course it is true," Isaac insisted. "Little do we care what goes on in the outside world."

"We think we are safe because we keep ourselves apart from the rest of the world," John said. "But I'm afraid that we are only fooling ourselves."

"Why do you say such a thing?" Jacob said.

"Do you not remember the incident where the Amish school-children were killed? Five young girls were killed, eleven more were wounded."

"*Ja,* I remember the killing of the Amish schoolgirls," Isaac said. "But the one who killed them was not Amish."

"You have made my point, Daad," John said. "He was a milk-man, an *ausländer*. Clearly, the little girls who were killed were not of his world, but that didn't save them. We are not of the world of the *Englische* and our Ordnung keeps us from them. But the

Englische have no such restrictions placed upon them. They come among us, they gawk at us, they take pictures."

"We can avoid them," Isaac said.

"No, we can't. We use the same money they use, and we do business with them. We sell them our pumpkins and corn, our milk and our honey. And I make furniture for them. We pretend that there are two worlds, but that isn't true. The only thing that makes us different from them are the rules we must follow, or not follow. I wonder how many of our people violate these rules but keep those violations to themselves. They come to church on Sunday morning, and they sing from the Ausbund, and they say their prayers, and they have the fellowship dinner, but they are nothing but a bunch of hypocrites."

"Be careful what you say, John," Isaac warned him. "You are close to blasphemy."

"I'm sorry, Daad," he said. "I'm sorry, Mamm. I must get to work." John nodded toward his brothers and sister. He looked at Leah for an extended moment, and the expression in his eyes said that he was trying to talk to her, trying to get her to understand.

To understand what?

Oh, John, she thought. *Why could we not have met at another time and in another place?* John was a prisoner of the Ordnung, which guided his life, and Leah was imprisoned by a false accusation that had all but destroyed her life. It felt almost as if John was someone she'd happened to see through the car window in heavy traffic. There was a momentary connection between them, then it was gone.

"What got into John?" Sam asked.

"I think because he lived with the *Englische* for so long that sometimes it is difficult for him to return to our ways," Isaac said.

"But look at Leah. Her whole life has been with the *Englische*. And now she is one of us," Sam said.

"No," Isaac said. "Leah is a good woman, but she is not one of us."

"But she is living with us, she dresses as we do, she attends church. Why do you say she is not one of us?"

Isaac looked directly at Leah. "Perhaps she could become one of us if, say, she married an Amish man, got baptized into the church, and renounced the outside world. But until she does that, she will never be one of us."

Leah could feel Isaac's eyes boring right into her soul. Could he read her feelings for John? Had John said something to him?

"We cannot spend the entire day gossiping like women. Come, boys, we must get started," Isaac said, breaking the connection between them.

Gossiping like women? That was a very sexist thing to say, and yet neither Emma nor Ada seemed to take offense. Isaac was right. She certainly was not of this world.

As Leah washed dishes, she considered some of the contradictory things about Amish life. The Amish were very religious, but they had no churches. She thought of her own religious upbringing. When she thought of church, she thought of a building with a steeple, whether it be a small, one-room country church or Christ Church Cathedral, with its stoles, altars, kneelers, stained glass windows, choirs, organs, and a paid priest.

"You are being very quiet," Ada said.

"Am I? I'm sorry, I guess I was just thinking."

"About what Daad said?"

"Yes."

"He thinks that maybe John is falling in love with you."

"Would that be so bad?"

"It would not be bad if you became Amish. But I think you could not do that."

"My mother was Amish."

"*Ja*, but she wasn't Amish when you knew her."

"There are just so many things about the Amish that I don't understand. For example, you can ride in a car, but you can't own a car. Why not?"

Ada chuckled. "Every young Amish person has asked that same question. We see the *Englische* young people driving around in cars, and we ask our parents and the bishop why we can't have a car."

"And has anyone ever given you a proper answer?"

"If we owned cars, our communities would disappear."

"Why do you say that?"

"Consider this. If we had cars, we could go easily into cities like Decatur, Springfield, St. Louis, or Chicago. Maybe even as far away as Los Angeles or New York. Now we can go no farther than a horse and buggy will take us. That keeps us together. Cars would allow more contact with *ausländer,* like you. And that could lead to men and women thinking of themselves as individuals, rather than as a part of the whole."

Strangely, Leah felt a little hurt at being referred to as an *ausländer*. It was just that she was beginning to feel as if they had accepted her.

"Is thinking of yourself as an individual bad?"

"*Ja.*"

"Now, see, I don't understand that, Ada. The thing I most admire about you, the thing the entire world admires about you, is your rugged individualism and self-sufficiency."

"But we are strong only as long as we as a people stay together," Ada said.

"All right, yes, I suppose I can see that."

When the dishes were done Ada hung up the dishcloth and drying towel.

"Today I am going into the field to help pick the pumpkins. Would you like to come?" Ada asked.

"Yes, I would."

"Good. As Daad always says, 'We can use an extra two hands.'"

Leah actually enjoyed being in the pumpkin field, amid the bright orange pumpkins. She had been with the Amish for a month and a half now, and they were so insistent upon muted colors, so determined that there could be nothing garish, and except for quilts, most of which they sold, there could be nothing that existed "just for pretty." The bright orange of the pumpkins was a vivid violation of that rule.

"I love the pumpkins," Leah said. "They are so beautiful."

"I like them too," Ada said. "I like the color."

"I thought Amish couldn't have colors like orange."

"But this is God's color," Ada said.

Leah nodded. "Well, you're right about that."

There was a long pause as the two women worked, then Ada spoke again. "Do you?"

"Do I what?" Leah asked, confused by Ada's question.

"Love him?"

Leah didn't need further clarification, but neither did she answer the question.

"Daad and Mamm are worried. They think that John loves you."

"I think I just remind him of what life was like on the outside."

"*Ja,* that is even worse," Ada said, but she walked back to the end of the wagon before Leah could answer.

Did she love him? Leah wondered. No, that was quite impossible.

John fitted two pieces of the desk together, then put a level on the top to make certain that it was perfectly even. He was having a hard time concentrating today—he couldn't get Leah out of his mind.

It was funny, because all the time he was out among the *Englische,* he'd made it a point never to get serious about any woman. That wasn't to say there had been no women in his life. Like Kitty, who worked at a bar that was just across the highway from gate six at Fort Campbell, in Kentucky. And Linda Sue, a waitress in Printer's Alley in Nashville. Neither Kitty nor Linda Sue had ever suggested that their relationship be anything beyond a temporary liaison. But his relationship with Cassandra Purvis, daughter of his battalion commander, had been a bit more troublesome. After a few casual dinners and movies, he drifted along with her for a while until he realized that he didn't really love her, certainly not enough to make this change in his life permanent.

It wasn't that they broke up so much as grew apart—they just stopped seeing each other as casually as they'd started. Then a young lieutenant came to see him one day, asking if he could speak with him in private. After much stammering, the soldier finally made it clear that he was hoping to pursue Cassandra himself. John gave the young man his blessing—but part of him envied his enthusiasm.

Lieutenant Kirby married Cassandra Purvis within three months of that discussion, and John felt lucky that he had not allowed himself to be caught up in anything like that. He came back to the Amish fully expecting to meet some young Amish woman, get married, and raise Amish children. What could possibly be wrong with that? But, though he had been back for two years, he had found no one. And how could he? No Amish woman could possibly see the world through his eyes—nor would he want to subject one to that. He had shared it with no one, but a great restlessness still resided in his scarred soul.

"Ah, but what about Leah?" he asked aloud. Then, embarrassed for fear he might have been overheard talking to himself, he looked around the shop hastily.

What about Leah? he wondered. She was beautiful, she was intelligent, and there was a worldliness about her. She could not be corrupted by him. Was this a test? It wasn't fair. All the while he had been out with the *Englische,* he had managed to avoid any emotional entanglements with an *ausländer.* But now, one had come to him.

This was not going to work. He could not—he would not fall in love with her.

John rose from the desk he was working on, then walked to the back door, opened it, and looked out across the alley. He saw Prodigal's head in the shadows of the stable. He had named him Prodigal to keep himself ever mindful that he was being given a second chance.

He wasn't sure that he was doing right by his second chance. Three months ago he had taken Sam to town, where the two of them changed into *Englische* clothes, then went to a movie. They saw the movie *Cars,* and Sam found the idea of talking cars so funny that he laughed until tears were streaming down his face. Sam did not tell Isaac for a long time after that, but then his conscience got the best of him, and he confessed his sin.

John thought his father would chastise him for that, but he didn't. And the fact that his father said nothing at all to him, even though he clearly knew of the violation, bothered John more than if his father had taken him to task.

He had taken Jacob out with him, also, but not to a movie. He and Jacob went to a Hooters restaurant. Jacob had never before seen women like the Hooters waitresses.

"Why do they call this place Hooters?" Jacob asked. "Are there owls here?"

"I think it's something like that," John replied with a smile. "What do you think of the ladies?"

"I would like to see Hannah Esh in such an outfit," Jacob said.

John laughed out loud. "That, little brother, you will never see," he said.

"John, when you were out among the Englische, *did you see many women dressing like these women?"*

"On the beach, you see women who are wearing much, much less than this."

"Oh, I do not think that would be good," Jacob said. "The Bible says, 'But I say to you that everyone who looks at a woman with lustful intent has already committed adultery with her in his heart.' I'm afraid that I would commit adultery every day."

"That is a sin that is hard to avoid when you are out among the En-glische," John agreed.

"Did you?"

"Like you say, it is hard not to when you see beautiful women, scantily dressed, day after day."

"No, I mean did you ever really—uh—not just lust in your heart? Did you ever—uh—actually do it?"

John chuckled. "Jacob, don't you know that's not anything you ever ask another person?"

"You're not another person. You are my brother."

"And I've already caused enough trouble by bringing you out like this. I'll not be responsible for putting lustful thoughts in your head."

"John?" Collins called from the front of the shop. "You want to step up here for a minute?"

John put down the sandpaper, removed his gloves, brushed the sawdust from his clothes, and walked into the front of the building.

"John, this is Kyle Sherman. He's opening a law office and is looking for furniture."

"What are you looking for, Mr. Sherman?"

"A desk, a credenza, and a table," the lawyer replied. "I'm going out on my own, you see, and I need some elegant furniture to impress potential clients."

"I showed him several pieces," Collins said. "But he wants furniture that's made especially for him."

"I'm not only a lawyer, Mr. Miller. I'm also an artist," Sherman said. "Like you," he added, taking in several of the pieces with a wide swoop of his hand. "And I know that when you create a piece of art especially for someone, it takes on a personality all its own. Do you understand what I'm saying?"

"You are asking if I understand the concept of anthropomorphism," John answered. "And yes, I do."

"Concept of what?" Collins asked, totally confused by the word.

"It means giving personality to an inanimate object," Sherman said. He cocked his head as he studied John for a moment. "How do you know that word?"

"It is as you said, Mr. Sherman. I am an artist. I give personality to everything I work with."

Sherman smiled and nodded his head. "Mr. Collins, I believe Mr. Miller and I are going to get along quite nicely."

"I have no doubt," Collins replied. "Everyone who has ever met him likes him. Say, did you know that lawyer fella who was murdered over there in St. Louis a couple of months ago?"

"Yes, I knew him quite well. It made quite a splash when it first came out, but it's about died down now."

"Have they found who did it?"

"They think they know who did it, but they haven't found her yet."

"It's a terrible thing," Collins said. "How soon will you want your furniture?"

"Whenever you can get it done. I don't like to rush art, or perfection."

John returned to the back of the shop and began working again. Was he going to stay this time? When he told Jonas Beachey that he was going back to his Amish family, Beachey accepted his decision without trying to talk him out of it.

Jonas Beachey and his wife, Kathleen, ran what could be called an underground railroad, an organization that helped ex-Amish in their transition into life among the English. They had left the life over twenty years ago and since that time had helped hundreds leave.

It had been Jonas who helped John, providing him with clothes and helping John get a birth certificate, social security card, and driver's license. They also helped John get his high school GED and arranged a student loan so he could go to college. Enrolling at SIU Carbondale, John decided to go out for basketball. He was discouraged by others who told him that all the players were athletic scholarship players. He tried out anyway and made the team. By his sophomore year he was on an athletic scholarship of his own, and by his senior year, he'd made all-conference.

Jonas and Kathleen kept up with John, providing him support and communicating with him by e-mail while John was in the army and in Afghanistan. Jonas made it clear to John that he was not going to proselytize one way or the other, that he wasn't out to destroy the Amish.

"And just as we have helped you leave the Amish, if you want to go back, we will help you with that as well."

When John left the army he wasn't even aware of the scars on his soul. He came back to visit the Beacheys, to share stories with them, most of which involved a dark humor.

"We sent a lot of Habibs to see their seventy-two virgins. But you know, I've been thinking about it, and I don't think there are seventy-two virgins waiting for them. I think there is just one virgin, and she is seventy-two years old."

John laughed a lot when he first got back, and he talked a lot, and he teased about people who had to deal with PTSD.

"I figure anyone who goes nuts after they get back was probably nuts to begin with," he told Jonas.

"John, have you ever heard that a light shines brightest before it goes out?" Jonas asked.

"What does that mean?"

"It means don't be so sure that everything you have gone through has had no effect on you."

For the next year John was unable to settle down. He traveled the country, taking a series of part-time and menial jobs—from washing dishes in Eugene, Oregon, to construction work in Phoenix, to working as a hotel night clerk in St. Louis. Then one night, he woke up in a cold sweat and lay in bed for a long moment, overpowered by a sensation of fear and grief. He left the very next morning to go back home. It wasn't that far a drive, and he wondered if he had been, subconsciously, working his way back all along. He stopped in Decatur, Illinois, put his car in storage, then hired a taxi to take him to his father's farm.

At first, John's father wouldn't accept him, but John quoted from the parable of the prodigal son.

"'I will arise and go to my father, and will say unto him, Father, I have sinned against heaven, and before thee, and am no more worthy to be called thy son. Make me as one of thy hired servants.'"

John's father listened, then picked up the story.

"'But the father said to his servants, Bring forth the best robe, and put it on him; and put a ring on his hand, and shoes on his feet: And bring hither the fatted calf, and kill it; and let us eat, and be merry: For this my son was dead, and is alive again; he was lost, and is found.'"

Isaac Miller embraced his son. "But I do not think you starved," he said with a smile, putting his hand on John's stomach. "And I'm not going to kill a fatted calf."

"I did not starve here, Daad." John moved his father's hand from his stomach to his chest, over his heart. "But I starved here."

Because he was returning home for good, John was accepted, not only by his parents, who rejoiced that he who was lost had been found, but also by the others in the community.

CHAPTER TWELVE

Y ou wanted to see me, captain?" Hellman asked, stepping into Captain Peach's office.

"Yes, Gary, have a seat. I was in the mayor's office this morning and he started asking me a lot of questions. Uncomfortable questions."

"Like what, captain?"

"Like what are we doing to solve the Carl Trevathan murder? Bring me up to speed on what's happening."

"We're still following leads."

"Hell, Gary, the whole world knows who did it. It was that female lawyer in his office who had the hots for him. When I say 'bring me up to speed,' what I mean is, do you have any idea where she is now?"

"No, sir, I don't have the slightest idea."

"Well, what have we done so far to try to find her?"

"We have interviewed every work colleague, every friend that we have been able to track down, high school and college classmates, but so far, nothing's gotten us any closer."

"She didn't just drop off the face of the earth."

"Captain, I'm not sure she's the one who killed Trevathan."

"Well, that'll be for the court to decide, won't it? It's our business to propose, the court's business to dispose. And what in heaven's name makes you think she didn't do it? She was the last person seen with him. We have the gun that killed him, and it has her fingerprints all over it. And she disappeared."

"She's running because she's afraid. But her fingerprints weren't on the magazine. How did she load the pistol? In fact, there were no fingerprints at all on the magazine."

"So she wiped them off."

"Did she? Why would she wipe her fingerprints off the magazine, but not off the gun? Doesn't that give you pause?"

Captain Peach stroked his chin. "No fingerprints of any kind on the magazine, you say? Well now, that is interesting. But if Leah McKenzie didn't do it, that puts us back to square one, doesn't it?"

"We aren't back to square one, captain. We never left square one."

Leah was still having a hard time adjusting to the early mornings. It wasn't even daylight yet and as she was cracking eggs for scrambling into a large bowl, she couldn't stop herself from yawning. She was startled when someone came up behind her and put his arms around her.

"It's good to see that you are in the swing of things," John said. She could feel his breath on her neck.

She turned toward him in surprise.

"John, what are you do—?" Leah started to say, but her question was stopped in midword when he kissed her.

At his kiss, she felt two things—thrilled by the touch of his lips, and frightened that someone would discover them.

"John!" she said, pulling away from him.

"Afraid we'll get caught?" John asked with a mischievous grin.

"Yes!"

"Admit it though, doesn't that make it a little more exciting?"

Leah laughed. "You are impossible. I think you're just pretending to be Amish."

"Speaking of being caught, you're making a mess on the floor. You'd better get that cleaned up before Mamm comes back in. I think I hear her now."

Leah looked at the floor and saw that beaten egg had dribbled off the large wooden spoon she had been using.

"Oh!" she said. She wet a cloth and got down on her knees to wipe up the floor. John, with another cloth, got down to help her.

Emma came into the room then, and seeing them both on their knees, asked, "*Was ist hier passiert?*"

Then, realizing she had asked the question in German, she asked again, "What happened here?"

"I splashed some egg onto the floor."

"I told her that you would beat her with a broomstick if you came in and found it," John said.

"John! Why do you say such a thing? No such thing would I do!"

Leah couldn't keep from smiling.

"Oh," Emma said. "A joke you were telling."

John laughed. "*Ja*, Mamm, a joke I was telling."

"Is not so funny this joke I think, to tell this poor girl that I would beat her."

"It's all right, Emma, I know that you wouldn't do such a thing."

"It is Isaac who will beat you," Emma said.

"What?" Leah gasped.

Emma laughed. "Now is joke I tell," she said.

Leah and John laughed with her.

"Thank you for beating the eggs. I will cook them now."

"Mamm, will you put a little cheese in the eggs?"

"*Ja*, if you like."

"I'll grate the cheese," Leah offered.

"That will be good. Ada is still milking."

Half an hour later the entire family was gathered around the table and the sun was just coming up. In that time the animals had been fed, the cows milked, the eggs gathered, and breakfast cooked.

They paused for the silent blessing of the food. During the blessing, Leah said a quick prayer of her own.

Dear Lord, please let the police find whoever it was that actually killed Mr. Trevathan. She finished her prayer just as the others were saying "amen."

"I think today with the corn we will be finished," Isaac said. "Tomorrow we will start bringing in the hay."

"Are we making a good crop of corn, Daad?" John asked.

"Ha!" Sam said. "Listen to the city boy ask about corn."

"Sam, I was picking corn when you were still in diapers," John said. "And I would farm now, if there was land enough."

"I know. I'm sorry," Sam said.

"Don't be sorry, just be quiet," John replied, and Jacob laughed at their youngest brother.

"If you had not left, my part of the farm would be yours," Jacob said. "I am sorry I have taken your birthright."

"Don't be sorry, Jacob. You are ten times a better farmer than I could ever be."

"That's what I said," Sam said.

John picked up a spoonful of scrambled eggs and catapulted them into Sam's face.

"Mamm, did you see what John did?" Sam asked as both Ada and Jacob laughed.

"Stop it. *Kleine Kinder ihr seid.* Like children you are!" But even Emma was laughing.

"Leah, today I'm taking the pumpkins in to the farmers' market. Also, I must buy some material to make another dress. Would you like to come with me?" Ada asked.

"Oh, yes, I'd love to go to town with you," Leah said.

"Ha!" Jacob said. "I think Ada takes you because she wants you to help unload the pumpkins."

"Of course I'll help her."

Almost as soon as she replied, Leah began to have second thoughts, but not because of the work of unloading the pumpkins. On the one hand, she desperately wanted to go to town; she needed to go to town, just to prove to herself that there was a world beyond this farm, beautiful though she thought it was. And she hoped she might hear something about her case.

But she was sure that her picture had been on TV by now, and there was always a chance that someone might recognize her.

When everyone else left the dining room, and only John and Leah remained, he kissed her again.

"John! Everyone is still around!" she said nervously.

"Do you think they have never seen a man and woman kiss before?"

"I think they have never seen their son and an *Englischer* kiss before."

"Admit it, you like the thrill of it."

John kissed her again, and giggling nervously, Leah twisted out of his embrace.

"John, please, now I *am* getting a little frightened."

"Are you going to be with Ada today?"

"Yes."

"Ask her about bundling."

"Ask her about what?"

"Bundling," John said.

"What is bundling?"

"Ask Ada. She will tell you."

When Leah went outside, Jacob, Sam, and Ada were loading the pumpkins, so Leah started helping. After the wagon was loaded, Sam began hitching up the team as Ada went into the house for any last-minute requests or instructions.

"Do you love John?" Jacob asked. The question came out of the blue and surprised Leah.

"What?"

"I said, do you love John?"

"I know what you said. What I want to know is why you would ask such a thing."

"I ask you because I think John loves you."

"I think you are imagining things, Jacob."

"No, I think I'm right. And that worries me."

"Why does it worry you?"

"Because you are an *ausländer,* and you can't marry John."

"Whoa, Jacob," Leah said, holding her hand out. "I think you've jumped way ahead of the game here. Nobody, and I mean absolutely nobody, has mentioned getting married."

"I think he would leave the church again for you," Jacob said.

"Jacob, I haven't come here to purloin John away from anyone."

"What does 'purloin' mean?"

"It means 'steal.' I have no intention of stealing him from the church."

"Maybe it would be better if John did leave the church."

"Why would you say such a thing?"

"John has been outside. He's seen things and done things that no Amish man has ever seen or done. I look at him sometimes, and I know that though he has come back to us, he has not come all the way back. Daad may be talking about having to castrate some pigs, but John is away in some distant place, like maybe St. Louis or New Orleans, or Timbuktu."

Leah chuckled. "Jacob, do you know where Timbuktu is?"

"No, but it must be someplace very grand, because I've heard of it."

"I'm sure it's a grand place, all right."

"Can I ask you something, Leah?"

"Sure. Ask anything you want."

"Do you have a tramp stamp?"

Leah laughed out loud at the sudden change in subject.

"Do I have a tramp stamp? No, I don't have one. But tell me, Jacob, where in the world did you hear about such a thing? And what made you think I might have one?"

"In town, once, at the farmers' market, some *Englische* boys were talking about girls, and they said every girl they knew had a tramp stamp. When I asked what that was, they just laughed. I still don't know what a tramp stamp is."

"It's a tattoo."

"A tattoo? They call a tattoo a tramp stamp?"

"It depends on where it is," Leah said. "A tramp stamp is . . ." Leah paused for a moment. "You're going to make me blush, Jacob."

"I'm sorry. I don't mean to embarrass you. But I really want to know why the boys laughed."

"When a woman gets a tattoo here"—she put her finger on her backside, just above the cheeks—"that is called a tramp stamp."

"Why would someone put a tattoo somewhere where nobody can see it?"

"You are missing the point, Jacob. When they put one there, it's an invitation for someone to see it."

"Oh?" Jacob thought about it for a moment. "Oh!" he said. "Oh, a girl who would do something like that would be, well, I don't know the word."

"Now you see where the tramp stamp gets its name."

"*Ja, ja,* I see," Jacob replied, laughing nervously.

Once the pumpkins were loaded, Leah and Ada climbed up

into the driver's seat and Ada picked up the reins. With a cluck of her tongue and a snap of the reins, they got under way.

The house was six miles from Arthur, which was about an hour and a half away by team and loaded wagon. Leah couldn't help but think that she could have made this same trip in her car in less than ten minutes. But, instead of getting impatient, she actually enjoyed the trip into town.

There was something therapeutic about watching the sway of the horses and the bob of their heads, and hearing the soothing clop of hoofbeats. She could also enjoy the scenery, from the greens, yellows, and browns of the fields, to the neat farmhomes with their barns and silos, to the bright orange of the pumpkins. And she had a greater appreciation of the wildlife, from the many red-winged blackbirds that decorated the fences, to the squirrels in the trees, and even to a fox that sat on the side of the road, watching as they passed by.

"Do you have a boyfriend, Ada?"

"*Ja,* I have a beau. You've met him."

"I've met him? Where?"

"At church."

Leah smiled. "Yes, I saw him. He was helping with the horses."

"How did you know?"

"I saw the way you and he looked at each other. I think John called him Caleb?"

"*Ja,* Caleb Brenneman."

"But when John and I went to the singing, you didn't go."

"Because we went somewhere else," Ada said. Leah saw that Ada was blushing and realized this was uncomfortable for her, so she didn't ask any more questions. To her surprise, though, Ada continued the conversation.

"Sometimes at night, after Mamm and Daad and my brothers have gone to bed, he'll come and shine a flashlight through the window of my bedroom. Then, when I see the light, I know that it is him. I go downstairs and let him in and we sit in the parlor."

"What do you do in the parlor?"

"Sometimes we play games. But mostly we just talk."

"And do you kiss?"

Ada's blush grew more pronounced, and she smiled in embarrassment.

"*Ja*, we kiss," she said.

"Ada, what is bundling?"

Ada laughed. "You are an *Englischer*. Where did you hear about bundling?"

"From John. He said I should ask you about bundling."

"John said that?"

"Yes."

"Is John your beau?" Ada asked.

"No, I . . ." She didn't finish the sentence.

"He took you to the singing."

"Yes, he did. But I think he just wanted to show me what it was like."

"No. I think he wouldn't take you to the singing and he wouldn't ask you about bundling if he didn't want to be your beau."

Leah thought of the kisses they had shared, but she didn't mention that to Ada.

"John is not like the others," Leah said.

"John was with the *Englische* for a long time. I was young when he left."

"Yes, he told me."

"He has not told us where he was while he was with the *Englische*. I think maybe something bad happened to him and he does not want to speak of it."

Leah was surprised to hear that. John told her he had been in the war and that the war had scarred his soul. She was pleased that he had told her, and she made a silent vow not to betray his trust in her.

"So what is bundling?"

"It is when a boy and a girl go to bed together."

"What? You mean, make love? Have sex?"

"No. There is no sex," Ada explained. "Bundling is condoned in the Old Testament. In the Book of Ruth it says that men and women should lie on the same bed, as lovers, without undressing."

"Have you and your beau ever bundled?"

"*Ja,*" Ada answered, again with an embarrassed smile.

"What is it like?"

"It is very . . ." Ada searched for a word. "Nice."

They came into town then, into traffic. It was funny; Leah had no problem driving a car in traffic, even out on 270 where cars did seventy miles per hour while practically bumper to bumper. But here, in the small town of Arthur, she felt extremely vulnerable to the traffic, even though it was light.

It didn't bother Ada at all, and she manipulated the loaded wagon skillfully, moving into a left-turn lane before turning with the light. Ada stopped at the farmers' market. The market was busy with several shoppers, cars, pickup trucks, and even another wagon. Someone came up to Ada.

"Good-looking pumpkins, Ada," he said. "How many do you have?"

"I have one hundred and twenty."

"Okay, I'll have Enoch come help you unload them while I go inside and write your check."

"Thank you, Mr. Quinn." Then to Leah Ada said, "You should get down and help Enoch carry the pumpkins to the bin. That is easier than bending over to pick up each one."

"All right," Leah said.

Enoch came with another, and the second man hopped up onto the wagon and helped Ada hand them down.

Leah was struck by all the beautiful colors at the farmers' market, the orange pumpkins dominating, but also green and red bell peppers, yellow squash, ears of brightly colored Indian corn, purple and white turnips, and decorative brown cornstalks.

When the wagon was unloaded, Ada and Leah climbed back in, then Ada drove it farther downtown, where she parked in a lot behind the Plain Fabric Shop. The lot was evidently there for that very purpose, because there were hitching posts scattered about. With the team secured, Ada and Leah went into the shop. A little bell on the door announced their entry.

"Ada," a woman said. "How good to see you." The woman was wearing a lace bonnet, but other than that, she seemed to be conventionally dressed.

"Grace, this is my friend Lena Lapp," Ada said.

That was the same way John had introduced her at the singing, so Leah didn't correct her. Besides, under the circumstances, the fewer people who knew her real name, the better it was. She knew that John and Ada had introduced her in such a way so they wouldn't have to explain why an *Englischer* was wearing plain clothes. But whatever the reason, it worked well for her.

"I have some new dark blue cloth in," Grace said. "It is sturdy. Also, it will be cold soon, and you will want something warm for the winter."

"Good, I will look at it."

"Ada, do you mind if I step out front?" Leah said.

"No, I don't mind. But be mindful of the tourists."

"The tourists?"

"Yes. They can be . . ." Ada looked for a word, and Grace provided it.

"Troublesome," Grace said. "They like to gawk at the Amish. Some have no manners at all."

"Oh, thank you. I'll be"—she paused, then used Ada's word—"mindful."

The bank was next door to the fabric shop, and in front of the bank was a newspaper stand. This would be the first time Leah had any opportunity to get some news from the outside world, and she went over to the stand. The paper cost fifty cents, and she dropped two quarters into the little yellow slot, then opened the door and pulled out a paper. On the front page, below the fold, she saw it.

Mystery Deepens on Trevathan Murder Case

Police have no new leads regarding the murder last month of Carl Trevathan, prominent St. Louis attorney. They are still looking for Leah McKenzie, who was a lawyer in Trevathan's firm and is the leading suspect in the case.

Leah read the entire story and, as she did so, felt a vise of fear grip her. She was sure that her father had read not only this story but all the other stories, all of which suggested that she had murdered Carl Trevathan because of unrequited love. She wished she could get word to her father that she was all right and that she was innocent.

"Oh, look, George. Now there's a picture you don't want to miss. There's an Amish woman reading the newspaper," a woman's voice said.

Leah looked up just as a middle-aged man held his phone out to take her picture. Quickly, she put the paper in front of her face.

"Isn't it quaint how much they dislike having their pictures taken?" the woman said as the two walked away.

"You know what I think? I think they don't mind at all. If they didn't want people gawking at them, they wouldn't dress that way."

CHAPTER THIRTEEN

Detective Sergeant Gary Hellman returned to the building occupied by the law firm of Blanton, Trevathan and Dunn.

"Hello, Mike," Hellman said as he came through the front door.

Since the murder, Hellman had been a frequent enough visitor to the law offices that he and Mike Stratton were on a first-name basis now.

"How you doing, Gary? Any new leads on who killed Mr. Trevathan?"

"Nothing new. We're still looking for Leah McKenzie."

"She didn't do it."

This was the first time anyone had ever made such a definitive comment about it, and the declaration caused Hellman to stop and come back.

"What do you mean, she didn't do it?"

"I mean she didn't do it."

"How do you know?"

"Because I saw her just after it happened. I took her home. I've never seen anyone as shook up. And as sad. She took it real hard."

"Mike, did you know that Blanton and Dunn are both suggesting that there was something going on between Miss McKenzie and Trevathan?"

"Something going on? You mean like them sleeping together?"

"Yes, something like that."

Mike laughed. "If you had known them, if you had seen them together, you would know that wasn't true."

"How were they, when they were together?"

"He sort of treated her like his daughter. She was real respectful around him, but she wasn't coming on to him."

"Did you say you took her home?"

"Yes, sir, I took her home, I even went up to her place and looked around for her, because she was too scared to go in."

"Did she have a gun?"

"A gun? No, sir, she didn't have any gun."

"You're sure of that?"

"Yes, sir."

"Was she carrying a purse?"

"Oh. Yes, she was."

"So there could have been a gun in her purse that you knew nothing about. Is that true?"

"No, she didn't have a gun in her purse."

"How do you know?"

"She was so upset that she couldn't find her keys. She handed me her purse and I found them. I opened up her apartment for her and took a look around. If there had been a gun in her purse, I would have seen it."

"Thank you, Mike, you've been a big help."

Hellman took the elevator up to the law offices. When the doors opened, he saw someone working on the brass letters that spelled out the name of the firm on the wall just behind the receptionist's desk. Instead of Blanton, Trevathan and Dunn, it was now just Blanton and Du, the final two N's not yet in place. Millie was directing the work, but she turned when the elevator doors opened.

"Detective Hellman," she said. "What brings you back here? Have you found Miss McKenzie?"

"No, not yet. I want to ask Mr. Blanton and Mr. Dunn a few more questions, if they're here."

"Yes, they are. Just a moment." Millie picked up the phone and touched a number. "Linda, Detective Hellman is here. He wants to speak with Mr. Blanton and Mr. Dunn. All right, thank you."

Hanging up the phone and flashing a smile, Millie invited Hellman to go on back. "You know the way by now."

"Yes, thank you."

When he went into the inner office area, Blanton and Dunn were waiting for him.

"Do you have some news for us?" Blanton asked. "Have you found her?"

"No," Hellman said. "I see you're taking down Trevathan's name."

"Yes, well, we bought Mrs. Trevathan out," Blanton said.

"And she's satisfied?"

"Three million dollars buys a lot of satisfaction. Now, Mr. Hellman, what can we do for you?"

"I'm trying to trace the path of the gun that was used," Hellman said. "I've talked to the people who were on the ninth floor when the doors were open. They said Miss McKenzie was sitting on the floor holding Trevathan's head in her lap. None of them reported seeing a gun. Also, when the doors opened on the bottom floor, none of the deputies from the U.S. Marshal's office recall seeing her with a pistol, either. Did you see one when you picked her up?"

"No, I did not see a gun," Blanton said. "Maybe Mr. Stratton did. He drove the car that day."

Hellman shook his head. "I've spoken to him; he says she didn't have a gun."

"And yet she obviously did have one, as the gun that killed Carl was covered with her fingerprints," Blanton said.

"That is true," Hellman said. "You're the one who turned the gun over to the police, aren't you, Mr. Blanton?"

"Yes. I figured that if our firm was going to represent her, then we owed it to her, and to the altar of truth, which we all serve, to share every pertinent piece of information and evidence. You have to know, though, Detective Hellman, that when I first saw the gun, I thought long and hard about making it available. But, in the long run, I do believe my client will be better served by the truth."

"Are you aware there were no fingerprints on the magazine?"

"No. Why would that be significant?"

"The gun had to be loaded, didn't it? How did she get the

magazine into the handle of the pistol without getting fingerprints on it?"

"I imagine she wiped them off."

"Why would she wipe her fingerprints off the magazine, but not off the gun?"

Blanton shook his head. "I don't know. I can't tell you that."

"How did you come by the gun?"

"I beg your pardon?"

"It's not a hard question, Mr. Blanton. Ballistics have proven that this was, indeed, the gun that killed your partner, so that puts this gun at the scene of the crime. But from the time it was used in the murder until you turned it over to the police, the location of the gun is a mystery. Nobody saw her with the gun at the federal court building. Mike Stratton took her home, and he said she didn't have a gun with her then."

"How does Stratton know she didn't have the gun? It could have been in her purse. I know I didn't see it."

"He looked in her purse." When he saw the puzzled look on Blanton's face, he explained, "She was too nervous to get her keys from her purse so he got them for her."

"Well, she obviously handled the gun at some point."

"That is the supposition, of course. But the bottom line, Mr. Blanton, is that we can only definitely put the gun in two places: at the scene of the crime, and in your hands when you turned it over to the police."

"Whoa! Wait a minute here! What are you suggesting? Have you forgotten that her fingerprints are all over it?"

"Except for on the magazine, and I'm still puzzled about that.

Perhaps if you told me how you managed to come across the gun, I could get a handle on it."

"Oh, well, that's easy," Blanton said. "I just, uh, took it from her desk."

"Why?"

"Because it is evidence, and like I said, I think that one who serves truth also serves his client."

"What I mean is, what made you think to look through her desk in the first place?"

"I don't know. I guess you could just call it a whim. Anyway, I looked through her desk, found the pistol, and turned it in. And since this office, and everything in it, belongs to me—to Mr. Dunn and me—it was certainly within my rights to search her desk."

"Yes, I suppose so," Hellman said. "I'm curious, though. How is it that you handled the pistol but none of your prints are on it?"

"That's easy. I knew that the pistol might have some evidentiary value, so I stuck a pencil into the end of the barrel and carried it that way."

"Yes, that would be the best way to handle it," Hellman agreed. "By the way, I've also learned that the reason she was at the federal courthouse that day was to deliver a report to Mr. Trevathan. Do you know anything about that report?"

Blanton shook his head. "No, not exactly. Jim, do you know anything about a report she might have been delivering to Carl?"

Dunn shook his head as well. "I don't know anything about a report. If she was delivering one to Carl, it wasn't something that I had anything to do with."

"Did you know that Mr. Trevathan was at the federal court-house that morning?"

"Yes, of course we knew."

"Why was he there?"

"He was filing a brief on a case we have before the federal courts."

"What case would that be?"

"Not a very interesting one, I'm afraid. It had to do with the illegal trading of stock in Bolt."

"Bolt?"

"An Internet company. Or at least it was. The founders of the company thought they had another Yahoo! or Google on their hands. Then they decided they could make more money selling stock than they could by providing services."

"You were representing them?"

"No, we were representing some people who had been taken by them. You don't think Bolt might have had something to do with Carl getting killed, do you?"

"Why do you ask? Do you think it might be connected?"

"I don't know. It could be, I suppose. Money does strange things to people."

"That would sort of take it out of the 'crime of passion' area, though, wouldn't it?" Hellman asked.

"If it were true," Blanton said.

"Was there a great deal of money involved in the Bolt case?"

"It depends on what you mean by a 'great deal of money.' I think the total was around a million dollars."

"I think a million dollars is a lot of money," Hellman said.

Blanton chuckled. "It is, I suppose, until you divide that up by five hundred litigants. That breaks down to only about two thousand dollars per person, before our fee. Detective Hellman, Bolt is one of the smallest of our cases; it is very unlikely that it could arouse enough anger or passion to cause someone to commit murder. In fact, had the case gone on, it would not have even been handled by a senior partner."

"And yet you said that Trevathan was at the federal courthouse to file a brief on that very case."

"Yes. I'm not sure why."

"Didn't the three of you work together?" Hellman asked.

"Yes, of course we did," Dunn replied.

"Is it likely that there would be a report of such significance that Trevathan wanted it personally brought to him, and yet neither of you know about it?"

"Linda?"

"Yes, Mr. Blanton?"

"Would you print out the entire file on the Bolt case for Detective Hellman?"

"Yes, sir."

"I'm doing this without a warrant, because I don't want to go through another court battle over this, the way we did with the computers."

"Thank you."

"I think you'll find, though, that there is nothing incriminating in the Bolt file. I hate to say it, but I still believe that Carl's getting killed was personally motivated, rather than business related."

"Mr. Blanton, are you not representing Miss McKenzie?"

"Yes, I am. Why do you ask?"

"Because I have given you a possible motive that has nothing to do with her, but you have dismissed it out of hand. Isn't that a rather strange way to act as her counsel?"

"I am an attorney, Detective Hellman. And as such, I am an officer of the court. I will construct the best defense I can for my client, but always within the bounds of truth."

"And you think the truth is that Miss McKenzie shot Trevathan."

"Yes, I'm afraid I do think that. But if you were to ask me whether I think she is guilty of murder, I would have to say no. I don't think Leah had any premeditated intention to kill Carl. And without premeditation, the charges should be no greater than manslaughter. And that is how I will plead her case. Assuming, that is, that she is ever found and the case is tried."

At that moment Linda came back into the office carrying a little faux-leather case, black with gold embossed lettering that read BLANTON, TREVATHAN & DUNN.

"Nice-looking case," Hellman said. "Do you want it back?"

"No, you can keep it. We just had five hundred of these made, and now we're going to have to do them all over again."

"Why?"

"The name is no longer correct. Detective Hellman, it has been over two months. Do you have any idea where Leah might be?"

"I don't have the foggiest notion," Hellman said. "It's as if the earth just swallowed her up."

It was as if the earth had just swallowed her up. Or at least, the hay had. Leah had come into the field with Ada to help Isaac, Sam, and Jacob harvest the sweet timothy. Isaac was driving the wagon, and Jacob and Sam were doing the pitching, tossing the loose hay into the back of the wagon. Leah and Ada were moving the hay to the front of the wagon. But a moment earlier Leah had fallen in the wagon, and within seconds, Jacob and Sam, who were tossing pitchforks full of hay into the wagon with practiced and well-oiled precision, had her covered with it.

"Help!" Leah called, but she was laughing, even as she shouted.

Ada reached down and, grabbing Leah's hand, pulled her back up. She laughed out loud.

"They covered me on purpose!" Leah said with mock outrage.

When the wagon was filled, Jacob and Sam crawled up to sit at the back of it with their legs dangling over the edge. Isaac drove the team of horses back from the field.

"My, I don't think I ever noticed before how much bigger these horses are than Daisy and Prodigal. They're even bigger than the horses that you used when we took the pumpkins to town."

"Yes, these are draft horses, Percherons, and they must be big and strong to pull heavy loads. And the plows in the fields."

Ada and Leah lay down on top of the hay and looked into the sky.

"Have you ever made pictures with the clouds?" Ada asked.

"Yes," Leah said. Even as she answered the question, she realized that she hadn't done such a thing since she was a little girl in the park with her mother. Had her mother done this? Had her mother stretched out on a pile of loose hay in a wagon and looked up into the sky to make pictures from the clouds?

"There is a horse pulling a buggy," Ada said, pointing to one cloud.

Leah laughed. "That's what you see?"

"Yes. What do you see?"

"I see a knight with a shield and a spear, seated on a white charger."

"What is a charger?"

"It's a horse. So I guess we see sort of the same thing."

"Yes, but what I see isn't just any horse. It is Caleb Brenneman's horse and buggy."

"Are you and Caleb going to get married?"

"He has asked me, but we have not yet gone to the bishop to discuss this."

"Do you need the bishop's permission to marry?"

"No, we do not need his permission to marry, but we do need his permission to schedule the wedding. In our church, the wedding season begins in November and continues until Christmas."

"Wedding season?"

"*Ja.* We have a marriage season. And the marriages all take place on Tuesdays and Thursdays."

"But it's only a few days now until November."

"*Ja.* Soon we will have to talk to the bishop. Then, after we are married, before we start our own house, we will spend the rest of the winter paying overnight visits to all of my aunts and uncles, and all of Caleb's aunts and uncles. It is our way of starting our married life together."

"Do your mother and father know you're planning to be married?"

"We have not spoken to them. We will speak to them and Caleb's parents before we speak to the bishop. But I think they know."

"How can they not know when he comes over to the house all the time?" Jacob said. "'Oh, kiss me, Ada. Kiss me,'" he teased.

Ada threw a handful of hay at him, and he and Sam laughed at their sister.

"I think soon you will be talking to the bishop as well. Hannah Esh won't wait forever for you to ask her," Ada said.

"Hannah Esh? Why, Jacob, you haven't said a word about having a girlfriend," Leah said accusatorily.

"I think maybe she is a girlfriend, but we have not spoken of marriage."

"Why not?"

"I don't know if I want to be married yet. I am not like Caleb, who will do everything Ada asks."

"Oh, I think you will when you marry her," Ada said.

"Ha! If we are married, I will see if she has a tramp stamp," Jacob said.

"A what?"

Jacob laughed out loud. "Ask Leah about a tramp stamp. She knows all about them. I think she even has one."

"Jacob, I do not!" Leah said, but she laughed with him.

Jason McKenzie turned the television off. The stories about Trevathan's murder were not appearing with as much frequency, but they still ran upon occasion, and one had aired that night.

"*Leah McKenzie is still the primary suspect, and her whereabouts are, as yet, unknown. Both local and federal law enforcement agents continue to search for her.*"

He wondered where Leah was, and he prayed that she was

all right. He wasn't worried about whether or not she had killed Trevathan, because he knew with every fiber in his body that she could never do such a thing. And, just as he knew that she had nothing to do with the murder, he had the feeling that she was all right, wherever she was. He did wish, though, that he could hear from her.

Although Jason had missed his wife every day since she died, he was glad she wasn't there now to have to go through this. Because Sarah's entire family had been lost to her when she and Jason were married, Jason and Leah had been her entire life. He didn't think she would be able to take what was going on now: the separation, the anxiety of wondering whether Leah was alive or dead, and the pain of having to listen to others accuse her daughter of having committed a murder.

Jason went to the photo album and began looking at pictures. He found the earliest picture he had ever taken of Sarah. She was wearing plain clothes.

It was 1986, and Jason, who was attending school at Millikin University in Decatur, Illinois, had driven with some friends to Arthur. The news was filled with stories of the Chernobyl nuclear reactor accident. That was when Jason saw Sarah for the first time, walking down the street with two other girls, all of them wearing the signature long dark dress, with apron and white lace cap.

"Lord have mercy," Jason said. "I've never seen a more beautiful woman in my life."

"Where?" the others asked, looking around.

"That girl in front of us. The one in the middle."

"Amish?"

"Yeah."

"Forget it. They won't even talk to the English."

"I'm not English."

"Yeah, you are. To them, anyone who isn't Amish is English."

Jason's friend's pronouncement proved to be correct, because when they passed the three Amish girls, Jason spoke to them. All he got in return was a shy smile.

But later that same day the situation changed, when someone riding a bicycle on the sidewalk ran over the girl who had caught Jason's fancy. By coincidence he happened to be just across the street from her when it happened. Rushing over to her, he picked her up, put her in his friend's car, and had him drive them to the medical center in Arthur. There, she was treated for a broken leg.

Jason learned where she lived and checked on her many times over the next six weeks. At first his visits were welcomed by Sarah's family. But as they came with more frequency and seemed to be developing into more than a relationship based on simple concern, Sarah's parents tried to break it up.

But it was too late. Jason was already in love with her, and she was in love with him. Then, in the middle of the night, Sarah snuck out of her house to meet Jason, who had brought outsider clothes for her to wear. They went to St. Louis, where they were married. Immediately shunned by her family and everyone else in Arthur, Sarah began a period of isolation that lasted for the rest of her life.

Looking through the photo album had been a bittersweet thing for Jason ever since Sarah had died. And now, with Leah gone who knows where and being accused of murder, looking at the photo album was even more painful.

And yet, he could not stay away from the pictures. Now that was all he had of either one of them.

Jason closed the album and looked at the fire burning in his fireplace. A trapped bubble of gas in one of the logs popped and sent up a small shower of sparks.

"Where are you, Leah?" Jason asked quietly.

CHAPTER FOURTEEN

After Leah went to bed that night, she saw a spot of light moving around on the ceiling. The light was coming from outside, and she was sure it was not an incidental event. Then, remembering that Ada told her that Caleb would announce his visits in such a way, Leah smiled. Getting out of bed, she walked over to the window and saw a familiar figure in the garden below.

"John!" she said in a loud whisper. "What are you doing?"

"Come down," John called. He turned the flashlight off.

Quickly, Leah got dressed, wishing that she had more attractive clothes to wear than just a plain dress. She picked up her sturdy high-top shoes and had a moment to mourn the heels she had been wearing when she came to this place. She started to put the shoes on, then decided it would be quieter to carry them down the stairs. She walked out onto the front porch and sat on the swing to put them on.

"Here, let me help you," John said. He lifted her leg, then slipped on the shoe, laced and tied it, then did the same thing with its mate.

Except for shoe salesmen, Leah had not had help putting on her shoes since she was a very little girl. And while the shoe salesmen did nothing for her, she felt a strong charge of sensual pleasure at John's ministrations.

"I believe you said on the night of the singing that you thought a date should be dinner and a movie," John said.

"I did say that, yes."

"Well, I can't take you to a movie. But I can take you out for dinner."

"Oh, I . . ."

"I'm sorry. I know this is rather sudden, and with no prior notice."

"It's not that. I would love to go with you, John. But you ate at the same dinner table as I did tonight and you know how much food was there. I don't think I could eat another bite."

"What about, on a cool night like this, a piece of hot apple pie with melted cheese and a cup of coffee?"

Leah smiled. "I think I could handle that. Do you know where we might get such a thing?"

"Yoder's Place in Arthur."

"What is Yoder's Place? And it's after nine o'clock. Will it still be open?"

"It's sort of a late-night hangout. People go there after movies and such. It's open until midnight."

"All right."

John led her out to the barn, where Prodigal was already hitched up to his buggy.

"You seem to have been pretty sure of yourself," Leah said. "You already have Prodigal hooked up. Hello, Prodigal." Leah squeezed the horse's ear as she had seen John do.

"It's not so much that I was sure of myself as it is that I didn't want to waste any time if you said yes."

John helped Leah climb into the buggy, then he got in and tucked a blanket around them, which brought their bodies into close contact. He snapped the reins, and Prodigal started out. For a few moments Leah allowed herself to just enjoy the feel of John's muscular thigh pressed against her own. The sensation warmed her to her very core, and she imagined a life in which she could stay there with John, a life where people still enjoyed the simple pleasures of late-night pie or singing at church.

But then Leah sighed and sat up a little straighter. As much as she liked him, she and John were from two different worlds—and Leah's mother and father had proved how difficult it was to bridge that gap. She just didn't see how she could be anything more than John's friend.

"John, I hope what I'm doing doesn't upset your parents. They have been very good to me; I wouldn't want to hurt them, or even make them angry."

"One thing about the Amish, Leah, is that parents and family tend to stay out of matters of courtship. They believe in giving people privacy."

"Courtship? Is that what we're doing?"

"Do you know another word for it?"

"No, I guess not."

Leah leaned back in the seat. Despite the cool night air, it was warm and cozy inside the closed buggy, but she didn't know if it was because of the blanket or her close contact with John. Prodigal was trotting along at a brisk clip.

"It's funny," she said. "I'm used to driving at seventy miles per hour, sometimes faster. But now I feel as if we're going fast."

"It's all a matter of perspective. And Prodigal is probably a little cool and wants to warm up."

"John, when you came back from Afghanistan, you didn't come home right away, did you?"

"No."

"What did you do between the time you left the army and when you came back here?"

"I drifted around a bit. I spent some time in Oregon and Phoenix. I was a night clerk at a hotel in St. Louis."

"Which hotel?"

"The Marriott at Union Station."

"Oh, I love Union Station."

"You know St. Louis?"

Leah caught her breath. Had she said too much?

"Yes."

"Oh, that's right. You said your mother was at Barnes Hospital when she died."

"Yes."

"What do you do in St. Louis? Do you have a job?"

"Oh, here comes a car! It's coming very fast!" Leah said. She feigned more fright than she was actually experiencing to avoid answering John's question.

The car was meeting them on the narrow, two-lane blacktop road. John pulled the buggy over to the side of the road, with the right two wheels actually on the shoulder.

"I don't worry about the cars I can see," John said.

The car flashed by, doing at least sixty, Leah thought, and the wind of the car's passing actually shook the buggy.

"Oh!" Leah said, and this time she wasn't feigning fright. "That fool driver has no business going this fast on this road."

"And it isn't even raining," John said with a chuckle.

"It isn't raining? Oh! You mean—John, I'm so sorry I nearly ran into you that night. Now that I'm on this side of it, I see how dangerous it can be."

"Yes, well, you didn't run into me though, did you? In fact, the only one hurt in that little episode was you. And I give thanks to God that you weren't badly hurt."

"I'm not much of a praying woman," Leah said. "But I have certainly given thanks to God that I didn't crash into the back of your buggy. I could have killed you."

"Think nothing of it. God was watching out for both of us that night."

When they reached Yoder's Place, they parked outside, along with a dozen or so cars.

"I see what you mean about this being a place for night owls," Leah said, pointing to the many cars. "There are a lot of people here."

"Be prepared. We are going to be stared at," John said. "I'm used to it, so it doesn't bother me, but I just want to warn you."

"I'll be all right," Leah said, though not with much authority.

John tied off Prodigal at a hitching post, and Leah smiled at the fact that in this day and age there were actually hitching posts in front of a business.

When they went inside, the place was crowded and very noisy.

"Yoder," Leah said. "Isn't that an Amish name?"

"Yes."

"And yet, there is clearly electricity here."

"The man who owns it isn't really named Yoder, and he isn't Amish. His name is Walker. He named the place Yoder's to attract tourists."

"Whoa, hey, get a load of the two freaks," someone said, and a man got up and took a few steps toward John and Leah. He appeared to be in his late twenties or early thirties. He had a scraggly beard that looked to be more the effect of a lack of grooming and personal hygiene than a planned beard. His hair was long, and he was wearing a ring in one ear. His bare arms were covered with tattoos of knives and skulls, and a swastika. He was wearing a ball cap that said SHIT HAPPENS. There were several empty beer bottles on the table where he had been sitting.

"What are the Amish doin' in here? Ain't you got your own places, where you can eat shoofly pie, and sauerkraut, and drink buttermilk?"

"Leave 'em be, Arnie," one of the others at his table said. There were two other men and two young women at the table. "The Amish are our neighbors, an' they ain't hurtin' nobody."

"I'm just curious is all. I thought all the Amish went to bed with the chickens." Arnie chuckled. "Hah, you know what I bet? I'll bet these two are married, but not to each other. Yes sir, you two are stepping out on your ol' man and your ol' lady, ain't you? What about it, honey?" he asked, getting right in Leah's face. "Don't you feel guilty? I mean, what with your husband back home in bed, and you out here catting around? Here your husband worked all day, growing corn, and plowing beans, and slopping hogs, and doing all those Amish things. And what are you doing? You're whoring around on him, that's what you're doing."

"Arnie, stop it," one of the others said. "Leave them alone."

"Sure, I mean, who am I to begrudge them having a little fun? I guess when you get right down to it, Amish aren't that different from anyone else. Just a bit more hypocritical is all."

"That's enough, Arnie, I mean it."

"John, come on, let's go somewhere else," Leah said.

"I'd be glad to," John replied. "If there was anyplace else to go. But except for a couple of bars, this is the only place open at this hour."

"A bar?" Arnie said. "Did you folks hear that? He's not only whorin' around, he's going to take her to a bar."

"Arnie, I'm tellin' you, let it go," one of the others said.

"You know what I read once? I read that Amish women don't wear anything under these long dresses they wear. Oh, they look prim and proper on the outside, but underneath, they don't wear panties or a bra. Is that right, honey?"

Arnie reached his hand out toward Leah as if to grab her breast. But John shot his hand out quickly and caught Arnie by his wrist. He began to squeeze.

"What the hell!" Arnie shouted. "Get your hand off me, you nineteenth-century freak!" Arnie threw a right cross at John's head.

Moving faster than Arnie could believe, John reached up and caught Arnie's fist in his hand.

"I . . . uh . . . let go! Let go! Let go!" Arnie called out. His voice was no longer belligerent and challenging but high-pitched and frightened. Now, with Arnie whimpering in pain, John forced him down into a chair. Only then did John let go.

"I've enjoyed our little game," John said. "But now, if you don't mind, I think my friend and I will have a piece of apple pie."

As John led Leah to a table, Arnie sat quietly, moving his hand and wrist slowly as if testing them.

"That freak nearly broke my wrist," Arnie said.

"Too bad he didn't," one of the others at his table replied.

"I'm sorry about that," John said as they sat down. "I'm afraid it wasn't very gentlemanly of me."

"Nonsense, sorry for what? You were forced into that."

"It would never have happened if I hadn't brought you to this place. I'm almost afraid to leave you alone long enough for me to go order the pie."

"I'll be fine," Leah said.

John walked up to the counter and ordered two pieces of apple pie with melted cheese and two cups of coffee. When he started to pay for them, though, the clerk refused his money.

"I'll have the waitress bring your order to your table, sir, and it's already paid for."

"What do you mean? Who paid for them?"

"One of the men at the table with that jerk wanted you to know that they aren't all like that."

John smiled. "Well, that was very nice of him."

A moment later a waitress brought the pie and coffee to them.

"Thank you," John said. Then he recognized her. "Rebecca?"

"Hi, John. I go by Becky now," she said.

"I didn't know you were working here. How are you doing?"

"I'm doing fine, thanks. I miss my family and my friends though." Becky brightened. "I have two kids now. A boy and a girl."

"Well, good for you."

Becky looked at Leah. "I don't think I remember you."

"This is Lena Lapp. She's from Missouri," John said, speaking quickly.

"It's good to meet you, Lena. I'm Becky Greene, though I used to be Rebecca Lantz."

"Lantz? Next door to the Miller farm?"

Becky's smile was rather melancholy. "He's my father."

"Becky is under *meidung*."

Leah did not have to ask what that meant. She knew that Becky was being shunned. "I'm sorry," she said.

"It's all right. I do miss my family and friends, but I love my kids. Oh, and Lena, don't let that ignorant creep bother you. Most of the English are nice people."

With a smile, Becky left the table and went back to work.

"She was nice," Leah said.

"Yes. There was a time when—well, let's just say that things might have turned out differently for both of us."

"You mean you and Becky?"

"'Rebecca' then. We were . . . good friends. But I had a hunger for more; I wanted an education, I wanted to see more of the world. I left, and shortly after I left, she met Howard Greene, and they got married. Howard is a deputy sheriff of Douglas County."

The thought of any officer of the law made Leah somewhat uneasy, so she just nodded.

"Yeah? Well, you can all just go to hell then!"

The loud voice came from Arnie, who was now arguing with

the others at his table. After a few inaudible words from the others, Arnie stormed out of the restaurant. The other patrons applauded.

"See?" Leah said with a big smile. "They aren't all like that."

One of the people who had been sitting at the table with Arnie came over to John and Leah.

"Sir, ma'am, I would like to apologize for the behavior of our, uh, friend. It was inexcusable."

"How can you be friends with such a person?" Leah asked.

"I've known him all my life. He wasn't always like this. Again, I would like to apologize."

"You have nothing to apologize for," John said. "You didn't do anything. Was it you who paid for the pie and coffee?"

"Yes."

"I thank you for that."

"It's the least I could do."

A moment later, as John and Leah continued their conversation over pie, Leah suddenly called out.

"John! The buggy is on fire!"

John got up and ran so quickly to the door that he beat everyone else out. Prodigal, who was still attached to the buggy, was whinnying and rearing in absolute panic.

"Easy, boy, easy!" John said as he quickly unhitched Prodigal and led him away from the buggy, which was now totally in flames.

"Ha! How are you going to get home now, Amish boy?" Arnie shouted.

"You? You did this?"

"Yeah, I did it, Amish boy," Arnie said. "You want to do something about it?"

Arnie snapped open a switchblade and held it out in front of him, moving it back and forth slightly like the head of a snake.

"Arnie, put that knife away!" someone shouted, for by now every one of Yoder's customers had come outside.

"Yeah, I'll put it away when Amish boy there takes it away from me," Arnie said. "You picked on the wrong man, Amish boy."

John turned back to his horse and began talking to him quietly to soothe the horse's fear.

"John! Look out!" Leah shouted as Arnie rushed toward John, his knife hand extended.

John spun around, then stepped to one side as Arnie advanced, much like a matador evading a charging bull. John reached out to grab Arnie's knife hand, then he twisted Arnie's arm around behind him and pushed it up until he pulled the arm from the shoulder socket.

Arnie bellowed in pain and John, utilizing the motion Arnie had already started, gave him a shove. Stumbling wildly, Arnie wound up in the flaming buggy.

Arnie screamed in pain, and John braved the flames to pull him out of the fire, though by now, Arnie's clothes were aflame. In panic, and burning like a human torch, Arnie started to run, but John knocked him down, then rolled him across the ground until the fire was out.

Arnie lay there with his clothes charred and his skin red from the fire, moaning in pain. Almost immediately thereafter a fire truck arrived and one of the firemen, seeing Arnie on the ground, squirted him with snow from a CO_2 extinguisher.

The police arrived at the same time and John leaned against the front of the restaurant, his arms folded across his chest. Leah stood next to him, not saying anything, but anxiously wringing her hands. After a few minutes of talking to the others, one of the officers came over to talk to John.

"Is it true? Did you throw Mr. Cole into a burning buggy?"

"Yes, I threw him into the buggy. It was burning because he set it on fire."

"Nevertheless, whether he started the fire or not, what you did could be classified as attempted murder."

"That isn't true," Leah said.

"I beg your pardon, miss?" the police officer said.

"You said this could be classified as an attempted murder, and I am saying that isn't true."

"How is it not true?"

"Mr. Miller was clearly responding to a situation of aggravated assault, and he was acting in defense of his own life. You see, officer, Mr. Cole not only committed arson by setting fire to Mr. Miller's buggy, he also attacked Mr. Miller with a knife. I think everyone here will testify to that. Mr. Miller, acting in defense of his own life, disarmed Mr. Cole. In the act of disarming him, Mr. Cole wound up in a burning buggy. If anyone is arrested it should be Mr. Cole, for arson, reckless endangerment, aggravated assault with a deadly weapon, and cruelty to animals, in that he put Mr. Miller's horse, Prodigal, in jeopardy."

"Don't go anywhere, Mr. Miller, until we check this out."

"How am I going to go anywhere?" John replied. "As you can see, my buggy has been burned."

It took about ten minutes for the police to interview the others, then the officer who had been talking to John returned.

"You can go. There will be no charges."

"Thank you."

"How are we going to get home?" Leah asked as the officer walked away.

"I have been doing some work on Mr. Stolfatz's buggy. It's down at Mr. Collins's cabinet shop, where I work. We'll borrow it," John said.

They were halfway home before John spoke about what had just happened.

"How did you know all that?"

"How did I know all what?"

"What you said to the police officer."

"John, it was clearly self-defense. I just told the officer what happened."

"You did more than just tell him what happened. You told it in very precise terms, using terms like 'aggravated assault' and 'reckless endangerment.'"

Leah chuckled. "John, those are good English words. And as you know, I am an *Englischer*."

"It was more than that," John said.

Leah didn't answer.

"Leah, what have you not told me?"

"I'm a lawyer, John."

"Why haven't you said so before?"

Leah laughed nervously. "Because the public opinion of lawyers is not very high, even in my world. I knew I was going to have a difficult enough time as it is fitting in with the others. I was afraid it would be much more difficult if everyone knew, or even guessed, that I was a lawyer."

John nodded, then he chuckled. "Well, I'm glad you decided to come out from under the basket tonight. I don't know what would have happened if you had not been there to plead my case."

"You would have been all right," Leah said. "It was such a clear case of self-defense that even without my being there, the police would have quickly realized that you weren't in the wrong."

"Nor was I in the right."

"Of course you were."

John held up his hand. "In the eyes of the church, I was not in the right," he said. "And I will have to answer for it."

"Answer for it? Answer how?" Leah asked, confused by the statement. "Why? John, you did nothing wrong."

"Matthew, chapter five, verses thirty-eight and thirty-nine. 'Ye have heard that it hath been said, An eye for an eye, and a tooth for a tooth: But I say unto you, that ye resist not evil: but whosoever shall smite thee on thy right cheek, turn to him the other also.'"

"Do you really know the Bible chapter and verse?"

"I love to read, and growing up, my choices in literature were generally split between the Bible, seed catalogues, and the *Farmer's Almanac*. The Bible won. But that was all right; there are a lot of good stories there." John chuckled. "You would be surprised at how many works of literature are inspired by the Bible."

"But this 'turn your other cheek' thing. Who is really going to hold you to something like that?" Leah asked.

"The church."

"All right. Suppose they do hold you to that—that impossible concept. How, I ask you, are they going to find out about it?"

"I'm going to tell them."

"What will happen then?"

"I will have to go before the elders, and then before the entire church to make atonement."

It was a little colder going back than it had been going into town, because their blanket had been destroyed in the fire. They sat very close to each other, John handling the reins with his left hand, his right arm around Leah, pulling her very close to him.

It was well past midnight by the time they returned to the Miller farm. John helped Leah down from the buggy, but when she started toward the house he called out to her.

"Leah, wait."

"Wait for what?"

"Until I get Prodigal unharnessed and into his stall. He has had a difficult night. I know that the fire frightened him. I think we should talk to him a bit to calm him down."

"All right," Leah said. She rubbed Prodigal's ear as John disconnected the harness.

"Bless your heart," Leah said quietly, soothingly, to the horse. "You don't have to be frightened now. You're home with friends who love you."

Prodigal dipped his head a couple of times.

"I'll be! I think he understood me."

"Of course he understood you. He likes you," John said.

Leah chuckled. "I like him, too."

Leah walked into the barn with John and Prodigal, and stood by as John put the horse into his stall.

"Is this where you live? Here in the barn?" Leah asked.

"Yes. Would you like to see my apartment?"

Leah knew that she should not. But she also knew that she was very curious. Curious, and something else. She felt a strong desire to see his apartment, and she knew that the desire wasn't just a matter of curiosity. It was something more, something primeval.

"You had better wait here until I light a candle," John said. "There are too many things to trip over in the dark of a barn and you could be hurt."

Leah waited by the stall as John disappeared. A moment later she saw the flare of a match, then she saw the light of a candle approaching her.

"This way," John said, putting his hand on her arm and leading her back to his apartment.

John lit a gas lantern, which illuminated his apartment as brightly as if it had been an electric light.

"Oh, my," Leah said, surprised by what she saw.

"Yeah," John admitted. "This is my little island of inequity in the Amish sea of righteousness."

She saw a bookshelf that was filled with books from writers such as Mark Twain, John Steinbeck, William Faulkner, Ernest Hemingway, James Jones, Herman Wouk, Pearl Buck, and Eudora Welty.

In addition, she saw a desk, and on the desk, a laptop computer.

"Am I seeing what I think I'm seeing?" she asked.

"Yes. I have permission from the bishop to use it," John explained. "I use it to keep records for the projects I am doing for Mr. Collins. It is battery powered, so I don't need electricity, and I take it in to work every day so it can be recharged."

"Are you online?"

"No. You have to have a telephone, or cable or satellite service, to be online, and of course, I have none of that."

"I had no idea your place was like this. Do your parents know? Do your sister and brothers know what your place is like?"

"They allow me my privacy," John replied. He opened a small, gas-operated refrigerator and took out two beers. "Would you like a beer?"

"You have beer?"

"Yes. Alcohol, used in moderation, is not against our Ordnung. After all, Jesus did turn water into wine, you know." He popped open the two cans, then handed one of them to Leah.

"You must read a lot."

"I enjoy literature," John said. He chuckled. "I'm not sure how that would go over with the elders. Actually, I am sure they would condemn it as being too worldly."

"John, are you happy living here?"

"Why do you ask that? I came back, didn't I?"

"Yes. But that doesn't answer my question. After being on the outside and experiencing all this"—she took in the room, the books and the laptop, with an inclusive wave of her hand—"are you happy being Amish?"

John took a swallow of his beer before he answered.

"It's something I need," he said. "It's something my soul needs."

"John, there are other churches. Being Amish isn't the only path to God. I know of no more godly a person than my mother. But she spent the last half of her life excommunicated from the Amish."

"I know," John said. "And I'm not one of those who think only the Amish will get to heaven. But my situation is a little different from most. As I said, my soul needs to heal, and for me, this seems to be the best way."

"Please understand, I'm not trying to turn you against your religion."

"'Square in your ship's path are Sirens, crying beauty to bewitch men coasting by: woe to the innocent who hears that sound,'" John said.

"Homer," Leah said with a chuckle.

"You know your classics. Your beauty is bewitching, Leah, but I'm not Odysseus, and you aren't a siren."

Leah laughed. "You never cease to surprise me."

"Nor, I hope, will I ever. I want to see you with your hair down."

Leah started to unpin it, but John held up his hand. "No," he said. "Unpinning a woman's hair and letting it fall is a very intimate thing. I would like to share that intimacy with you."

John stepped closer to her, gently removed her *kapp,* and began to unpin her hair. It was funny; Leah had never considered that to be an intimate thing before, let alone a sensual thing. But as she stood there, feeling his hands in her hair, feeling the locks tumble down to her neck, she found it extremely sensual, so much so that she began breathing in short, shallow gasps.

When her hair was lowered, John held his hands to her cheeks and looked at her. Leah could tell by the longing in his eyes that he was going to kiss her. More than that, she knew that she was going to kiss him back, so she started it, by wrapping her arms around his neck, then pressing her body against his, lifting her head, and parting her lips. For just a moment, Leah questioned herself. Perhaps she really was a siren.

Then she was aware of his lips parting against hers and when she felt his tongue dart into her mouth, her blood turned to molten fire. This kiss, it seemed, started where the last kiss had left off. She remembered that kiss, in the moonlight, on the night he had taken her to the singing. It had been more than a mere kiss; it had been deep and surprisingly intimate.

She had not been in charge that time and found herself even less so now, not of John, not even of her own emotions. Then, as the kiss continued, her body grew limp in his embrace, completely subservient to his wishes. She lost herself in the kiss, testing its limits to see how far it would take her. She began spinning, spinning, spinning into a bottomless vortex.

"John," she said, her lips moving against his, the word lost in the depth of the kiss.

"John" was the only word she spoke, but what did it mean? John what? *John, stop? John, go on? John, I want even more?*

Leah knew that if John wanted to he could lay her down right there, on this bed in this room and in this barn, and she would allow him to take her. No, she wouldn't just allow him to take her, she would willingly give herself to him. And even if someone, having seen them return home, happened to come out to the barn and check on them, even if they found John and Leah in bed together, she wouldn't care. All self-restraint, all caution, all fear was gone, and at this moment she knew that she wanted to give herself to him, more than she had ever wanted anything in her life. She waited for him to make the first move, prayed that he would make the first move.

John had tightened his fingers in the silky spill of her blond hair, then did what Leah could not do. He found the strength to gently tug her head back to break the kiss. She stared up at him with eyes that were filled with wonder and as deep as her soul.

"John, I . . . ," she started to say, but she found herself utterly unable to speak. And her knees grew so weak that she could barely stand and he had to steady her. "I had—better get back to my own room."

"Are you sure?"

No, I'm not sure, she wanted to shout. But from some reserve of strength that she didn't even know she had, she found the will to nod her head.

"Yes. I'm sure."

"All right. I've no intention of forcing myself on you."

"You wouldn't have to force yourself on me," Leah said. "I am yours for the asking—but I pray that you don't ask. Not now. It would—complicate things."

"Indeed it would," John said. He came to her again, only this time all he did was give her a chaste peck on the forehead. "Go," he said. "Please go before I ask."

Jason McKenzie almost didn't see the picture at the back of the paper. There was a photograph of an Amish woman looking at a newspaper.

Amish Keeping Up with the News, the caption read.

Jason had never forgiven the Amish for what they did to his wife, but this picture caught his attention. He couldn't be sure—it wasn't a head-on view of the woman, it was in profile. But he could almost swear that it was Leah!

There was no information with the picture, other than the caption. So he called the newspaper office to see what he could find out.

"This is Joyce Kimble," said the officious-sounding voice that answered the newsroom phone.

"Miss Kimble, in today's issue, there was a picture of an Amish woman. What can you tell me about that picture?"

"Not much, I'm afraid. I don't even know what picture you're talking about."

"Don't you read your own paper?"

"When I can. Mostly I read my own articles. Just a moment, let me call it up." There was a pause, then she spoke again. "Yes, here it is."

"Who is the woman in the picture?"

"I don't know. It isn't tagged. I'm not sure I could tell you if I did know."

"Can you tell me where the picture was taken?"

"Well, we have several Amish settlements in Missouri: Seymour, Jamesport, and Clark for example. I imagine it was taken at one of those locations, though I have no way of knowing."

"Well, who took the picture? Let me talk to the photographer."

"I'm afraid I can't help you there, either. The picture was submitted through our reader e-mail address, and they didn't request a credit."

"Why would someone take a photograph and have it published in a major newspaper without taking credit for it?"

"I don't know, sir. May I ask why you are so interested in this picture?"

"I, uh, just found the subject interesting," Jason said. "I'm sorry I bothered you."

"That's quite all right," Joyce said.

* * *

When the caller hung up, Joyce called over to one of the other reporters. "When a call comes through the exchange, we don't get the
caller ID. Is there any way to get it?"

"Sure, we can go to the main trunk and get it. Why?"

"I don't know, there was something peculiar about that call.
Call it a gut instinct."

The reporter Joyce was talking to rubbed his finger alongside
his nose. "Ah, the old reporter's itch, right? Joe Pulitzer himself
would be proud of you."

"Will you help me find the number?"

"Sure. But if it's some big story, you're going to owe me, big-
time."

"I'll take you to lunch."

"I'd rather take you to breakfast. After."

Joyce laughed. "Larry, if I took you up on that you would go
into shock."

CHAPTER FIFTEEN

On the following Sunday Leah prepared to go to church with the others, but this morning there was not the usual good-natured banter among the family as everyone prepared to go.

"It's my fault," Leah told Isaac and Emma. "If I hadn't agreed to go to town with him, none of this would have happened."

"Leah, you cannot take on the sins of others," Isaac replied. "Only Jesus Christ can do that, and He did so when He was crucified."

"What will happen to John?"

"That is not for me to say," Isaac said. "The bishop will present the case and the elders will vote upon it."

Jacob came in then. "Daad, the buggy for you, Mamm, Ada, and Leah is hitched and ready. I will ride in with John."

"If he is shunned, you will not be able to ride back with him," Isaac said.

"*Ja*, I know."

* * *

Word had already reached all the other church members that there would be a discussion on *meidung* for John Miller that day. Accordingly, Caleb Brenneman had been chosen by the church to speak against John. This was going to be very difficult for him, because Caleb and John had been lifelong friends, though that friendship had been tested when John left the church to go to college and then into the army. Also, Caleb was betrothed to John's sister, Ada. But Caleb would not avoid the duty once it had been assigned to him.

John's brother Jacob would speak for him.

"Jacob will do the best he can," John told Leah just before they went into the Brenneman house, where the service was to be held. "But after hearing the way you talked to that policemen the other night, I sure wish I could use you as my advocate."

"I would be glad to speak for you, John."

"You cannot. Women can have no voice in our church."

John reached out to take Leah's hand and Leah wished, with all that was in her, that she could kiss him. He let her hand go and then, with a wan smile, went inside. As Leah waited to go in with the women, she perceived, out of the corner of her eye, that someone was staring at her. Turning, she found herself looking directly at her grandmother.

"Grandmother?" she said quietly.

Miriam Lapp turned away from her and went into the church meeting.

Leah had attended church meetings often enough now to be somewhat familiar with the proceedings. She knew which side to go to and where to sit. What surprised her about this meeting was seeing a chair in the middle aisle where the preacher normally stood to give his sermon. She wondered what the chair was for, then she took a short breath as she saw its purpose.

John came in and sat in the chair with his head bowed and his eyes closed.

Oh, Lord, Leah prayed. *Be with John and give him the courage to face this. And give Jacob the words to defend him.*

The deacon, minister, and bishop came down the stairs as before, but this time Jacob and Caleb were with them.

The bishop stood. "My brothers and sisters, *meidung* is a hard thing, but it is one of the most hallowed tenets of our church. We are told in Romans 16:17: 'Now, I beseech you, brethren, mark them which cause divisions and offenses contrary to the doctrine which ye have learned; and avoid them.' And in First Corinthians 5:11: 'But now I have written unto you not to keep company, if any man that is called a brother be a fornicator, or covetous, or an idolater, or a railer, or a drunkard, or an extortioner; with such an one no not to eat.' And in Matthew 18, verses 15 through 17: 'Moreover if thy brother shall trespass against thee, go and tell him his fault between thee and him alone: if he shall hear thee, thou hast gained thy brother. But if he will not hear thee, then take with thee one or two more, that in the mouth of two or three witnesses every word may be established. And if he shall neglect to hear them, tell it unto the church: but if he neglect to hear the church, let him be unto thee as an heathen man and a publican.' And finally, in Matthew 18:18: 'Verily I say unto you, Whatsoever ye shall bind on earth shall be bound in heaven: and whatsoever ye shall loose on earth shall be loosed in heaven.'

"Our obligation is clear. And now there comes before us one who was shunned before."

The bishop pointed toward the chair. "John Miller, son of Isaac and Emma Miller, you are called to answer for your sin against God and this church."

Bishop Hershberger sat down then, and Caleb got up. He pointed a finger at John.

"Friday evening this man went into town to a place called Yoder's."

There was a buzz of conversation among those in the congregation.

"I'm sure that many of you have heard of Yoder's, and perhaps you have even seen it as you pass by. In case you do not know about it, I will tell you. The man who owns it is not named Yoder, and he is not Amish. He uses the name—he uses us—as a means of making money from the *Englische* who want to gawk at us, and take our pictures, and ridicule us. You can buy beer at Yoder's, and whiskey. And you see all sorts of ungodly people there.

"John took an *Englische* woman to Yoder's with him. He is not married to the *Englische* woman, but they rode together in his closed buggy.

"It is bad enough that John went with an *Englische* woman to such a place, but what makes it worse is what he did while he was there. While he was there, he got into a fight with an *Englischer*."

"An Amish man, fighting?" someone said aloud, shocked by the suggestion.

"We are a peaceful people! We do not fight!" another shouted.

"He got into a fight, and he seriously injured the *Englischer*. I am told that the *Englischer* went to the hospital with second-degree burns over much of his body.

"I submit to you that are here gathered, that such a thing is a serious enough violation of our Ordnung that John Miller should be banned."

Caleb sat down, and Leah looked over at Ada. She was crying, as was Emma. And the expression on Caleb's face was one that reflected his extreme distaste for having been forced to play this role.

Jacob stood then, and for a long moment he just looked at John.

"John," he said. "Are the accusations made by Caleb Brenneman true? Did you go to Yoder's?"

"I did," John answered.

"And while you were there, did you get into a fight with an *Englischer*?"

"I did."

"Was it your intention to fight him?"

"No."

"Did he set fire to your buggy?"

"Yes."

"Is that why you fought him?"

"No."

"Did he attempt to attack you with a knife?"

"Yes."

"What did you do?"

"I took the knife away from him."

"And then what did you do?"

"As I was taking the knife from him, he was shoved into the carriage."

"By 'he was shoved,' do you mean you shoved him?"

"Yes."

Now the buzz of conversation among all in the congregation was intense.

"You have been called before the bishop, the elders, and this body to answer for that," Jacob said. "How did the bishop learn of your transgression?"

"I told him," John said.

"Did you tell him out of a sense of pride, because you prevailed over the *Englischer* who attacked you?"

"No. It was out of a sense of contrition that I confessed to the bishop," John said. "I am truly sorry for having offended God, and for having offended my brothers and sisters of this church. I detest my sin."

"And have you prayed to God for forgiveness?" Jacob asked.

"Ich bete, dass Gott mein demütiges Bekenntnis zu akzeptieren, und dass Er vergibt mir. I pray that God accept my humble confession, and that He forgive me."

Jacob nodded, then he turned to the bishop and the elders.

"You have heard from John's own mouth his humble contrition and his prayer for forgiveness. If God can forgive him, are we not doing God's service by also forgiving him?"

After both Caleb and Jacob addressed the church and the elders, the bishop rose.

"John, you have defied the Ordnung before, haven't you?"

"I have."

"You left the church when you were eighteen. You lived with the *Englische*?"

"Ja."

"And while you were living with the *Englische,* what did you do?"

"I went to college, then I went into the army."

"The army?" someone in the congregation said. "An Amish man in the army?"

"And while you were in the army, what did you do?"

"I went to officer candidate school, and I became an officer."

"And did you go to war?"

"Yes."

Again, there was a buzz of disapproval from the congregation.

"And did you not think that you were violating the law of God by taking up the sword?"

"Bishop, there is biblical precedent for this. In Romans 13:4, it says: 'For he is the minister of God to thee for good. But if thou do that which is evil, be afraid; for he beareth not the sword in vain: for he is the minister of God, a revenger to execute wrath upon him that doeth evil.'

"I took the sword against those who committed evils so foul that even to relate their sinful deeds would be an abomination to the good people of this church."

"Did you kill others with this sword?" the bishop asked.

John hung his head and pinched the bridge of his nose.

"Answer my question, John Miller!" the bishop demanded, his voice now booming through the small room. "Did you kill others with this sword?"

"Yes," John called back, his words as loud as the bishop's. "Yes, bishop, with the sword I did smite the evildoers. I killed others."

"Oh, John, no!" Emma cried. Leah read the intense pain in John's face at having to reveal the secret he had kept from all but her.

"How many did you kill?"

"I don't know."

"You don't know? Are you telling us, John Miller, that you have killed so many that you don't even know?"

"I'm not saying that. I'm saying that in a firefight there is much confusion. Bullets are swarming by your head like bees, and you are returning fire. You are also responsible for your men, some of whom are being killed as they stand beside you. And sometimes you call in fire missions for artillery, or you request suppression by close air support. When you do that, even though your finger isn't on the trigger, you have initiated the action by your request, so, in a real sense, you are responsible for those deaths as well."

"What did you feel when you killed, John Miller?"

John looked out over the congregation, measuring the expressions in the faces of all present. Some of the expressions were of horror, some of contempt, some of worried support, and a few were even of morbid curiosity.

"What did you feel when you killed, John Miller?" the bishop repeated.

John recalled the response he'd once heard a sniper give a reporter who had asked the same question, in just as hostile a tone.

"What do you feel when you shoot someone?" the reporter had asked.

"Recoil," the sniper had answered laconically.

But how would John answer the bishop's question?

When he killed the men who had decapitated the woman and her husband, and crushed the arm of their young son, he felt rage, then intense personal satisfaction as he saw each of them fall.

But each time he killed it took a toll on his soul, and even now it was difficult for him to live with the knowledge that he had taken the lives of other human beings.

John looked up at the accusing stare of Bishop Hershberger. The last question the bishop had asked still resonated, and the eyes of all present were fixed upon him, waiting for his answer.

"It is not a matter of what you feel when you shoot someone. At the time it is a matter of self-preservation and you kill so that you aren't killed. It is a reflexive action, and you feel nothing. I could say things to you like 'fire mission requests,' 'kill zone,' 'targets of opportunity,' all of it spinning around in your head while bullets whiz by, bombs are bursting, and men are screaming out in their death agonies. But none of that will mean anything to you, none of it will mean anything to anyone in this church.

"But those are things I live with every day, those are things I dream of every night. And when I am alone with God, I beg Him to ease the pain on my soul that I cannot."

"Have you asked God to forgive you?"

"Every day of my life, I ask God to forgive me," John replied.

"Bishop Hershberger, if I may speak?" Jacob said.

"Yes, you may speak."

"John, when you returned, I know that you spoke to Bishop Eicher. Did you speak to him of these things?"

"Yes," John replied.

"And what did he say?"

"He asked me to pray for forgiveness, and he told me he would pray for forgiveness as well."

"Why did we not know of this? I am your brother. Why did I not know of this?"

"Bishop Eicher said that it would not be right for me to burden others with the transgressions I would have to live with every day."

"Did Bishop Eicher say you should be banned?"

"He said he would not bring it up before the elders because no punishment could be greater than that which I am experiencing every day."

"Bishop Hershberger, Bishop Eicher, who has since passed, listened to all John had to say. He measured the contrition that was in John's heart and found him repentant. And Bishop Eicher welcomed John back into the church.

"I think these questions you ask now have nothing to do with what we are discussing. We are discussing what happened in Arthur last week."

"I disagree with you, Brother Jacob," Bishop Hershberger replied. "If, in the hell of war, John Miller developed a taste for doing violent things, then we can understand why he threw the *Englischer* into the burning buggy."

"Witnesses have stated that the *Englischer* attacked him with a knife. It was to defend himself."

"The Bible tells us to turn the other cheek."

"And in Ecclesiastes 7:17, it says, 'Don't be foolish, why should we die before our time?' I believe that when John defended himself, he was following the word of the Lord."

"We have heard the case presented against John Miller by Caleb Brenneman, and we have heard him defended by Jacob Miller. After the church service the elders will meet, and a decision will be made."

The chair in which John had been sitting was returned to the men's side, but it was placed in a position that kept it separate from all the other men. The regular church service continued then, and after the sermon, but before the fellowship meal, the bishop, pastor, deacon, and elders gathered to decide John's fate.

As the women put the food on the tables for the fellowship meal, no one but Leah would talk to John. But because Leah was not a member of the church, no one said anything to her about approaching him.

"You shouldn't be with me," John said.

"Why not? I'm not Amish. Besides, you haven't been found guilty yet, have you?"

"You are used to thinking in the way of the English court," John said. "There a person is presumed innocent until proven guilty. Here, we are presumed guilty until proven innocent."

"What do you think they will decide?"

"I don't know," John admitted truthfully.

Then, the bishop and the elders, who had been meeting in another room in the house, rejoined the others. Bishop Hershberger held up both his hands, and everyone knew that a decision had been reached and was about to be given.

"Hear now the decision of the elders," Bishop Hershberger announced in a loud and commanding voice.

All conversation stopped, though outside the Brenneman house, squeals of laughter could be heard from children who were playing under a maple tree.

"John Miller. Stand and listen to the decision that has been made by church elders."

John moved out into an open area and stood there so all could see him.

"John Miller, you have violated the Ordnung by the violence

you showed when you threw an *Englischer* into a burning buggy. It has been decided by the elders that you will be shunned."

"Oh, no, please!" Emma called out.

"Shh, woman," Isaac said, though he spoke the words quietly and put his arm around his wife.

"If, within six months, John Miller, you have shown repentance, you will be welcomed back to the church."

"Six months?" Jacob said. "Bishop, six months? Isn't that a long time for one offense?"

"It is not one offense, Jacob. You heard from his own mouth his confession that he had committed murder."

"But he did not commit murder, bishop. He was at war. He was wielding the sword against evil, as it says in Romans thirteen!"

"An Amish man has no business being in a war," Bishop Hershberger said.

"But Bishop Eicher had already heard John's confession and welcomed him back into the church. You cannot punish him again for something about which he has already been forgiven."

"It is not for man to forgive, but for God. Do not question my authority, Jacob Miller, or you, too, will be before the elders."

"It's not—"

"Jacob!" John said sharply. "Let it be."

Jacob nodded, then sat down.

"Now," Hershberger said, the frown on his face replaced with a broad smile. "We will eat, *ja*?"

John waited until everyone else helped themselves, then he went to the tables where the food was laid out and filled his own plate. Afterward, he took his plate and a chair, then, while everyone else ate and visited, he sat alone in his chair in the corner, with the plate balanced on his lap.

Leah got her plate and walked over to join him.

"Leah, if you ever want any chance of being accepted by your grandmother, don't be here with me right now," John said. "Please."

"I don't care whether I'm ever accepted or not," Leah said. "This wasn't fair. None of this was fair."

"Fair has nothing to do with it. You, of all people, should know that. Didn't you see what happened to your own mother?"

"John, I—"

"Please, Leah, it would be best for both of us if you don't stay with me now. At least, not here, while we are at church. At home, it will be different."

Leah smiled. "You mean you can eat with us at home?"

"I can eat with you. Not with anyone else."

CHAPTER SIXTEEN

J ohn, I heard about you losing your buggy," Collins said when John went to work Monday morning. "I'm sorry."

"It was a good buggy. It once belonged to my grandfather."

"I have one in my garage at home that I'll sell you cheap," Collins said.

"You have a buggy?"

"I bought it eight years ago from Miriam Lapp when her husband, Joseph, died. It's been collecting dirt, spiderwebs, and probably a few birds' nests over the years, but I imagine you could put it back in shape without a lot of effort."

"You have Joseph Lapp's buggy?" John asked, showing a great interest in the news.

"You better believe I do. Come on, get in the car, I'll drive you over there and let you take a look at it."

"Thanks."

John fastened the seat belt when he got in.

"I have to warn you, the buggy doesn't have seat belts," Collins said, laughing.

"That's all right. If I really need seat belts, I can always take a set off my SUV."

"What? You're teasing me."

"No. I almost wish that I were, though. The cost of storage is beginning to build up."

"I thought Amish couldn't have a car."

"We can't. That's why I keep the car up in Decatur."

"I'll be. I knew that you were gone for a while, but you don't ever talk much about it, and I never figured it was my place to ask."

John didn't reply.

"Well, anyway, I gave Mrs. Lapp a thousand dollars for the buggy, but like I said, this was eight years ago. I'll let you have it for five hundred dollars, if you think it's worth it."

The buggy was exactly as Collins had described it, dirty, covered with spiderwebs, and it even had a couple of old, long-abandoned birds' nests. But structurally and mechanically, it was very sound.

"What do you think? Is it worth five hundred dollars?"

"It's worth at least a thousand dollars."

"Really? Well, how about that? Oh, but I said five hundred dollars, so that's all I'll charge you."

"Suppose I give you seven hundred fifty dollars? You'll be getting more than you asked for, and I will be getting a bargain."

"All right," Collins said. "It's a deal."

* * *

It took John two days to clean and repaint the buggy. But when he was finished with it, it looked like a brand-new one. He wanted to take Leah, his mother, and his sister for a ride in it, but he couldn't. He had been banned by the church, which meant that, though he could ride in a buggy being driven by an Amish member, he could not give Amish members a ride in his buggy.

"But it is all right for you to ride with him," Ada told Leah. "You are not Amish."

"But not in his new buggy. It's a closed buggy, and at the hearing, Caleb used that against him," Leah said.

"You mustn't be upset with Caleb," Ada said. "He only did what the bishop and elders told him to do."

"I know. And I could tell by the expression on his face that he took no pleasure in it."

"I have discussed this with Father, and he says that because you are *Englische* that the Ordnung about riding in a closed buggy does not refer to you."

"Good. I would not like to turn him down if he asks. I think the shunning is very hard for him."

"It is hard for all of us who love him," Ada said.

"Then why do you do it? Why was my mother shunned, to live the rest of her life apart from her family, not even allowed to come home when her father died? Why will my grandmother not accept me? Why do a gentle people have such a cruel component?"

"You don't understand," Ada said. "This is not done out of cruelty, it is done out of love."

"Out of love? I watched my mother suffer this forced estrangement for her entire life, and you say this is something that is done out of love?"

"Yes," Ada said. "Don't you see? When someone sins against the church, it is the same as sinning against God. We do this so that they may see the error of their ways and repent. We do this to save their immortal soul."

"My mother was a good Christian woman. I do not believe her soul was lost. I know that she is in heaven."

"I pray that she is," Ada said. Then she smiled. "But I have news for you. Caleb and I have spoken with his parents and with my parents. We will speak to the bishop today and schedule when we may be married."

"Oh, Ada, I am so happy for you!" Leah said. "Do you have any idea when it will be?"

"*Ja*. I think it will be the first Tuesday in December. You will still be here?"

"Yes, I will still be here." Leah had no idea whether she would still be there or not. But Ada was so pleased that Leah didn't want to say anything that might detract from her happiness.

The next Saturday morning John asked Leah to come with him.

"Where are we going?"

"Bring your English clothes with you," John said.

"My English clothes? Why?"

"Where we are going, I think it will be less trouble if we both wear English clothes."

"John, please, I've already gotten you into trouble once. I don't want to be the cause of your getting into trouble a second time."

"You didn't get me into trouble the first time," John said. "And for the six months I am shunned, I look at it as sort of a mini-*rumspringa*."

"*Rumspringa*?"

"*Rumspringa* is a coming-of-age experience that we go through before we are baptized into the church. During *rumspringa,* we can experience the English way of life; we can go to bars or nightclubs, drive cars." He looked over at Leah with a broad smile. "And we can date non-Amish people."

Leah laughed. "Somehow, John, I get the feeling you're misinterpreting the meaning of the shunning."

"Well, the bishop has his point of view and I have mine."

"Where are we going?"

"The first place we'll go is to the shop where I work. We'll change clothes there."

"A lot of good that will do," Leah said with a chuckle. "As soon as we drive up in a buggy, don't you think that might give a few people a clue?"

"We'll leave the buggy there," John said.

It was the middle of November, and this was the coldest night so far, but it was amazingly warm in the buggy because John had installed a propane gas heater.

"You didn't have this in the other buggy, did you?"

"No. But when I was reconditioning this one, I decided to put one in. It feels nice now, but on cold, snowy days, it is almost a necessity. Oh, you might find this interesting. This buggy once belonged to your grandfather."

"Really? Cool! I'm riding in my grandpa's buggy."

"Of course, I souped it up, made a hot rod out of it."

"A hot-rod buggy. What a concept."

"Absolutely. Why, I can go from zero to ten miles an hour in ten seconds."

John and Leah both laughed.

"John, how are you doing?"

"What do you mean?"

"Your shunning. Is it very hard on you?"

"It would be worse—much worse—if I didn't have you."

"John—don't count on me to be here forever."

John reached over and put his hand on Leah's leg. "I know you aren't going to stay here forever—maybe not even much longer. Frankly, I'm surprised you've stayed as long as you have. But, as long as you are here, I intend to take advantage of it."

"But your parents, your sister, your brothers."

"I can't eat with them, I can't do anything for them, but we do talk. And I still live in my apartment in the barn, which satisfies the guidelines of the *bann,* in that I am not living under the same roof."

They rode on in silence for a few minutes, the only sound Prodigal's hoofbeats clopping hollowly on the blacktop pavement and the whirring of the wheels.

"The only thing I feel really bad about is that I won't be able to attend Ada and Caleb's wedding."

Leah put her hand on John's. "I'm sorry you won't be able to go as well." She smiled. "Were you surprised that they decided to get married?"

John laughed. "Surprised? When Caleb was sixteen and Ada was eight, she told me she was going to marry him. I don't think she ever looked at anyone else but Caleb."

"I hope they have a long and happy marriage."

"They are Amish," John said.

"Does that mean their marriage will be long and happy?"

"It means they are Amish," John said without any further explanation.

Arthur was filled with its usual Saturday-morning traffic of cars, trucks, buggies, and wagons.

They pulled up to a large, hangar-like building. The sign out front said COLLINS FINE FURNITURE. Beneath that sign was another: CUSTOM FURNITURE, MADE BY SKILLED AMISH ARTISANS.

"This is where I work," John said.

"Let me guess. You're one of the skilled Amish artisans," Leah said with a smile.

"Sort of."

"What do you mean 'sort of'?"

"I'm the only skilled Amish artisan."

"Oh, it's open," Leah said in surprise.

"Yes. Glen does most of his business on Saturdays."

They drove around behind the shop, where John disconnected Prodigal, then put him in his "parking space" in the barn behind the shop. John pushed the buggy into the barn as well.

He led Leah into the shop through a back door. This was the construction area, and Leah could smell fresh wood and paint. Storage racks stood along the wall filled with pieces of wood of all sizes and types. There were also several pieces of furniture in various stages of construction.

"That's what I'm working on now." John pointed to an executive desk.

"John! That is beautiful!" Leah said. She ran her hand over its surface, feeling the smooth texture. Her father would really love something like this. "What would something like this cost?"

"About twenty-six hundred dollars," John said. He laughed. "There isn't room for it in your bedroom. Besides, I'm doing this one for a special customer. You might know him. He is a lawyer from St. Louis named Kyle Sherman."

Leah took in a quick breath. She did know him—she had even argued a case against him. She also knew that he would be well aware of her status as a wanted fugitive.

"Do you know him?"

"There are a lot of lawyers in St. Louis. I don't know every one of them," Leah said, trying to pass it off lightly. She hadn't exactly denied knowing him, she just hadn't acknowledged it. "But back to this desk, or rather, one like it. I wasn't thinking about it for me, I was thinking about it for my father. Though I have no idea how I would get it to him."

What was she thinking? Getting it to him wasn't the problem. Making contact with him, any kind of contact, was the problem, because she was sure that her father's phone was tapped and that he was being closely monitored.

It was ironic, she thought. In her own way, and because of the situation, she was as much under a *meidung* as her mother had been.

John pointed to an office. "That's my office; you can change in there," he said.

"Where will you change?"

"I'll change in there after you have."

"Ha! Why all the privacy? You've seen everything I have to show," Leah teased.

"Don't tempt me, woman," John said with a broad smile.

Leah was still smiling as she went into John's office, then stripped out of the plain clothes and pulled on the panties and skirt she had been wearing the day she arrived there. As she finished dressing, she combed her hair out, then looked down at herself. Seeing herself in these clothes took her back to St. Louis and her troubles there.

What was happening there now? It had been nearly three months since she left. How desperately she wanted to call her father, not only to let him know that she was all right, but also to find out what was going on.

When she walked back out into the shop area she saw the expression of appreciation on John's face. "You are beautiful," he said, almost reverently.

John went in to change next, and Leah sat in a leather cushioned chair as she waited. He reemerged very soon after wearing dark blue trousers and a white sweater over a shirt the same color as the trousers.

These clothes, much more than his Amish wardrobe, displayed his muscular body, broad shoulders, and narrow waist. She had already come to the conclusion that he was a handsome man, but seeing him in English clothes allowed her to evaluate him against standards she was familiar with—and he came out very well in the comparison.

John looked up at the shop clock and saw that it was two minutes until nine.

"We had better get out front," John said. "I arranged for a car to pick us up at oh nine hundred."

Leah laughed. "Oh nine hundred?"

"Sorry. I got out of the Amish mode and slipped back into military mode. Of course, I mean nine o'clock."

Leah started toward the front of the shop.

"No, let's go out back and around," John said. "It wouldn't be good business for customers to see the Amish artisan dressed like them."

"All right."

Neither Leah nor John was wearing a sweater or jacket, and Leah shivered.

"It will be warm in the car," John said. "And I promise we won't be outside anywhere."

At nine o'clock sharp the car arrived.

"Route 121 in Decatur," John said.

It was six miles from the Miller house to Arthur, and thirty-five miles from Arthur to Decatur. But the trip from Arthur to Decatur by car took less time than their drive into Arthur that morning.

"Right here," John said when the car reached a fenced-in area. On the other side of the fence sat boats, camper trailers, and RV units.

"Will you be wanting me to pick you up later, Mr. Miller?" the driver asked.

"No, thank you, Tom. This will do it," John said as he paid the driver.

John and Leah got out of the car, and as Leah watched it drive away, she couldn't help but wonder what John had in mind. She followed him through a gate in the fence, across a gravel-covered area, and into a small office. John showed a man behind the desk a paper; the man looked at it, then picked up the phone and dialed a number.

"Jimmy, bring number forty-four around front."

He hung the phone up, then pointed to a couple of chairs. "Have a seat," he said. "It'll be around in a moment."

The man left the office so that only John and Leah remained. The television was on, and one of the cable news programs was playing. A very attractive blond-haired woman was giving the news.

". . . said that they expect construction on the new building to be completed within six months.

"In St. Louis, the murder of high-profile lawyer Carl Trevathan remains unsolved after three months."

Leah's heart leapt to her throat.

"Mr. Miller, you want to step out here a moment?" the lot manager asked, sticking his head in through the front door. "We'll need you to look over the vehicle and sign off that there is no damage."

"I'll be right back," John said to Leah.

"Detective Gary Hellman, the lead investigator for the case, spoke with our own Brian Kelly."

"The early reports were that this was a murder of passion," the reporter said. "I believe the theory was that it was a case of unrequited love. Leah McKenzie felt betrayed because Carl Trevathan wouldn't get a divorce so he could marry her. Now I'm not so sure that is the case."

"Oh? Are you telling me that you have other suspects?"

"No. Unfortunately, we still have only one suspect, and that is Leah McKenzie. But I think the motive may be something much more involved than a romance gone bad," Detective Hellman said.

"Can you share with our viewers what that might be?"

"Because it is an ongoing investigation, I'm afraid I can't say too much about it," Hellman said. "But I will say that it has to do with money. A lot of money."

"Concerning one of the firm's clients?" Brian asked.

"I can't go any further than that."

"Anything you want to say to our viewers that might help your case?"

Leah gasped as she saw her picture flash up on the TV screen. It had been taken at an office celebration last year, and she knew it had to have come from Keith Blanton.

"This is a fairly contemporary picture of her."

"Do you really expect her to still look like that?" Brian asked. *"I mean, she could quite easily have dyed her hair, cut it short, and bought contacts that would change the color of her eyes."*

"Yes, she could, and she probably has. But for right now, this is all we have to go on."

The picture returned to a full one-shot of the reporter, who stared into the camera as he gave his sign-off.

"That's all we have up until this point, Midge. The St. Louis metro police and the FBI are working hand in hand on this case, but they are baffled, because so far, not one lead has turned up that would suggest where they might find Leah McKenzie."

"Do the police suspect foul play as far as Miss McKenzie is concerned?" Midge, the beautiful studio anchor, asked.

"I asked about that very thing, and Detective Hellman said that it was a distinct possibility. The point is, Leah McKenzie disappeared almost three months ago, and since that time there hasn't been the slightest hint as to where she might be. And as you know, in this age of cell phones, ATM machines, and iPads, it is virtually impossible for someone to drop off the face of the earth."

"What was the feeling Hellman gave you off camera?" Midge asked. *"Is it his gut feeling she is still alive?"*

"You know, Midge, I think it is his belief that she is still alive. And

here is another gut feeling that may surprise you. Though he continues to name her as the number one suspect, I got the sense he isn't totally convinced that she did it."

Leah felt a sudden leap of hope over the reporter's almost casual remark.

"Leah, come outside," John called to her, sticking his head in through the front door.

Leah followed John outside, thankful that he had not been there during the TV report.

"What do you think?" John asked, pointing to a shining red SUV.

"What is that?" she asked.

"Why are you asking me? You're the one who lives with the English. It's a Ford Explorer."

"I know what kind of car it is; what I mean is, is it yours?"

"It is," John replied. "Bought and paid for. I keep it here because there isn't a facility in Arthur that can store it. Get in."

John held the door open for her, and she slid into the passenger seat as he hurried around to the other side.

"Where are we going?"

"I've got the day all planned," John said.

"All right, let's hear it."

"Do you like Chinese food?"

"Yes, I love it."

"Good. We'll start there."

It had been several days since Joyce Kimble got the telephone call asking about the picture of the Amish girl in the newspaper. She got the telephone number of the person who called her, but when she called the number back, nobody answered. She did a reverse number check and learned that the call had been made from a pay phone on Woodson Road.

She had passed it off as idle curiosity until that morning, when she was in her apartment having a late breakfast and watching television.

Joyce looked more closely as she saw a picture flash up on the TV screen. It was a picture of Leah McKenzie.

Joyce thought there was something very familiar about that girl's face. Where had she seen it before?

Then, it dawned on her.

Moving quickly to her computer, Joyce downloaded a picture of Leah McKenzie, then the picture of the Amish woman that had run in the paper several days ago. She printed them both out, then, holding them side by side, studied them closely.

She couldn't be sure, but there was enough similarity between the two pictures that she would not rule out their being of the same person. This would bear looking into.

CHAPTER SEVENTEEN

At lunch, Leah ordered wonton soup and sweet-and-sour pork. John had wonton soup, egg rolls, and Szechuan beef.

"Until I left, I had never heard of Chinese food," John said as he deftly used chopsticks.

"Really? How can you not have heard of Chinese food?"

"Well, I knew there were people in China, and I knew they must have eaten something. But I didn't know there was an entire industry of Chinese food being served in America. And now I love it."

"I like it as well," Leah said.

"It is sort of nice to be out without having everyone stare at you, isn't it? It's not really so bad in Arthur, except for the other night. But the farther away you get from the Amish base, the more apt you are to be stared at."

"John, do you intend to stay with the Amish for the rest of your life?"

John had a piece of bamboo shoot clamped between his chopsticks, about to transfer it to his mouth, but he stopped and put it back on his plate, then looked across the table at her.

"Why do you ask that?"

"You have to admit, you aren't like all the others. You aren't like Caleb. You aren't even like Jacob."

John was silent for a moment.

"I never was like them."

"So, that brings me back to my original question. Are you going to stay with the Amish for the rest of your life?"

"I don't know. I hope the rest of my life is a long time."

"Why haven't you ever gotten married?"

"I didn't want to get married before I experienced a bit of life. And when I came back, all of the eligible women were already married."

"Like Rebecca?"

John nodded. "Yes, like Rebecca."

"I'm sorry, I have no business prying into your personal affairs."

"Sure you do. We're friends, and we're spending time together. I don't mind answering some personal questions. I might have a few of my own."

Leah flinched. Had she opened Pandora's box?

"I'll ask you the same question you asked me. Why have you never married?"

"I was in law school while all my friends were settling down. Then I was too dedicated to my career to think about anything like getting married."

"And that brings up my next question. For someone who is as dedicated to her career as you are, how is it that you can, or would, take so much time off? You've been here for quite some time now."

"Are you getting tired of me?" Leah flashed him a smile, delaying until she could come up with a suitable answer.

"I mean, is it really just to try to reestablish a relationship with your grandmother?"

"Among other things."

"If you don't want to talk about it, I'll shut up."

"The lawyer I worked for, Carl Trevathan, was killed. He had a wonderful family, it was very tragic—I just needed some time off."

"I understand," John said.

Though John didn't know the entire story, Leah got the idea that if he did know everything, he really would understand.

"It's not just that he was killed, it's—"

"John Miller!" someone said, coming over to the table then. "I haven't seen you since college! Where have you been keeping yourself?"

"Eddie Webb," John said. "It's been a while. I'm back in Arthur. What are you doing now?"

"I'm a dentist down in Benton."

"I thought you were going to go to medical school."

"Why? Malpractice insurance eats up all your profits. Dentistry is the way to go. Your wife?"

"A friend," John said. "Lena, this is Eddie."

Eddie stuck his hand out toward Leah, then he looked at her more closely.

"Lena?"

"Lapp," Leah said.

Eddie shook his head. "No, that name doesn't ring a bell. But I would swear we've met somewhere."

John laughed. "What line are you going to use next? 'Do you come here often?'"

Eddie chuckled nervously. "I guess it did sound like that. But someone as pretty as she is probably gets hit on all the time, anyway. Well, it was nice talking to you. I'll be on my way." He stared long and hard at Leah again, then shook his head. "I could swear I've seen you somewhere before."

Leah gave a quick prayer of thanks that John had not introduced her by her real name.

"Hope you don't mind that I didn't use your real name," John said after Eddie had left. "But if he really did know you from somewhere, I wasn't ready to share a lot of 'remember when' talk. Today, you're all mine."

Leah laughed. "Why, John, are you jealous?"

"No, I could never be that. Proverbs twenty-seven, verse four: 'Wrath is cruel, and anger is outrageous; but who is able to stand before envy?'"

"You have a verse for everything?"

"I'm a simple man, Leah. I need a TO and E."

"You need a what?"

"TO and E, table of organization and equipment. It's pretty much your guidelines for the military. For me, the Bible is my guideline."

"Well, I can't argue with that."

John looked up toward a wall clock. "We need to get a move on if we don't want to be late."

"Late for what?"

"You'll see."

Leah asked no more questions but wondered what John had in mind after they left the restaurant. She became even more curious when he turned into the campus of Millikin University. The curiosity was satisfied when she saw a sign that read BASKET-BALL TODAY.

"A basketball game!" she said.

"I told you I love basketball. Not quite March Madness, I'll admit. And I didn't go to school here, but I sneak up here from time to time to watch Big Blue play."

John bought tickets and they went inside. Leah found the arena's storied wall of fame, and as John went to the refreshment counter, she searched the photos of former college champions until she spotted the one she had been looking for, in the track and field section:

Jason McKenzie

Three-mile run—15:01

1987

John came over to her carrying a big tub of popcorn and two root beers.

"You can't enjoy basketball without popcorn and root beer."

"That's true," Leah said.

"What are you looking at?"

"That," Leah said, pointing to one of the photographs.

John looked at it, then did a double take. "Jason McKenzie?"

"My father," Leah said. "He went to school here."

"Well, I'll be. And I see he was quite an athlete. Fifteen oh one for a three-mile run? That's a very good time. Oh, I guess that means you'll be cheering for Millikin in the game today."

"Yes. Unless they're playing Wash U."

"We're safe. They're playing Greenville College."

It was then that Leah understood how John was dressed. The blue and white of his shirt and pants matched the blue and white colors of the Millikin basketball team.

It was a good game, going into double overtime before Big Blue pulled out a win. John and Leah cheered along with everyone else. She loved cheering for her dad's alma mater, and in fact she loved the whole afternoon. It was great fun, more fun than she had had in a long time.

Back in Arthur, Sam was in the loft of the barn, moving hay around, when he slipped on some loose hay and fell to the ground below. He reached out to break his fall and felt an intense pain in his arm. When he sat up, he saw a bulge just under the skin.

Holding his left arm with his right, he went into the house, where Emma and Ada were preparing supper.

"Sam, you may as well get washed up," Emma said. "Supper is nearly ready."

"I think I broke my arm, Mamm," Sam said.

"Glory be, you have!" Emma said. "Ada, get your *daad*. He has set many a broken bone."

Ada hurried on her errand and when she came back a short while later, Emma already had a splint ready, along with several strips of cloth.

"Jacob, hitch up Daisy and go into town to look for John. He should be told about this," Isaac said as he took Sam's arm in his hands. "This is going to hurt," he said. "But we have to reset the bone, or you'll never be able to use your arm again."

"I'm ready, Daad," Sam said, bracing himself for the ordeal.

"The very idea," Marv Jensen said. He spoke aloud, even though he was the only one in the car. "Just who does he think he is, firing me like that?"

Jensen reached down into the cup holder, which at the moment held half a bottle of Johnnie Walker whiskey. He took another drink and noticed, without much concern, that he was driving a little over eighty miles per hour on Highway 133, which was a narrow, two-lane blacktop road. No problem; he was an excellent driver, and he always had been. He sped by a yellow triangular sign so quickly that he didn't even notice the horse and buggy in silhouette.

"I made his company. Me!" Jensen said. "Before I came along all he had was a print company that was going broke. I'm the one who built the website for him, and I'm the one who started offering website building as a service."

Jensen took another swallow.

"All right, so I got angry and cussed out one of his customers. Big deal. He wouldn't have even been one of his customers in the first place if I—"

That was when Jensen saw the buggy in front of him.

"What the hell?" he shouted as he slammed on the brakes.

* * *

When the basketball game was over, John and Leah drove out to Decatur Lake and sat there for a while, just looking out over the water.

"What made you decide to become a lawyer?"

Leah chuckled. "Abbie Carmichael."

"Who was she? A teacher? Neighbor? Relative?"

"She's nobody real. She was a character, an assistant district attorney on the TV show *Law and Order*."

"What do you mean?"

"I was hooked on that show when I was young. I saw this woman lawyer standing up against the men, getting the better of them, and I thought, that's what I want to do. So, when I graduated from high school, I decided I would become a lawyer."

"Good for you."

"What about you? It must have taken courage to leave home the way you did, especially knowing what the consequences would be."

"More curiosity than courage, I think," John said. "Then it turned out that it wasn't something I wanted to do after all."

"I'm curious, John. How did a boy, growing up Amish, ever get it in his mind that he wanted to be in the army in the first place?"

"I didn't start out wanting to be in the army, but I did want an education. And I'll be honest with you, I don't know where that came from."

They talked until it got dark, then John started the engine. "It's time for our next phase," he said.

"What would that be?"

"Come on, aren't you enjoying the surprises?"

"I have to admit I am," Leah said with a laugh.

A few minutes later, John parked in a parking lot near a building sporting a neon sign—the Purple Crackle.

"What is a purple crackle? Or maybe I should say, what is the purple crackle?" Leah asked.

"It's a nightclub. Good meals, a convivial bar, and dancing."

Leah chuckled. "You've fit a lot into one day."

After a dinner of prime rib and wine, John invited Leah onto the dance floor.

"It's been a long time since I've danced," Leah said.

"That's all right. I never have danced."

"What?"

"It's just not anything I ever got around to doing."

"Then how do you know you can dance?"

"I'm sure I can't. But I've been watching and it looks to me like people are just holding on to each other and sort of moving a bit in time with the music. How hard can that be?"

"You're right. How hard can it be?"

Just as they got up another song started, this one very fast, and John turned around and led her back to the table.

"You don't want to try that one?" Leah asked.

"I don't want to even think about trying it."

It was two more songs before there was another slow dance, and this time John and Leah did get on the floor.

As they danced, Leah wasn't sure whether they were dancing or not, but they did seem to be moving together. What they were doing, and of this she was very aware, was holding their bodies together. Leah could feel every inch of his body on hers, pressing against her, arousing the most delightful sensations. Resting her head on John's shoulder, she allowed herself to relax against him, swaying with the music. For tonight, she could pretend that she wasn't in hiding, that John wasn't Amish, that they were just two people on a date, falling in love.

It was nearly midnight when they left the Purple Crackle.

"Are we going back tonight?" Leah asked.

"That's a loaded question, isn't it?"

"How so?"

"If we don't go back tonight that means we'll be out all night."

"Yes."

"Together."

"Not necessarily," Leah said.

John chuckled. "Oh, now you're going to use logic, are you?"

"You don't think logic is called for?"

"Not necessarily," John said, duplicating her earlier answer.

"What do you suggest?"

"We could save money, and stay warm, by bundling."

"Bundling?"

"You did ask my sister about it, didn't you?"

"I did."

"Well?"

Leah looked across the car at him. His face was darkly visible by the light from the instrument panel. They passed a car, and for just an instant, his face was brightly lit—a flash in the night—then in darkness again. "I don't know, John."

"What is it you don't know?"

"I'm not Amish. And you've been on the outside. I don't know if we could bundle without . . ."

Leah didn't have to finish the sentence. "Trust me," John said.

"I'm not worried about trusting you. I'm not sure I can trust myself."

"Then trust me." John turned off the road, into a motel. He drove up under the entry portico, and Leah waited in the car as he went inside to get a room.

Should she do this? She knew her idyll in Arthur couldn't last forever—and she hated lying to John. But at the same time, he seemed so sure of her, sure enough for both of them. And if the worst happened, wouldn't she regret not taking this chance to steal a few more hours of romance with the most amazing man she'd ever met?

John came out a moment later with the motel key card and she knew it was too late to change her mind.

There was only one king-sized bed in the room. John sat down on the edge of the bed and began taking off his shoes.

"What are you doing? I thought you bundled with all your clothes on," Leah said.

John smiled. "We are allowed to take off our shoes."

"Oh."

Leah sat down and pulled off her high heels. "I have to confess that the shoes I've been wearing for the last two months are a lot more comfortable than these."

"I'm sure they are."

"What now?"

John pointed toward the bed. "Lie down here."

Leah got into the bed, then scooted way over to one side.

"This is only going to work if we are both in the middle," John said. "Otherwise, when we start bundling, we might fall off."

"All right." Leah moved into the middle of the bed, then turned onto her side to watch as John got in bed beside her.

"Like this?" she asked.

"Yes, like this."

John reached out to touch her cheek, then her lips. Her lips were quivering, whether from excitement or from fear as to where this was leading, she didn't know. John moved his hand down over her chin to tilt back her head. Now she found herself looking up at him as he brought his mouth down toward her. Her lips met his, and they shared a kiss that was deep and demanding. Then his lips left hers and moved to the smooth underside of her chin, then down to her throat. The feeling of his mouth and tongue on her neck, oddly soft and rough at the same time, was so intense that she could scarcely keep from crying out. She closed her eyes, surrendering herself totally to the sensations she was experiencing.

John lifted his mouth away from her and wound his left hand into her hair. Leah was still a virgin, though she had engaged in some heavy necking before, furtive gropes at college fraternity parties while loud music played and others were making out nearby. How unlike those meaningless and ultimately embarrassing incidents this was. She closed her eyes, afraid to keep them open for fear he could see, reflected in them, her naked desire. She could smell the disinfectant that had been used to clean the sink, the detergent in the bed comforter, and the pheromones of his masculine fragrance.

Then abruptly, he stopped.

"Maybe we had better—" John started, then stopped and took a deep breath. "Maybe we had better just lie here." John's voice was husky, aching, and sexy.

No! No, don't stop, please don't stop! Leah wanted to scream. But she said nothing. He lay on his back and put his arm around her so that her head was on his shoulder. After a while he began kissing her again, but this time his kisses, instead of being demanding, were tentative, caring, and oh so gentle.

"If that was bundling," Leah said, "it's a heck of a secret the Amish have kept from the English all these years."

"That was bundling," John said.

Leah was awakened the next morning by the smell of coffee. Turning over, she saw John putting sugar and creamer into one of the cups.

"Good morning," Leah said.

"I have noticed at breakfast that you use cream and sugar in your coffee," he said.

"Yes."

"I thought maybe we would have a cup of coffee here, then go down to the lobby and see if they are still serving breakfast."

"Still serving? My goodness, what time is it?"

"It's almost nine."

"Church!"

"Unless you want to go to a Protestant church here in town—uh, I assume you are Protestant—there won't be any church for us today."

"I'm Episcopalian," she said.

"Was your mother Episcopalian? I mean after she left the Amish."

"Yes."

John poured two cups of coffee, stirred hers, then brought it over to her. "That must have been quite a change for her."

"I suppose it was, but she was very active in the church. I think she enjoyed it."

"I expect, with her background, she would have been very active in any church."

"John, what about your missing church today? Is that going to get you into more trouble?"

"Well, how much more trouble can I get in? I'm already banned for six months. Even if I do go to church, I have to sit over in the corner, all by myself, like I did when I was delinquent in grade school."

Leah laughed out loud. "You didn't!"

"Oh, I'm afraid I did. But it was all Caleb's fault. When I dropped the frog down the back of Rebecca's dress, Caleb told on me."

"I'll be. You always were a rebel, weren't you?"

"I guess I was." John picked up the phone and called the desk. "Are you still serving breakfast? Okay, thank you."

"Are they?"

"We can eat for an hour."

"You mean breakfast will be out for another hour?"

"No, I mean I plan to go down there now and start eating, and eat for an hour."

Leah laughed.

*   *   *

With only sweet rolls and dry cereal it wasn't that satisfying of a breakfast, and Leah actually found herself missing the sausage, fresh-baked bread, scrambled eggs, fried potatoes, and stewed apples that were the standard fare in the Miller house.

"Not much of a breakfast, is it?" John asked. "Shall we go somewhere else?"

"I'm all right with this, unless you need more."

"Yes," John said. "I need more."

Leah got the idea that he wasn't talking just about food.

CHAPTER EIGHTEEN

The sheriff's car looked out of place parked among all the buggies that were sitting in front of the Miller house. One buggy, or what was left of the buggy, had been deposited in a smashed pile over in front of the barn. The wheels were broken and the cab flattened. There was blood on the shafts of the buggy.

There were several people gathered inside the house, relatives, friends, and neighbors of the Millers. Deputy Kinsdale was talking to an ashen-faced Isaac.

"The driver's name is Marvin Jensen. He was drunk, and though we have no way of knowing exactly how fast he was going, he left a very long set of skid marks."

"Where is he now?" Isaac asked.

"We have him in jail."

"Was he hurt?"

"No. His air bag deployed. But when a four-thousand-pound

car hits a three-hundred-pound buggy and a nine-hundred-pound horse, the person in the car isn't going to suffer that much, air bag or no."

"I am glad he was not hurt."

"Yeah, well, that's the difference between you and me, Mr. Miller. If it had been my boy I would have wanted the son of a bi—" Then, remembering where he was, Deputy Kinsdale altered his sentence. "If it had been my boy he ran over, I don't think I could be as kind."

"I don't think he did it on purpose."

"Maybe not. But he got drunk on purpose, and he drove while he was drunk on purpose, and he was speeding on purpose. What about the horse? We've got him—"

"Her. Daisy was a mare."

"Yes, sir. Well, we've got her picked up. The county can dispose of her if you wish."

"No. We have a graveyard here, where we have buried four generations of horses. And Daisy was a very good one. If you would, bring her back and put her behind the barn. I will take care of her after the funeral."

"Yes, sir," Deputy Kinsdale said. "Mr. Miller, I'm really sorry about what happened to Jacob. Some of my friends in town knew him, and everyone says that he was a fine young man. You just have to wonder why things like this happen to good people."

"*Ja*, he was a good boy," Isaac said. "It was God who called him home."

Kinsdale went over to Emma and Ada, both of whom were weeping quietly, and holding his hat in his hand, he spoke to them.

"Mrs. Miller, you have my deepest sympathy."

"*Danki.*"

"And you were his wife?" he asked Ada.

"Sister."

"I'm so sorry, miss."

"Thank you for taking the time to visit us, deputy," Ada said.

"I'm just sorry that it had to be under such circumstances."

As Deputy Kinsdale left the house, he met the hearse from the undertaker, bringing the body home.

John made the decision to drive back to Arthur, rather than leave the car in Decatur. Glen Collins now knew about his car, and John was certain he could keep it in the barn behind the shop if he wanted to. John had been keeping it in storage in Decatur so he wouldn't be tempted to drive it. It was an "out of sight, out of mind" thing. But, since he was facing a six-month *bann* anyway, he saw no reason why he couldn't bring the car back to Arthur.

"I won't go so far as to rub it in anyone's face," he told Leah. "I'll leave the car in Arthur and drive the buggy back and forth to work."

"That's good," Leah said with a smile. "I think Prodigal would be hurt if you suddenly quit using him."

"Prodigal gets to you, doesn't he?"

"And Daisy too. It's funny, they each have their own personality. Prodigal is sort of bold, manly, and Daisy is sweet and demure."

"Animals do have their own personalities. People don't quite understand the relationship we have with our horses. They think they are beasts of burden only; they don't realize they are practically members of the family."

As they were driving back to Arthur, John turned on the radio.

"Do you want me to try to find something?" Leah asked. She

wasn't just being helpful; she wanted to avoid any news program, just on the possibility that her name would be mentioned.

"No need, I keep it set where I want it," John said.

As the radio came on, Leah recognized Symphony Number Nine, *From the New World*. "Oh, I love Dvorak," she said.

"You asked me once what I missed from living with the English, and I told you it was March Madness. I've already added Chinese food to that, and now I will add classical music. I really miss that. I had never even heard one piece of classical music until I was in college, and I fell in love with it."

"I love it too," Leah said. She was pleased to learn that she and John shared the same passion for classical music.

When they reached Arthur, John parked the car in the barn beside the buggy. He had a key to let them go inside the shop, where they changed back into plain clothes.

It was a nippy afternoon, but the propane heater in the buggy kept them as comfortable for the hour-long drive out to the farm as they had been in the car on the way back from Decatur.

"I very much enjoyed this weekend, John," Leah said. "Guilty though I feel."

"I told you—"

"I know, Odysseus, you've tied yourself to the mast so I can't harm you. But I feel guilty anyway."

"If anyone is guilty, it is I, Edward Rochester to your Jane Eyre."

"Don't tell me you've read Charlotte Brontë? Is there no end to your list of surprises, John Miller?"

"Which do you like best, vanilla pudding or rocky road ice cream?"

"Rocky road."

"Because of the . . . ?" John teased.

"Surprises," Leah replied, laughing.

They drove on in silence for a while longer, then Leah asked the question that was on her mind.

"John, where are we going?"

"We're going back to the farm."

"That's not what I mean."

John sighed. "I know that isn't what you meant, Leah. But I was taking the coward's way out."

"Don't, please. I want an answer. Where are we going with this—this relationship?"

"Where do you want it to go?"

"No, that isn't fair. You're turning the question back on me. I asked first."

"Leah, I think it is no secret that I have very strong feelings for you."

"You can have strong feelings for a political philosophy. I need a more definite answer than that."

"I love you, Leah," John said. "Is that definite enough for you?"

"Yes."

"How do you feel?"

"I love you too," Leah said. "So, where does that leave us?"

"I don't know. We are as star-crossed as Jake Barnes and Lady Brett Ashley in Hemingway's *The Sun Also Rises,*" John said.

"What?" Leah asked. "John, the war, you weren't . . ."

John laughed. "No, I'm whole. I meant that allegorically."

"John, you've told me your past. I think we've come to the point to where I have to tell you of my past. I lied to you when I said I had come here to try to establish a connection with my grandmother.

I mean, yes, I do want to do that, but that isn't what brought me here."

"You told me you weren't running away from a husband. Please tell me that wasn't a lie."

"I'm not running away from a husband."

"From an abusive boyfriend?"

"No, it's nothing like that. It's something worse."

John set his jaw, then took a breath to wait for the revelation, whatever it might be. "All right. I'm listening."

"I told you that I'm a lawyer. I work for, or rather *worked* for, the firm of Blanton, Trevathan and Dunn. Actually, I was a direct assistant to Mr. Trevathan, who was one of the most wonderful men I have even known."

"Trevathan, the man you said died."

"Yes. Three months ago, Mr. Trevathan was at the federal courthouse building, and he asked me to bring a file to him on the twenty-fourth floor. I did so, but the moment the elevator doors opened, I saw a man shoot him. Mr. Trevathan staggered into the elevator and hit the down button. By the time we reached the bottom floor, Mr. Trevathan was dead." Leah was quiet for a moment.

"There is more to the story?" John's question was gentle, sympathetic.

"Yes. About a week after that, I was going into Mr. Blanton's office to tell him something that Mr. Trevathan said just before he died, something that made absolutely no sense to me. As I got close to the office, I overheard him and Mr. Dunn talking. From the way they were talking, it made me think that somehow they were involved with Mr. Trevathan's getting killed. Then, Mr. Blanton said that they were going to make me the fall guy. They were going to claim that I killed him because of some romantic entanglement. They had my fingerprints on the gun that killed him."

"How did they get that?"

"There was a gun in Mr. Trevathan's desk when I cleared out his personal effects. I had never known him to keep a gun, and seeing it there surprised me, so I picked it up and took it to Mr. Blanton. It turns out that was the murder weapon, though how it got there, I don't know. And now it has my fingerprints all over it. Anyway, I left that day, and I've never been back."

"Maybe it's all blown over by now," John said. "Maybe they've found the real killer."

"No," Leah said with a shake of her head. "When we were in the storage yard picking up your car, I saw a news clip on television. They're still looking for me."

John reached over to grab Leah's hand. "They won't find you here," he said.

"They may not find me, but I'm going to turn myself in. I can't run from this for the rest of my life."

"If you are serious about that, I will go with you," John said. "If for no other reason than to supply moral support."

"I just wish I knew what Mr. Trevathan meant by those last words."

"What were his last words, do you remember?"

"Oh yes. I remember. '*Ad astra per alia porci*.' It's obviously Latin, but not any legal phrase I've ever heard."

"That's because it isn't a legal phrase," John said. "It means 'To the stars on the wings of a pig.'"

"What?"

"That's what '*Ad astra per alia porci*' means. 'To the stars on the wings of a pig.'"

Despite herself, Leah laughed. "Now, tell me, John, why in the world would you know something like that?"

"Are you a fan of John Steinbeck?"

"I've read him. *Grapes of Wrath, Of Mice and Men*. Why do you ask?"

"I didn't discover literature until I was in college, and John Steinbeck became a personal favorite of mine. A professor once told him that he would be published when pigs fly. So Steinbeck adopted that as his personal motto and he used it on every book he ever wrote."

"Why in heaven's name would Mr. Trevathan say something like that as his last words?"

"I don't know, but it must be something important or he wouldn't have said it."

"It makes even less sense now that I know what it means."

They reached the Miller farm then, and Prodigal turned into the long driveway that led up to the house. That was when Leah and John saw more than two dozen buggies parked outside.

"What is all this? Are they having church in your folks' house today?" Leah asked.

"No. At least not that I know. And it would be a little late for that, anyway. It's almost four o'clock."

"Why do you think there are so many people here?"

"I don't know, but I don't like it," John replied, a worried tone creeping into his voice. He snapped the reins to urge Prodigal into a rapid trot, then headed for the barn. "Sorry, Prodigal, I'm going to have to leave you hitched up until I find out what's going on here," he said.

Leaving the buggy, John and Leah walked quickly from the barn to the house. There was a low buzz of conversation going on when they stepped inside, but, upon seeing John, everyone grew quiet.

"What is it?" John asked. "What is going on here?"

"Where have you been, John?" Bishop Hershberger asked, coming through the crowd to confront him.

"What is going on, bishop? Where are my parents? Why is everyone here?"

"Everyone is here because of your brother Jacob."

"Jacob?" John's voice was tight and filled with concern. "What about Jacob?"

"Jacob is dead. He was killed in an accident yesterday. A car hit the buggy. Jacob and the horse, Daisy, were both killed."

"No!" John shouted loudly. "No!"

John started through the house, toward the parlor. Everyone parted to let him through.

"Mamm! Daad!" he shouted.

"Where were you, John?" Emma asked, her eyes red-rimmed. "Sam broke his arm, and Jacob was going into town to try to find you."

"Mamm, I'm sorry, I—" John opened his arms to hug his mother, but she held up her arm to stop him.

"No, I cannot," she said with a catch in her voice. "The *bann*." Then she, Isaac, Ada, and Sam, his arm in a sling, turned their backs to him.

*   *   *

Not since her mother had learned of her father's death and knew that she could not go to the funeral had Leah seen as much pain as she was seeing on John's face.

John stood there for a moment, staring at the backs of his family, then he turned. When he did so, everyone else in the house, except Leah, turned their back to him.

CHAPTER NINETEEN

A cold rain started falling early Monday morning, which was the day of the funeral. John was in the room that had been Jacob's bedroom in life, standing beside the varnished, stained, and oiled pine coffin as he looked down upon the mortal remains of his brother. Jacob Miller, wearing white trousers and a white shirt, was lying in a coffin that had no side handles. There was no lining inside. Except for the coffin, which rested on sawhorses set up against the back wall, the room was completely empty of all furniture.

John had spent the entire night in the room with the coffin, the only one present. This time with Jacob was necessary for him, because once the funeral started, he would have to stay alone in a separate room. When relatives, friends, and neighbors filed by for their last view of the body, and to pay their condolences to the rest of the family, John could not be there with them.

During the last three days, friends and neighbors had taken over all the burdens of the Miller family, from preparing meals and washing dishes to feeding the animals and milking cows, even to making all the arrangements for the funeral.

When the first mourner arrived, John left the house, then went into his apartment in the barn, closed the door, and lay on the bed with his hands laced behind his head. He couldn't attend this funeral, but as he lay there, lost in sorrow, he recalled a previous funeral that he had attended.

Actually, it wasn't a funeral, it was a memorial service, but the deceased meant almost as much to him as Jacob, for the deceased had been a part of the peculiar brotherhood to which John belonged at the time, the brotherhood of arms.

Before Master Sergeant James E. Wyatt's body was shipped back to be buried in his hometown, the battalion held a memorial service for him in the Helmand River Valley in Afghanistan.

John thought of the memorial service and recalled standing in front of his company as U.S. flags and guidons snapped in the breeze. A member of the division band raised a bugle to his lips to reverently play "Taps," the call that had put to rest millions of soldiers, from Custer's gallant slain to those who had fallen in Iraq and Afghanistan.

Leah was torn. She wanted to be with John because she knew how hurt he was, and she wanted to comfort him if she could. But she also knew, instinctively, that right now he might prefer to be alone. And she wanted to provide what solace she could to Emma, Isaac, Ada, and Sam. Ada, Leah saw, was being comforted by Caleb. How sad it was, Leah thought. Caleb and Ada were soon to be married, but that happy occasion was now overshadowed by the death of Ada's brother.

The house had been prepared for the funeral by friends and neighbors, and the biggest room in the house, the parlor, had benches arranged for the mourners. People began gathering slowly and silently until well over two hundred were present, more people than could be accommodated by the one room. Those mourners who could not be seated were scattered throughout the rest of the house.

At exactly nine o'clock, Pastor Lantz removed his black hat. When he took off his hat every other man in the house took his off as well.

Elam Lantz opened with a prayer.

"Oh, Lord Jesus Christ, you, our redeemer, who willingly gave yourself up to death so that all who believe in you might be saved and know eternal life, we commend Jacob Miller into your arms of mercy, in the belief that he will have a place of happiness, light, and peace in the kingdom of your glory, forever. Amen."

As Pastor Lantz continued with the service, the cold wind outside began blowing harder, and Leah could hear the window rattle in its frame. Glancing through the window, she saw that the gusts were whipping up dust and debris. All the horses looked miserable as they stood out in the blustery cold.

Lantz continued to talk, pointing out that Jacob was regular in attending church and could always be counted upon to help others.

"He was the kind of man we need around us, and he is here no more. But God needs such men as well, and our brother Jacob has been called home to the Lord."

After Lantz, Bishop Hershberger spoke, carrying on for over an hour in German and English, sometimes mixing the two languages in the same sentence. He reminded everyone of the certainty of death and that their only path to heaven was to be right with God.

"We should be thankful that it was Jacob, and not John, who was killed," the bishop said. "For Jacob was a welcome lamb of our community, a faithful follower of our Ordnung, a member, in good standing, of our church. Jacob's brother John, on the other hand, has been cast away from us. John is a lost soul, a man who, should he die before he serves out his penance, will surely not see the Kingdom of God, but will be cast into the burning fires of hell, there to writhe in torment for all eternity."

Leah seethed with anger. How could this person, supposedly a man of God, say such things about John in front of his parents?

"Mark well this lesson!" the bishop shouted. "Be like Jacob, who will spend eternity with the Lord and will see and welcome his loved ones again, not like John, a pitiful lost soul!"

Leah looked over at Ada and Emma. They were crying, and she knew that because of the bishop's words, their weeping was as much for John as it was for Jacob. Why would the bishop do that? Why would he double the sorrow felt by the family in this time of mourning?

After all the words in the house had been spoken and there was a final viewing of Jacob's corpse, the coffin was closed and carried outside. There was no hearse as such, no polished ebony vehicle trimmed in silver. Instead it was a one-horse spring wagon with the seat pushed forward. Because of the cold rain a canvas cover was placed over the coffin to keep it dry. The mourners stepped into their buggies, then formed a long line to follow the body to the *graabhof*—the graveyard. The procession moved very slowly, no faster than a man would normally walk.

Leah debated with herself whether to stay behind and go see, and perhaps try to comfort, John or go to the cemetery with the family. She decided that it would not look good if she stayed behind, so she went in the same buggy as Isaac, Emma, Sam, and Ada. Because Daisy had been killed in the same accident that killed Jacob, the buggy was drawn by one of the plow horses. It made the buggy stand out among all the others, because the horse pulling it was so much larger.

When they reached the cemetery, the horses were tied to the hitching posts, then everyone climbed down from their buggies and gathered around the open grave.

The first thing Leah noticed was that there was no tent or canopy with folding chairs for the family. They stood in the cold drizzle along with everyone else. Also, there was no carpet of artificial grass around the grave, over the pile of dirt, or down into the grave. The coffin, supported by two stout poles, was carried to the open grave and placed over it, the two poles providing the temporary resting place for the casket. Ropes were looped around the coffin at the head and feet, then the pallbearers lifted the pine box while others withdrew the poles it had been resting on. After the poles were removed, the coffin was lowered slowly into the open grave, and the ropes were removed.

One man stepped down into the grave, his action surprising Leah, and when she looked down inside, she saw that he was standing on a wooden frame that had been built around the coffin. Short boards were passed down to him, the boards the same length as the grave. Putting the boards on the frame, he built a partition over the top of the coffin.

Then the four pallbearers, who Leah later learned were the same ones who had dug the grave, began to close it. She could hear the loud thumps of dirt as it fell on the boards that covered the casket. When the grave was half-filled, the men with the shovels stopped and removed their hats. Every other man present removed his hat as well.

The mourners began to sing.

> *Oh, I can almost see the lights of that City,*
> *I see them gathered all around the great white throne;*
> *Through faith in my Savior and His wonderful love,*
> *Oh, I can almost see the lights of home.*

When the song was over they finished covering the grave, then pounded down the mound of soil so that it was smooth, with no large dirt clods left. After that, everyone turned away from the grave and returned to the buggies. They would be going back to the Miller home, there to have a dinner that had been provided by friends and neighbors.

"Emma, do you think it would be all right if I took some food to John?" Leah asked.

"*Ja, Liebchen,* of course. We are to shun him, not starve him," Emma said. "Miriam Lapp made chicken and dumplings. That has always been John's favorite. I think he would very much appreciate it if you took them to him."

"Miriam, my grandmother?"

"Ja, deine grossmamm."

A moment later, carrying a plate of dumplings, green beans, baked chicken, and a roll she had put on a tray with a second plate, Leah went over to Ada, who was standing with Caleb, apart from the others.

"Ada, I understand that my grandmother made the dumplings. Please tell me how I can say thank you to her in Pennsylvania Dutch."

"'*Vielen dank fur die Knodel, Grossmamm,*'" Ada said.

Leah repeated it as best she could. "Do you think she will understand me?"

"Ja, she will understand. Are you taking food to John?"

"Yes. If he will eat."

"Are you going to stay and eat with him?"

"Yes."

"Then I think he will eat."

Leah saw her grandmother sitting at the end of a table, eating with the Brennemans. Still holding the tray, she walked over to her table, and her grandmother looked up at her.

"Vielen dank fur die Knodel, Grossmamm. I know that the Miller family greatly appreciates your kindness in this time of their sorrow."

"Du bist ein gutes mädchen zu mir danken, Leah."

Even though Leah knew that a smile was inappropriate in this time of grieving, she could not help but smile. Her grandmother had responded to her. It was in German, yes, but the words sounded gentle, and she added Leah's name. She actually called Leah by name!

"You are a kind girl to think of them, and to thank me," Leah's grandmother said, repeating it in English this time.

"You are taking food to John?" Aaron Brenneman asked.

"Yes. *Ja,*" Leah said.

"That is good."

Sam was standing near the door and when he saw Leah coming toward it carrying a tray with two plates, he hastened to open it for her.

"*Danki,* Sam," she said.

Sam smiled. "You are becoming one of us, Leah."

Leah returned the smile, then stepped outside. The icy drizzle had stopped, but it was still cold. At least the wind was no longer blowing.

Leah hurried through the cold, across the distance between the house and the barn. There was enough ambient light in the barn that Leah had no trouble making her way through to John's room at the back. She kicked once on the door.

"John? John, it's me, Leah. I have food."

The door opened and John stood there for a moment looking at her. She was unable to fathom the look in his eyes. Did he feel she had betrayed him by staying with the others that day? Did he hold himself accountable for Jacob's accident? She was about to hand him the tray, then leave, when a broad and genuinely warm smile spread across his face.

"There are two plates. I take it that means you are going to eat with me?"

"Yes, if you don't mind the company."

John laughed, a short, almost bitter laugh. "Asking me today if I don't mind the company would be like asking a man in the desert if he wouldn't mind a glass of water. Please, Leah, come in."

John stepped back from the door and made a sweep of his arm by way of invitation.

"Ah, chicken and dumplings. My favorite."

"So your mother said," Leah replied, then she smiled. "Oh! And guess who made them! My grand—" Leah started, then stopped when John's answer interrupted her.

"Miriam Lapp."

"How did you know?"

"Leah, you have missed many things by not knowing your grandmother. And one of the things you have missed is her cooking. Especially her chicken and dumplings. She is known for it." John took a bite. "And, I am glad to say, she has not lost her talent."

"Oh, John, guess what! I learned from Ada how to say '*Vielen dank fur die Knodel, Grossmamm,*' and she answered me! She answered me in German and in English. She said I was a kind girl to think of them, and to thank her."

"Well, it's easy to see why. Evidently she felt sorry for you, because of your pitiable attempt to speak in Pennsylvania Dutch."

"Oh, is it really that bad?"

John chuckled. "I was just teasing you. I think it is wonderful that she spoke to you. Maybe she is beginning to have second thoughts."

"Would you take me to see her again?"

"Ha! You forget, I'm shunned now. It would do no good for me to take you there."

"Oh, yes, I almost forgot. And I also forgot to bring us something to drink."

"What about root beer?"

"You must like root beer; that's what you bought at the basketball game."

"It ought to be against the law to make any kind of soft drink but root beer," John said.

"Luckily for you, I like it as well."

John opened the door to the little half refrigerator and pulled out two cans of root beer. He popped the tabs, then handed one to Leah.

"Did you go to the graveyard for the burial?" John asked as they ate their meal.

"Yes."

"As soon as everyone leaves, I'm going."

"Would you like me to go with you?"

"It will probably be dark by then. Are you afraid of graveyards in the dark?"

"No, of course not, at least not as far as I know. The truth is, I've never been in a graveyard in the dark."

"Well then, this will be a new experience for you, won't it? If you go with me, I mean."

"Yes, it'll be a new experience, and yes, I will go with you."

"You'll need a coat. It will be even colder tonight."

"All right."

"Keep a watch for me. I'll shine my flashlight in your room again."

"I'll be waiting."

Leah had almost given up, because it was after ten o'clock when she saw the flashlight beam coming in through her window. Grabbing her coat, she left to meet John. She passed by Jacob's empty room as she walked quietly through the upstairs hallway to the head of the steps and, thinking of him, felt another quick stab of sorrow.

It was funny; until just over two months ago, she had never even heard of Jacob. Now she was deeply saddened by his passing.

She stopped out on the front porch to put on her shoes. The clouds had all moved away, and now the night sky was filled with stars except for the area right around the moon. The moon was so bright that night that it projected a rather large halo of lighter sky around it.

As she laced up her shoes, she wondered if she should buy a pair of galoshes. It hadn't snowed yet, so she hadn't needed them, but if she stayed in Arthur much longer, she would.

"Hi," John said. "I've got Prodigal hitched up, and I've started the heater, so it should be warm enough."

"Warm, yes, that sounds good."

Prodigal whickered as they approached, and he stamped a foot.

"I promise, boy, we won't keep you out in the cold too long," John said as he helped Leah in, then climbed in himself and picked up the reins. Prodigal moved out at a rapid trot, as if knowing that would warm him up some.

They reached the cemetery much faster than had the funeral procession that morning. John drove right up to the grave, where the freshly mounded dirt gleamed in the moonlight. There was no tombstone as yet.

"Is this your family plot?" Leah asked.

"We don't bury by family plots. We bury in chronological order. That grave"—he pointed to one just to the left of the fresh mound of dirt—"belongs to Mary Wagler. She died about four months ago. Whoever dies next will lie here, just on the other side of Jacob."

John walked right up to Jacob's grave and stood there for a long moment with his head bowed. Leah stayed back and remained quiet. Finally, after about five minutes, John turned away from the grave.

"All right, we can go back now. Thank you for coming with me."

"I'm glad you wanted me with you."

John didn't say anything until they were out of the cemetery and on the road leading back to the Miller farm. Then he chuckled.

"Once, when Sam was about two years old, he fell asleep in church. Mamm told Jacob to take him out to the buggy and stay with him.

"Jacob took him out but saw a baby rabbit run into the barn, so he put Sam in the first buggy he saw and started out after that baby rabbit. Well, the next thing you know, he had completely forgotten about Sam.

"It turned out that the buggy Jacob chose belonged to Mr. Zook, and Mr. Zook didn't stay for the fellowship dinner. Not noticing Sam, Mr. Zook hitched his horse up to his buggy, and off he went, with Sam asleep in the back.

"When Mamm came out to get Jacob and Sam for the fellowship dinner, neither one of them was in our buggy. Then she saw Jacob, still chasing that baby rabbit, and she asked what he had done with Sam. That's when Jacob panicked. He started running around, peeking into every buggy, trying to find Sam, and when Mamm and Daad asked him whose buggy he had left Sam in, he had no idea. All he knew, he said, was that it was a black buggy."

Leah laughed. "A black buggy?"

John laughed with her. "A black buggy. That is what he said."

"What happened?"

"Once Mr. Zook got home and started unhitching his horse, Sam woke up and was sitting in the front seat, calling for Mamm. Well, there were at least four others about Sam's age then, so Mr. Zook started going around trying to find which family Sam belonged to. In the meantime, Daad was going from house to house trying to find Sam. They crossed paths a couple of times before they finally connected.

"For a long time after that, Jacob had Sam convinced that he had done it on purpose, and if Sam didn't do what Jacob wanted him to do, he would give him away again, only this time he would put him in the car of an *Englischer.*"

Both John and Leah were laughing hard by the time he finished with the story. And though it could have seemed a bit incongruous—laughing so uproariously while coming back from what, for John, at least, was a graveside funeral service—Leah knew that John needed it. They both did.

CHAPTER TWENTY

J ohn, would you take me to see my grandmother again?" Leah
asked the next day.

"I'll take you, but I'll have to remain in the buggy."

"Oh."

"It's all right, I don't mind. I've got the heater to keep warm, and
I'll take a book to read."

"You're sure you don't mind?"

"I'm sure I don't mind."

"Thanks."

An hour later, as John remained in the buggy, Leah, hesitantly, anxiously, knocked on the door of her grandmother's house. Mary answered.

"Leah!" Mary said with a welcoming smile.

"Hello, Mary. I thought I might try one more time to visit with my grandmother. She spoke to me at Jacob's funeral; I hope that's a good sign."

"Come in, Leah," Miriam called from the kitchen.

Leah felt a surge of joy.

"Thank you," she said.

"Mary, get Leah a cup of coffee and a piece of cake."

Because of the breakfasts the Millers served, the last thing Leah wanted was something else to eat. But because it was being offered by her grandmother, there was no way she was going to turn it down.

A few minutes later, after Mary had also taken coffee and cake to John, who was waiting in the buggy, Leah and her grandmother sat down together.

"Thank you so much for talking to me today," Leah said.

"Tell me, child, about your mother," Miriam said.

"She was the most wonderful mother in the world," Leah said.

"Was she a devout woman?"

"Oh, yes, she was the most devout person I ever knew. You would have been very proud of her, Grossmamm. She lived her life for the Lord, and there is no doubt in my mind that she is with the Lord today, and reunited with her father."

Miriam wiped tears from her eyes.

"I know, Leah, that you find our ways hard. To shun your mother as we did was the hardest thing I ever had to do. But the Ordnung must be obeyed if we are to be true to the church and keep our covenant with God."

"But you're talking with me."

"Do you think I wanted to turn you away that first day? I spoke with the bishop; I begged him for permission to accept you as my granddaughter. And he agreed that because you did not leave the church, the Ordnung does not apply to you." Miriam smiled through her tears. "I am very happy that you are my granddaughter."

For the next hour, Leah and her grandmother talked. Miriam told Leah stories from her mother's past, stories that Leah had never heard before. And Leah told her grandmother about her mother, after she left. Leah did not tell of the heartache her mother experienced because of the shunning; she could see no reason for introducing such an unpleasant subject now.

When it was time to leave, Miriam walked to the front door with Leah.

"When you leave us, do not forget me," Miriam said. "You can write letters to me, and when you wish, you may come visit me."

"*Danki*, Grossmamm," Leah said.

When Leah got back into the buggy, she was beaming with happiness.

"It would appear that the visit with your grandmother was a successful one," John said.

"Yes, it was a wonderful visit. Thank you, John," she said. "Thank you for bringing me today."

News of the upcoming wedding of Caleb Brenneman to Ada Miller was published in the Sunday service, with the wedding to take place the following Tuesday. The Miller house, which had so recently been a place of sorrow, now became a place of joy as everyone prepared for the wedding and the feast that would take place immediately after. Celery, a big part of Amish wedding customs, was gathered and placed in vases all around the house. Walnuts and hickory nuts were cracked; floors were scrubbed.

On the day of the wedding cooks began arriving by seven in the morning. Caleb, as custom dictated, cut off the heads of the chickens, ducks, and turkeys that would be used for the meal. The women washed and dressed the fowl, made stuffing, and baked pies. By nine o'clock, when the guests arrived, the house smelled wonderfully of roast chicken and golden pastry.

Bishop Hershberger gave the sermon, focusing on marriages in the Old Testament, as well as the story of Adam and Eve and the wickedness of man and the flood. He also spoke of the correctness of Noah's household in that none in his family married unbelievers.

"There can only be trouble, pain, and sorrow by marrying outside of the church," the bishop said, and Leah, who was sitting in the back, was certain that the bishop was staring directly at her as he spoke the words.

Finally, as noon approached, the seemingly interminable sermon ended, and Bishop Hershberger called for Caleb and Ada to come forward.

"You have now heard the ordinance of Christian wedlock presented. Are you now willing to enter wedlock together as God in the beginning ordained and commanded?"

"Yes," both Caleb and Ada answered.

"Caleb, do you believe in your heart that Ada is the one chosen for you, by God, to be your wedded wife?"

"Ja, ich bin."

"Ada, do you believe in your heart that Caleb is the one chosen for you by God to be your wedded husband?"

"Ja, ich bin."

"Caleb, do you here promise your wedded wife, before the Lord and His church, that you will never desert her, but will care for her and cherish her though she may become sick, until God Himself shall separate you?"

"Ja, ich werde."

"Ada, do you also promise your wedded husband, before the Lord and His church, that you will never desert him, but will love and obey him until God Himself shall separate you?"

"Ja, ich werde."

Caleb and Ada joined their right hands together and the bishop continued: "The God of Abraham, the God of Isaac, and the God of Jacob be with you and help you fulfill His blessings upon you, through Jesus Christ. I now pronounce you husband and wife."

After the wedding the singing began, though by custom, neither Caleb nor Ada joined in—it was considered a bad omen to sing at one's own wedding. After the singing came the meal, at which each single boy would have to select a single girl to share the meal with him. For the boys who already had girlfriends, this was merely another opportunity for them to be together. But for the boys and girls who had no such arrangement, it was sometimes embarrassing to find a partner.

Caleb and Ada sat in the corner, the *ecke,* a place of honor. They exchanged greetings with their many guests while everyone enjoyed a bounty of roast beef, roast chicken, turkey and duck, dumplings, beef gravy, chicken gravy, mashed potatoes, coleslaw, prunes, fruit salad, cookies, cakes, and pies.

After the meal, the final song was sung. This was "Guter Geselle," or "Good Friend."

*   *   *

Just as he had missed the funeral for his brother, so too did John miss the wedding of his sister. Again, Leah brought him food, and they sat and ate together in his room.

"I'm sorry you couldn't come to the wedding," Leah said.

"Ah, the best part of a wedding is the food, and even better is to share good food with someone special. This food is good, and you are special, so what more could I ask for?"

As the two ate together, there was a light knock on the door and John got up to answer it. On the other side he saw a smiling Caleb and Ada.

"We asked the bishop," Ada said. "He told us we could come to you, to receive your blessings."

"The blessings come with a kiss," John said.

"*Ja*, I know that," Ada said happily.

John took his sister in his arms, hugged her and kissed her. Then he shook hands with Caleb.

"For what they are worth, coming from a sinner such as I, you have my blessings, and my wish for a long and happy life and marriage," John said.

"Thank you," Ada said, now wiping away tears.

"And, Ada and Caleb," Leah added, "from an *Englischer*, you have my blessings as well."

"*Sie sind ein Englischer, ja, aber ich denke, im Geist sie von uns sind.*"

"She said you are English, yes, but in spirit you are one of us," John translated.

"I won't disagree with that," Leah said as she hugged Ada.

* * *

When Frank Stone knocked on the door of Jason McKenzie's condo, Jason opened it quickly.

"You said you had some information for me?" Stone asked.

"Yes, come in," Jason said.

Once inside, Jason handed over a copy of *Everyday Magazine* and pointed to the picture of an Amish woman reading a newspaper.

"That is Leah," he said.

"Are you sure? I mean, I've got some photographs of her and this doesn't look like her."

"I know my daughter," Jason said. He tapped the picture with his finger. "This is Leah."

"So she's what, gone Amish?"

"It isn't that big of a stretch," Jason said. "Her mother was Amish."

"You don't say. Do you have any idea where this picture might have been taken?"

"I suspect it was taken around Arthur, Illinois," Jason said. "She's never been there, but that is where her mother was from, so it seems logical to me."

"Have you told the police?"

"No, I haven't told anyone. And I'm afraid to go over there myself. I know that I'm being watched. If I tried to make contact with her the FBI would be on us like a duck on a June bug. But I don't think anyone would be watching you."

"Yes, that's right. Nobody would connect me with her."

"Do you have an office, Mr. Stone?"

"Yes. It's on Clayton Road."

"This is what I want you to do. Go find her, and when you do, call me. We'll set up some sort of code that lets me know you have her. You can bring her to your office, and I'll be there."

"Do you have any idea where she might be in Arthur?"

"Mr. Stone, her grandmother's name is Lapp. Miriam Lapp. Leah has never met her grandmother, but my guess is that she's gone there."

"Thanks, Mr. McKenzie, you've been a big help."

"No, thank you, Mr. Stone. All I want is for my daughter to come back and be safe. I know she didn't kill Mr. Trevathan, and I'm sure if she'll just come back home, we can get this all worked out."

"I'll find her," Stone promised.

"I'll be damned!" Blanton said, slapping his hand on the desktop. "So, that's where she went, is it?"

"That's where her old man thinks she went. I'm going to go over there tomorrow, and I'll bring her back."

"No, I don't want her back."

"What do you mean, you don't want her back?"

"I want her—how can I put this? I want her taken care of."

"Taken care of?"

"Permanently."

"That's going to cost you more than a hundred thousand dollars."

"Be in my office tomorrow morning. I want to introduce you to your partner."

"I work alone."

"This is too important a job for you to work alone."

"Who is this person you want me to meet?"

"Just be here tomorrow morning by seven."

"Seven o'clock? That's pretty early, isn't it?"

"I want you here before office hours. We don't need curious eyes and ears around when we discuss the business at hand."

"You did hear me say that it was going to cost more than a hundred thousand dollars, didn't you?"

"How does a quarter of a million sound?"

Stone smiled. "That sounds good. That sounds damn good. Wait, you said you wanted someone else with me?"

"A quarter of a million apiece."

"Damn! It's worth half a million dollars to you to get rid of this woman?"

"Yes."

"You still haven't told me who I'm going to meet."

"I'll make the introductions tomorrow. Just know that he has a vested interest in seeing this through to its conclusion."

"A quarter of a million dollars?"

"Yes."

Stone smiled and ran his hand across the top of his bald head. "All right. I'll be there."

After all the excitement of the wedding day, it was difficult for Leah to fall asleep when she finally got in bed after midnight. By now all the guests were gone except for Caleb, who, since he was Ada's husband, was no longer considered a guest. As was the custom, Caleb and Ada were spending their wedding night in the bride's home.

Leah had been to many weddings in her life, but never one like this one. It was reverent and joyful, but it lacked all the pomp and circumstance that Leah had gotten used to. No organ music, no wedding march, no bride in white with a long train, no bridegroom and groomsmen in tuxedoes, no driving away from the church in a car decorated with "Just Married" signs.

Ad astra per alia porci.

"To the stars on the wings of a pig," John had said.

Why would Mr. Trevathan say . . . ? Suddenly Leah sat straight up in bed.

"Martin Pigg!" she said aloud.

Getting up, she dressed, then opened the dresser drawer, and found the thumb drive that contained the file she had printed out and taken to Trevathan on the day he was killed. Moving quickly and silently down the stairs, she picked up a flashlight that was by the door, then went out into the barn. As she walked through the barn, using the flashlight to light her way, Prodigal came over to the edge of his stall and looked at her in curiosity.

"Hello, Prodigal," she said. "I just need to see John for a few minutes."

Prodigal snorted and dipped his head a few times.

Leah knocked lightly on John's door.

"John? John, it's me, Leah."

"Leah?"

"Yes. Open the door, please, I need to talk to you."

"Just a minute."

Leah waited a moment, then the door opened. John was backlit by the glowing lantern he had lit inside. Even so, she could see that he was wearing trousers and an undershirt.

"What is it?"

"I know the key to it all now. It's Martin Pigg."

"What?"

"When you told me what '*Ad astra per alia porci*' means, I didn't make any connection at first. But now I know exactly what he was saying. He was telling me that the key is Martin Pigg."

"Who is Martin Pigg?"

"Our firm—that is, Blanton, Trevathan and Dunn—has been working on the American Capital Management case."

"The what?"

"I can't believe you haven't heard of it. It's almost as big as the Bernie Madoff Ponzi scheme. American Capital Management is accused of fraud regarding a pension fund that has wiped out the life savings of thousands of Americans. Martin Pigg is the CFO of ACM. And here's the worst part," Leah added. "Our firm represents Martin Pigg. He's our biggest client and we bill him at least five million dollars a year on the books.

"I'm thinking now that not only have we been representing him, but maybe we've been involved in the fraud and have probably been raking in a great deal more money off the books. I can't believe Mr. Trevathan just learned about it. The only thing I can think is that he must have suddenly developed a conscience over the firm's involvement and was going to expose the fraud. That's why Blanton and Dunn had him killed."

"Is there any way you can prove that?" John asked.

"I think so," Leah said. She held up the thumb drive. "This is the file Mr. Trevathan wanted me to bring him. Let's call it up on your laptop and have a look at it."

"We can't. The battery is down. But we can go into town in the morning."

When Frank Stone arrived at Blanton's office the next morning, Blanton and Dunn were waiting for him. There was a third man in the office as well. The pinched face and hair that looked as if it had never seen a comb belonged to someone Stone recognized—Vernon Garner. When Stone was a policeman Vernon Garner had been well-known as a hit man, though nobody had ever been able to get anything on him.

"He sure doesn't look like a hit man," Stone said one time when Garner had been brought in for questioning. "He looks like someone who just stepped down off a tractor."

"You want him to look like Charles Bronson or Clint Eastwood, maybe? Somebody like that comes toward you, you're naturally a little on edge. But if a guy in overalls chewing on a piece of straw comes at you, you think nothing of it," one of the other policemen said.

This morning Garner was in Blanton's office sitting on a leather chair in the corner. He was wearing bib overalls, and he had a battered hat on his knee.

"Since you two are going to be working together, I figured I should introduce you."

"I know Mr. Garner," Stone said. "Or perhaps I should say I know of him."

"Then you know his work."

"Yeah, I know it."

"I trust you do not find that off-putting."

"For the kind of money you're talking about, I wouldn't find him off-putting if he was Mahmoud Ahmadinejad himself," Stone said.

"Good. I will be waiting to hear from you. Call as soon as you have completed the job."

"All right," Stone said. He looked over at Garner. "My car is outside."

"We'll go in my pickup truck," Garner said.

"Okay," Stone agreed. "That's probably better anyway. My car is a little flashy, a pickup truck will fit in better in farm country."

"You know anything about farming, Stone?" Garner asked.

"Not a thing."

"I farmed till I was thirty years old. Then I figured there had to be an easier way to make a living."

As the two men walked toward Garner's truck, Stone considered this man beside him. He was small, and Stone was certain that an average-sized teenage boy could handle him in a fistfight. He looked helpless, almost pathetic. And yet, Stone knew that this very thing was his secret weapon.

Garner's truck was an extended cab, at least ten years old, and the paint was starting to fade.

"I don't mean to cast aspersions on your truck, Garner, but are you sure this will get us there?"

"It'll get us there," Garner said. "Oh, watch out for that spring on your side of the seat. I've got a blanket over it, but if the blanket moves around, you're liable to get stuck."

"Thanks, I'll be on guard," Stone said.

When Garner started the engine, Stone could tell by the way it purred that the looks of the truck had nothing to do with the way it ran.

"This is a '98 Dodge Ram with a 2010 engine," Garner explained. "I don't like my trucks to look too fancy, but I do like them to run good."

Stone took it as a reminder that there was more to Garner than met the eye.

CHAPTER TWENTY-ONE

I s my car running?" Leah asked.

"Yes, there's nothing wrong with it."

"What do you say we take it into town? I know you can ride in cars with others, and I'm an *ausländer,* so I can't see that it would cause any problem."

"I can't see that it would either," John said. "I've been wanting to ride in your car anyway. But if you're going to do this, I think you should change into your other clothes. I think an Amish woman driving a red convertible would call a little more attention to us than we would like."

"All right, I'll be right back," Leah said.

Half an hour later, once more wearing her English clothes, Leah came back out to the barn. In her absence John had cleared away everything behind the car so she could back out without any difficulty. As they drove away, Leah saw Isaac and Emma on the porch, watching them leave.

"I hope I'm not making things worse for you," Leah said.

"Don't worry about it," John said. "Right now, let's worry about getting your situation taken care of."

As Leah and John were heading into town, Frank Stone and Vernon Garner were pulling up in front of Miriam Lapp's house in Garner's pickup truck. A young girl, approximately fifteen years old, answered the door.

"*Ja?* Can I help you?"

"Is this the Lapp home?" Stone asked.

"*Ja.* I am Mary Lapp."

"I am looking for Leah McKenzie," Stone said.

At that moment an older woman came into the room.

"Are you Miriam Lapp?" Stone asked.

"*Ja.*"

"Mrs. Lapp, we're looking for your granddaughter, Leah McKenzie."

"Why are you looking for her?"

"Something has come up in St. Louis. An emergency. We must take her back at once."

"*Mary, sag ihnen nichts. Ich traue ihnen nicht.*"

Mary didn't know why her grandmother didn't trust these two men, but she knew that her grandmother was very wise about people, so she assured her she wouldn't give them any information.

"*Ich werde ihnen sagen nichts, grossmamm.*"

"What is this?" Stone said. "Speak English. Where is Leah McKenzie?"

"Please, leave my house now," Miriam Lapp said.

"Leave your house? What will you do if we don't leave? Call the police? Oh, no, you can't do that, can you? You don't have a telephone," Stone said, and he laughed demonically.

"You know what I think, Stone? I think they do know where she is, but they just ain't tellin' us," Garner said.

"I think you're right. Where is she?" Stone asked again.

Miriam put her arm around Mary and pulled the young girl to her. But her lips remained closed.

"Where is she?" Stone said, speaking the words much louder now.

It was now obvious that Miriam wasn't going to answer.

"What are we going to do?" Garner asked. "I don't believe this wrinkled-up old bag is going to talk to us."

"Oh, yeah," Stone said with a nod of his head. "She's goin' to talk to us, all right. Aren't you, Mrs. Lapp?"

"Please leave my house now."

"Leave your house, huh?" Stone punctuated his remark with a brutal slap to the old woman's face.

Miriam's head snapped back, and her eyes began to water. Her cheek glowed red where he had hit her.

"Stop that!" Mary shouted. "You leave my grandmother alone!"

"Sure," Stone said. "All she has to do is tell us where Leah McKenzie is."

Stone slapped Miriam again, harder this time than he did the first time.

"No, please!"

"If you don't want to see your grandma beat up, all you have to do is tell me where I can find Leah McKenzie."

"What do you want with her?" Mary asked.

"Well now, that's none of your business, is it?" Stone replied. He hit Miriam yet again, and this time his blow brought blood to the old woman's lip. It also caused her left eye to puff up and swell shut.

"You know what I think? I believe you could beat this old battle-ax senseless and she still wouldn't tell you anything," Garner said.

"You have any other ideas?" Stone asked.

"One."

"What would that idea be?"

"I'll show you."

Garner withdrew his pistol and held it to Mary's head. He pulled the hammer back.

"Mrs. Lapp," he said in a silky-smooth voice. "I'm only going to ask you this one time. And if you don't answer, I am going to blow this girl's blood and brains all over your nice clean floor. Now, where can we find Leah McKenzie?"

"*Nein, nein, bitte nicht schiessen, nicht schiessen!* Please, don't shoot!" she repeated in English.

"Are you ready to tell us where we can find Leah McKenzie?"

"*Ja*, with the Millers she is staying."

"Thank you," Garner said. He lowered the hammer.

"Well, that's more like it. I guess you had the best idea after all, Garner." Then to Mary, Stone asked, "Where is the Miller house?"

"It is two miles that way," Mary said, pointing. "You will see their name on the mailbox, out on the road."

"Thank you, you have been most helpful," Stone said. "Oh, if you've got some ice, you might wrap it up in a cloth and hold it to your grandma's eye. It will help keep some of the swelling down."

It wasn't hard to find the Miller house. As Mary had said, the name was on a mailbox that stood out on the road. Garner turned up the long road that led up to the complex, a big white house, a weathered barn, and a silo. A young man of about eighteen came toward them. His arm was in a sling.

"Would you be named Miller?" Stone asked, trying to smile as pleasantly as he could.

"*Ja.* Sam Miller."

"Sam, my name is Frank Stone. I'm a friend of Leah McKenzie's father. He's had an accident, and I've come to find Leah and fetch her home. I'm told this is where she's staying."

"*Ja*, this is where she is staying. But she is not here now."

"Oh? Where is she, could you tell me that?"

"She and my brother John went into town."

"Do you know where they were going?"

"No, but they went in Leah's car. It's a red convertible, so you might look for that. I don't think there's any other car in Arthur like it."

"Thanks, son, you've been a big help," Stone said.

As they got back in the truck, Stone chuckled. "If she's in that car, we've got her. I mean, how hard is that going to be to find?"

"It might be harder than you think," Garner said. "Red Mustangs aren't all that rare."

"How many will have a Missouri license that says 'Le-Gal'?"

"Ha! That does make it easier."

* * *

At that moment Leah and John were in John's office at Collins Fine Furniture. John's laptop was plugged in, and they'd called up the material on Leah's thumb drive.

> Information for Agent Robert Coker
>
> May 17—Learned today that our client, MP, has been
> falsifying documents to hide a one-hundred-million-dollar loss.
> I approached K and J to point this out, only to learn that our
> firm not only knew about it but is complicit in it. Following is
> a report on the specific losses and how they have been
> covered.

"'MP.' That's Martin Pigg," Leah said as she began reading through the report. "Oh, my, I should have taken time to read this before. This is very incriminating. I had no idea this was going on. Listen to this."

Leah began to read from the screen. "'I have seriously underestimated the amount of money involved in Martin Pigg's scheme. It is nearly one billion dollars, fifty million of which has been channeled through Blanton, Trevathan and Dunn. God help us; we could all wind up spending the rest of our lives in prison.'"

She looked up at John. "You know what that means?"

"Sounds to me like it means your bosses were headed for prison if this got out."

"Yes, and it was about to. I'm sure now that the reason Mr. Trevathan was at the federal court building was to turn this documentation over to someone."

"And you say you got a message from him to bring it to the courthouse?"

"Yes."

"I wonder why he didn't take it himself."

"I don't know. Maybe he was afraid that Mr. Blanton or Mr. Dunn would see it on him."

"Turns out it didn't matter whether they saw him with the report or not. They obviously knew what he was doing, or they wouldn't have had him killed."

"We've got to get this report into Agent Coker's hands," Leah said. "I need to make a telephone call."

John pointed to the phone on his desk. "Be my guest," he said. "Or rather, be Mr. Collins's guest. Do you know the number?"

"I know a number that I think will eventually get me to him."

Agent Coker was just leaving his office for lunch when the phone rang. He considered letting it go to voice mail but decided to take it.

"Agent Coker."

"Agent Coker, if I tell you that my name is Leah McKenzie, will that mean anything to you?"

"It will if you are who you say you are."

"Back in July, you testified in a case I was involved with. It was the ATAP Bond and Securities case, and had to do with interstate transportation of stolen bonds. Do you recall that?"

"Yes."

"Afterward, you asked me to have dinner with you."

"All right, I'm convinced you are Leah McKenzie. What can I do for you, Miss McKenzie?"

"I have the report that Mr. Trevathan was going to give you. I would like to e-mail it to you. Then I want to come see you. I believe the information in this report will help clear my name."

"All right, e-mail it. And, just so I'm up front with you, I intend to call Detective Hellman and get him in on this as well."

"Good."

"Where are you now?"

"I'd rather not say just yet. But I will be coming in to see you within the next twenty-four hours."

"All right. You send the report, then come see me, and we'll see where this leads us."

"Look for the subject line '*Ad astra per alia porci.*'"

"What?"

"'*Ad astra per alia porci.*' I'll explain later."

"All right, Miss McKenzie, I'll be looking for the e-mail."

When she hung up the phone, Leah e-mailed Coker the entire file from the thumb drive.

"When are you going?" John asked as they left the furniture shop and started toward her car.

"I think I'll go today," Leah said.

"Are you coming back?"

This was the question Leah had been dreading. Was she coming back? She had made some progress with her grandmother, and she didn't want to walk away from that. And there was also John.

What about John? If she was honest with herself, she would have to confess that she was in love with him. There was no way of denying that. But where would that love lead? Where could it lead?

Before Leah could answer John's question, two men who had

been standing by a pickup truck parked behind Leah's car started walking toward them. When Leah saw them approach, she gasped.

"John! He's the one who killed Mr. Trevathan!" she said breathlessly.

Garner, the one she'd pointed out, showed his pistol, though it was covered with his hat so that only Leah and John could see it.

"How about you two folks get into the backseat of my truck? We're goin' to take a little ride."

"You don't need him," Leah said. "I don't even know him. He works in the furniture store; I was looking at a desk."

"Now ain't that somethin', John Miller. Here she is, livin' at your house, and she claims she doesn't know you. You must not have made much of an impression on her. Both of you, get in the truck now. We're going to take a little ride."

"Where are we going?" Leah asked.

"It's like the song says, missy. I'm goin' to open the door to heaven or hell."

"Why are you doing this?"

"Money, sweetheart, money," Stone answered. He chuckled. "Most bosses, when they don't like something their employee is doing, are satisfied with firing them. Mr. Blanton and Mr. Dunn want you dead and they are willing to pay a great deal of money to have the job done."

With Garner driving and Stone keeping his gun on the two in the backseat of the pickup, they drove out into the country.

"Hey, Garner, look over there. There's an old barn with no house nearby. Why don't we take them there?"

"Good idea," Garner said.

Garner turned from the blacktop road onto a narrow dirt lane. Dust roiled up from behind the truck as it moved quickly between two now-denuded cornfields. They stopped in front of the barn and the dust cloud enveloped them for a moment before dissipating. Then, at gunpoint, Stone ordered John and Leah to get out.

"All right, inside you go," he said, pushing them toward the barn. He tried the door and it opened. "Ha, what do you know? It's not even locked."

"We've no need to lock doors," John said. "We don't steal from each other."

"Yeah, well, whatever is in here is safe from us. We aren't goin' to steal anything either," Stone said.

The inside of the barn was illuminated only by the wedge of light that came in through the open door and those bars of dust-mote-filled sunlight that streamed in through the gaps between the boards. The barn smelled of hay and animal.

John knew the barn. It belonged to Abram Beiler, and last summer, John had done some work for him on his buggy here. He remembered also that there had been a piece of dowel left over about the length and heft of an ax handle. And when John looked toward the wall, he saw it exactly where he had put it.

"Oh, John!" Leah said in a frightened voice.

"Don't hurt us," John said, his voice pleading. "Please don't hurt us."

"Ha, that's all you've got? Beggin' us not to hurt you?" Stone mocked. "What do you think about that, missy? You didn't think that your Amish boyfriend was really going to protect you, now, did you? You know it's against their religion to hit anyone. He's just going to stand by and watch it happen."

"If you are going to shoot us, shoot us in the back of the head, so at least we don't have to see it coming," John said as he turned his back and walked over toward the wall.

"See what I mean?" Stone said with a chuckle. "All right, farm boy, we'll accommodate you. I wouldn't want it said that we don't have a heart." Then to Leah he said, "You get over there with him."

Leah stepped over beside John and sensed the two men coming up behind them. She braced herself for a bullet in the back of the head.

"Oh, there is one more thing," John said easily.

"What's that?" Stone asked.

"I'm not exactly like all the other Amish."

"What do you—"

Even as Stone was asking the question, John grabbed the dowel and whirled around as if swinging a baseball bat, taking both of the armed men down before they could react. Then, with both of them on the ground, he reached down quickly and took their guns. He also took a cell phone from one of them and handed it to Leah.

"Call nine-one-one. Tell them we are in the old Beiler barn on Beiler Road," he said.

"Did you kill them?"

"No. But they are going to have headaches for a while."

CHAPTER TWENTY-TWO

There were two deputies' cars outside the Beiler barn. The presence of the cars with their flashing red and blue lights had drawn more than a score of curious people, both Amish and English, to the barn. They watched as two men, both with bruises on their faces, were marched out of the barn in handcuffs.

"If you two men will testify that you were sent by Blanton and Dunn, it will go easier on you," Leah said.

"I don't know what this woman is talking about. We weren't sent here by anyone," Stone said. "My name is Frank Stone and I'm a private investigator. We were just trying to find this woman to collect the one-hundred-thousand-dollar reward that's out for her."

"What one-hundred-thousand-dollar reward?" one of the sheriff's deputies asked.

"Check her out," Stone said. "Her name is Leah McKenzie."

"Is that your name?" one of the deputies asked.

"Yes."

"Wait here." The deputy slipped back into his car, then tapped her name into his on-board computer. He gasped as he saw what came up.

Leah Nichole McKenzie

Unlawful Flight to Avoid Prosecution—First-Degree Murder

Reward: The FBI is offering a reward of up to $100,000 for information leading directly to the arrest of Leah Nichole McKenzie.

Leah Nichole McKenzie is a suspect in the murder of Carl Trevathan in a federal court building in St. Louis, Missouri.

McKenzie is a well-educated lawyer who speaks fluent French. She has no known ties outside the city of St. Louis but may be in possession of a handgun and should be approached with caution.

When he came back out of the car he was holding a pair of handcuffs. "Miss McKenzie, you are under arrest. You have the right to remain silent. Anything you say or do can and will be used against you in a court of law. You have the right to speak to an attorney. If you cannot afford an attorney, one will be appointed for you. Do you understand these rights as they have been read to you?"

"Yes, I understand them."

"Turn around please."

"Deputy Kinsdale, is it absolutely necessary that she be put in handcuffs?" John asked.

"Don't be giving me a hard time, John," Deputy Kinsdale said. "I'm just doing my job."

"I'm coming too," John said.

"Not in this car, you aren't."

John stood by, helpless and frustrated, as he saw the deputy hold his hand on top of Leah's head and help her into the backseat of his car.

"John, *was ist das*?" Beiler asked.

"Why have they taken the *Englische* woman?" another asked.

John watched the two deputy cars drive away. Then, noticing that the pickup truck was still parked where Garner had left it, he hurried over to it and looked inside. The keys were in the ignition.

John jumped into the truck.

"John, no, you can't drive!" someone shouted.

"Watch me," John shouted back.

Putting the truck in gear, he spun the wheels as he hurried away from the others, following the two sheriff's cars.

As he knew they would, the deputies took Stone, Garner, and Leah to the county seat at Tuscola. On the way there John used the cell phone he had taken from the two men to call Glen Collins.

"Collins Fine Furniture."

"Mr. Collins, I need Kyle Sherman's telephone number," John said.

"Sure, just a moment."

John waited, then Glen Collins came back on the line. "Here it is: 314-555-1718. You having a problem with a piece of his furniture?"

"No, I just need to talk to him," John said without giving any more information. He punched out of that call, then called the number Collins had given him.

A moment later he had Kyle Sherman on the line.

"John, how is my furniture coming along?"

"Just fine, Kyle, just fine. But that isn't why I called. I need your legal services."

"My legal services?"

"Yes." John explained the situation to him, telling him that Leah had been hiding out with the Amish for the past few months. "She didn't do it, Kyle, and she has proof," John concluded.

"I never thought she did it anyway," Kyle said. "I know Leah McKenzie, personally and by reputation, and there is absolutely nothing that would suggest she would ever do such a thing. But you say you have proof? That's very good. What do you have?"

"Get in touch with an FBI agent named Robert Coker," John said. "Today, Leah sent information to him that will exonerate her."

"All right. Where is Leah now?"

"She is in a sheriff's car right in front of me. They are taking her to jail in Tuscola."

"I'll get in touch with Agent Coker. If what you're saying is true, we'll have her out before dark."

"I'm telling you, there is a one-hundred-thousand-dollar reward for that woman, and I want it to go on record now that I am the one who found her," Stone shouted as soon as they went into the county jailhouse.

"You don't have anything on us," Garner said. "What are you putting us in jail for?"

"Attempted murder."

"We weren't going to murder anyone, I tell you. We were just trying to collect the reward."

"Then why did you take them to the Beiler barn?"

"We didn't take them there."

"We have witnesses who saw them get into your truck," Deputy Kinsdale said.

"You sit there," one of the deputies said to Leah. "It's been a while since we've had a female prisoner; we're going to have to get the cell cleaned up."

Almost immediately thereafter, John came into the building.

"John!" Leah said, thankful to see him.

"I've called my lawyer friend in St. Louis," John said. "And I asked him to call Agent Coker."

"Good. John, I'm sorry I got you into this mess."

The telephone rang.

"Don't worry. It isn't going to be a mess for long."

"All right, Agent Coker, if you say so," Leah and John heard the sheriff say.

The sheriff hung up the phone, then came over to Leah. "Miss, if you'll stand up and turn around, I'll get those handcuffs off you."

"Thanks," Leah said, complying with his request. "Was that Robert Coker?"

"Yes, it was. He asked me to hold off on doing anything with you until he got here. He's flying over."

"Do you have an airport here?"

"Ha!" the sheriff said. "He won't be needing an airport—he's coming by helicopter. He'll be landing right across the street in an hour and a half."

Two hours later, Leah, John, Kyle Sherman, and Agent Coker were sitting at a table in the Courthouse Café.

"I've had you released to my custody," Coker said. "As soon as we get back to St. Louis, we can arrange bail."

"How are we going to St. Louis?"

"I'm going to rent a car."

"Could we go in my car? I'm going to want it with me, anyway. I'll let you drive."

"Sure, I see no problem with that. By the way, that material you sent me? It is dynamite. It not only involves Blanton and Dunn in the Martin Pigg case, it has enough information to make the case against Pigg. How did you come by that information, anyway?"

"That's the file I was delivering to Mr. Trevathan on the day he was shot. He asked me to print it out, then delete the file. I violated his orders, because instead of deleting it, I copied it."

"You said you printed out the file—what did you do with it?"

"I gave it to Mr. Blanton. I hadn't read it yet, so I had no idea what was in it. In fact, I didn't read it until this morning, so I had no idea that all this time I had the evidence that would exonerate me."

By noon the next day Leah was free on bail, and the first thing she did was drive out to Chesterfield to her dad's office. Jason McKenzie's secretary Suzie Bailey's eyes opened wide when she saw Leah, but Leah put her finger to her mouth to shush her.

"Is it safe for you to be here?" Suzie asked.

"Absolutely safe," Leah replied. She opened the door into her dad's private office and saw him standing at the window, looking out.

"Hello, Dad," she said.

"Leah!" Jason shouted happily, literally running across the room to her. They embraced, and he held her for a long time until, with a start, he jerked back from her. "Is it safe for you to be here?" he asked.

"Absolutely safe. I didn't do it, Dad, and I have the evidence. I'm out on bail now, but as soon as all the evidence has been reviewed, I have no doubt that any charges that have been filed against me will be dropped."

"I knew you didn't do it, darlin'," Jason said. "From day one, I knew you were innocent. I just wanted to hear from you, is all."

"I couldn't communicate with you. Not until I found some way to prove my innocence."

"Were you in Arthur?"

"Yes! How did you know?"

"I saw your picture in the paper wearing plain clothes."

"My picture in the paper?"

Jason walked over to his desk and opened a drawer, then removed a newspaper. "This one," he said.

Leah looked at the paper, then gasped. "Oh! I know when and where this picture was taken!" she said. "But it was just an old couple who took it. I never had any idea it would turn up in the newspaper."

"I'm about to go to lunch," Jason said. "Have you outgrown a hamburger from Dove's? I know you used to love them when you were younger."

"Some things you never outgrow," Leah said.

Half an hour later, Leah and her father were in Dove's eating the huge specialty hamburgers and enjoying the unending supply of French fries when her cell phone dinged that a text message was coming in.

"So you have your cell phone turned on again, do you? Do you have any idea how many times I tried to call you?"

"I threw my old cell phone into the river. This is a new one I just picked up this morning," Leah said as she accessed the text message. "This is from my lawyer. My hearing is in the morning."

"Your hearing? You're going to trial that quickly?"

"If everything goes right tomorrow, there won't be a trial," Leah said. "Dad, I want you to come with me. I'm going to need you for moral support."

"You just tell me where to be, and I'll be there."

Kyle Sherman met Leah and her father in the front of the court-house. "I have news for you," he said.

"What news?"

"Keith Blanton and James Dunn have both been indicted for collusion and participation in securities fraud, investment advisor fraud, mail fraud, wire fraud, money laundering, false statements, perjury, making false filings with the SEC, and theft from an employee benefit plan. In addition, Garner, in return for taking the death sentence off the table, has agreed to testify that Blanton and Dunn hired him. There won't be anything to this hearing but going through the motions. Oh, and someone else is here, come to give you support."

"Who?"

"He's waiting in the courtroom. Come on, the hearing is due to start in about five minutes."

Leah saw him as soon as they stepped into the courtroom. John was standing just inside the door, dressed in plain clothing.

"John!" she said happily.

"John?" Jason asked.

"Dad, I want you to meet a—a very good friend of mine. This is John Miller. John knows my grandmother. I've been living with John's family, and I don't think I could have gotten through all this without them."

"It is good to meet you, John, and I thank you for all that you and your family have done for Leah."

"It is good to meet you as well, Mr. McKenzie. And I would do anything in the world for Leah."

"Oh?" Jason replied.

"Come, Leah, we need to get in there," Sherman said.

Leah and Sherman went to the defendant's table in front of the courtroom. Leah saw Agent Coker and Detective Hellman sitting in the front row.

"All rise!"

Everyone stood as the judge came into the room. He sat down, then indicated that everyone else could do the same.

"Mr. Prosecutor, your opening remarks?" the judge said.

"Your Honor, I defer my opening remarks and ask that the defense speak."

"Mr. Sherman, do you have any problem with that?"

"No, Your Honor, Mr. Gilmore and I have discussed this."

"Very well, you may proceed."

"Your Honor, Vernon Garner has signed a confession stating that he is the one who killed Carl Trevathan. In his confession he names Keith Blanton and James Dunn as his coconspirators, in that they hired him to do the job. The motive was the involvement of the firm in the Martin Pigg fraud case, in which more than a billion dollars of investors' money was mishandled, misused, and stolen. Blanton, Trevathan and Dunn, while representing Martin Pigg, profited to the tune of fifty million dollars, and we have documented proof of that.

"In addition, we have signed statements from Garner and from Frank Stone stating that they were hired by Blanton and Dunn to murder Miss McKenzie, to prevent her from exposing their participation in Pigg's Ponzi scheme."

"What?" Jason shouted, his voice pained. "Stone was going to kill her? My God! I told him how to find her!"

"Order! Order!" the judge shouted.

"Your Honor, may I request a five-minute recess?" Sherman said.

"Court will recess for five minutes," the judge said.

"Go to him, Leah," Sherman said.

Standing quickly, Leah hurried through the knee-high banister back to where her father was sitting with John.

"Sweetheart," Jason said, his face white and reflecting the horror of what he had done. "I'm sorry, I had no idea! Stone said he was working for Blanton to find you, to help you. I was so desperate to find you, to know if you were okay. I thought I was . . . helping . . ." His voice trailed off.

"It's all right, Dad," Leah said. "Really, it's all right."

"My God, to think that I could have gotten you killed. I will never forgive myself."

"Really, Dad, it's all right."

Jason stood up and put his arms around her, drawing her close to him.

"Dad, you'll see, it has all worked out for the best."

"I . . . I'm so sorry."

"Mr. McKenzie," John said. "You only did what any father who was worried about his daughter would do. Please, don't punish yourself."

Jason nodded.

"I love you, Dad," Leah said before she turned and walked back up to the front of the courtroom.

A moment later, the judge called the court to order, and Kyle Sherman resumed his opening statement.

"Your Honor, in view of the evidence already presented, and of the statements signed by both Garner and Stone, I request that all charges against my client be dropped."

Sherman sat back down.

"Mr. Prosecutor?" the judge said.

George Gilmore stood. "Your Honor, due to overwhelming evidence, as well as signed statements that suggest that Keith Blanton and James Dunn are the guilty parties in this case, and pursuant to an agreement my office has already worked out with Mr. Sherman, we are in one hundred percent agreement that all charges against Miss Leah McKenzie should be dropped."

"What is the current status of Blanton and Dunn?" the judge asked.

"Blanton and Dunn have both been arrested and are in custody," the prosecutor replied. "And James Dunn has already signed a confession implicating them both in the murder."

"Detective Hellman, do you have anything that would contradict the prosecution's submission for withdrawal of charges?"

"I do not, Your Honor."

"Agent Coker, will the federal government be making any charges against Miss McKenzie?"

"The federal government has no charge against Miss McKenzie."

"Does anyone present see any reason why Miss McKenzie should be disbarred?"

"No reason, Your Honor," the prosecutor replied.

"Miss McKenzie, there are no criminal or civil charges against you. Your license to practice law remains *in esse,* and you are free to go."

"Thank you, Your Honor."

Leah received a quick hug from Kyle Sherman, then she hurried back to hug her father again. Then, almost hesitantly, she and John hugged.

"Miss McKenzie, on behalf of the city of St. Louis, I want to apologize for putting you through this ordeal," Detective Hellman said, approaching Leah and the others. He smiled. "And if it is any consolation, I never was fully convinced that you were guilty. But I hope you understand that I had to follow the investigation to the end."

"I understand fully, Detective Hellman. Apology accepted," Leah said. "And, as they say, every cloud has a silver lining. Because of this . . . ordeal, I was able to get in touch with a part of my life that had always been a mystery to me. And I will always be thankful for that."

After lunch with John and her father, Leah drove John back home. They listened to classical music on the satellite radio, almost as a protective barrier against the elephant riding in the car with them.

Finally John reached up to turn the radio off.

"We are going to have to face it, Leah," he said.

"I know."

"So we may as well get it out into the open now."

"Yes."

"Of course, it all depends on whether or not you still feel about me as I do about you. And I will tell you flat-out that I love you."

Leah was silent for a moment, then, hesitantly, she responded. "You know that I still love you."

A big smile spread across John's face.

"Great!" he said. "I'll talk to the bishop and see if he will allow us to get married, even though I am under the *bann*. I think I can talk him into it."

"John."

"We can live with my folks until we get our own place."

"John," Leah said again.

"You know who will be the happiest of all? Your grandmother."

"John, please, don't do this!" Leah said, speaking more harshly than she intended.

"Leah, what is it?"

"I can't marry you."

"What? Why not? I love you, and you said that you love me. What more do we need? Why can't you marry me?"

"You know why I can't marry you."

"No, I don't know."

"You're talking about getting permission from the bishop, you're talking about my grandmother—all that means you expect me to become Amish."

"Yes," John said. "I suppose that is what I expect."

"I can't do that."

"Why can't you? You have lived with us for almost three months. You have made a connection with your grandmother. I thought you liked living among the Amish. I thought you liked the people."

"I do like it, and I do like the people. But I can't stay there. I just can't. Surely you can see that. I have a career, a life. And after what happened with my mother, I think it would break Dad's heart if I were to join the Amish. You've lived outside; you know what it's like."

"Yes, I know what it is like. And I chose to return," John said.

"Did you?"

"What do you mean by that?"

"John, you have your own car, you have a computer, you have a library of books and a store of memories, good and bad. You are trying to live with one foot in the Amish culture and one foot on the outside, and you can't do that."

"It has worked well so far."

"You mean you've gotten away with it so far, but the time is going to come when you will have to choose one or the other. If you and I are to have a life together, it won't be with the Amish. But I leave that up to you. I won't ask you to leave the church. I won't complicate the choice that you're going to have to make."

"Leah . . ." John didn't finish the sentence, and Leah didn't prod him to do so.

They drove in silence the rest of the way back to the Miller farm. As soon as they got there, John, without another word, walked from the car to the barn without looking back.

Ada, Caleb, Sam, Emma, and Isaac came out from the house to greet her.

"What happened?" Ada asked.

"All charges have been dropped," Leah replied with a relieved smile.

"Oh, I am so happy for you. So, what do you do now?"

"Now? I'm going to St. Louis to try to get my life back."

"And John?" Ada asked.

Leah looked toward the barn. Then, turning back toward Ada, she felt the tears streaming down her cheeks, though she wasn't weeping aloud.

"As I said, I'm going back to St. Louis to try to get my life back."

"And John is staying here?" Emma asked.

"I will not take him away from you."

"Do you love him, Leah?" Emma asked.

"Yes, I love him with all my heart. And he loves me. But . . ." She took in the farm with a wave of her hand. "I can't compete against this. And I cannot, and I will not, compete against God."

It had been six months since Leah left the Amish, and with money invested by Annie Trevathan, Leah opened her own law office. Marilyn Summers and Linda Martin came with her.

Bringing Marilyn and Linda proved to be a boon for her business, because between the two women, they had files on every client that Blanton, Trevathan and Dunn had represented. And they managed to bring nearly all of them over to Leah once she hung out her own shingle.

Leah kept up with the Pigg case and knew that Keith Blanton and James Dunn had both pleaded out to avoid the death penalty and were now serving thirty-five years in the penitentiary. Because Frank Stone cooperated fully with the prosecutor, he got only five years. Vernon Garner's lawyer had managed a plea bargain for him that kept away the death penalty, and Garner was serving life plus thirty-five years.

At the moment Leah, Marilyn, and Linda were in the office eating lunch from Chinese take-out boxes.

"Leah, can I ask you a question?" Marilyn asked as she clutched a shrimp between her chopsticks.

"Is it the same question?"

"Yes. But you've never given me an answer. Why aren't you dating?"

"I told you, I don't have time for that right now. I'm concentrating on getting my practice started."

"Getting your practice started?" Linda said with a little laugh. "Are you kidding? You were at full speed the day you opened your doors."

"Thanks to you two," Leah said.

"So, back to my original question. You're getting a little long in the tooth now, kiddo," Marilyn said.

"What?"

"I'm just saying," Marilyn said quickly. "You're going to have to find someone someday. You don't want to wind up an old maid, do you?"

"Maybe the right man hasn't come along," Leah said.

"How are you going to know when you have the right man if you never spend time with one?" Linda asked.

"I knew."

"What?"

"I'll know."

"That's not what you said. You *did* meet someone, didn't you? What happened? Where is he now?" Marilyn asked.

Before Leah could respond, a familiar voice interrupted. "I'm here, standing in the doorway."

"John!" Leah cried, astonished.

"Sir, you should wait in reception," Marilyn said.

"It's okay, Marilyn," Leah said. "I'll deal with this gentleman."

"Are you sure, because—" Marilyn started, then she saw the way the two were looking at each other.

"Marilyn, I think we're in the way here," Linda said.

"Oh, uh, yes. Uh, if you need us, Leah, we'll just be, that is, uh, we'll just leave you two alone."

"Thank you," Leah said, though she had not taken her eyes off John since he came in.

John was wearing khaki trousers, a white shirt, and a blue blazer. His hair was cut short, and he wasn't wearing a hat.

"Out among the English, I see," Leah said.

"Yes."

"Another mini-*rumspringa*?"

"Not mini. This time it is for good."

"You're leaving the church?"

"Yes."

"Why now? Why didn't you leave when you were first banned?"

"It was a matter of personal honor. I needed to serve out the *bann;* I needed the cleansing," John said. "On the day the bishop said I was once again welcome, I told him I was leaving for good."

"Oh, John. What about Emma, Ada, and your father? How did they take it?"

"Better than I thought they would," John said. "Daad said that I couldn't be half-Amish and half-English, that I was going to have to be one or the other. So I chose to leave."

"I see."

"Leah, I've signed a contract with St. Louis Custom Furniture Company. You wouldn't marry an Amish carpenter, but what about an English cabinet maker?"

"You did all this to marry me?"

"Yes."

"Oh, John, please tell me you haven't been seduced by the siren's song."

John stepped up so close to Leah that their bodies came in contact. He put his hand on her cheek and turned her face up to his.

"Of course I was. How could I resist? It is the most beautiful song in the world," he said. "Will you marry me, Leah?"

"Yes," she said, but her answer was buried in his kiss.